I0773052

Through Stormy Skies

Copyright © 2025 by Hallie Anne

All rights reserved.

No part of this publication may be reproduced, distributed, or transmitted in any form or by any means, including photocopying, recording, or other electronic or mechanical methods, without the prior written permission of the publisher, except as permitted by U.S. copyright law.

No generative artificial intelligence (AI) was used in the writing of this work. Without in any way limiting the author's exclusive rights under copyright, any use of this publication to "train" generative artificial intelligence (AI) technologies to generate text is expressly prohibited.

The story, all names, characters, and incidents portrayed in this production are fictitious. No identification with actual persons (living or deceased), places, buildings, and products is intended or should be inferred.

Published by Aspen & Ivy Press

Cover Design: Yummy Book Covers

1st Edition published in November 2025

eISBN: 978-1-965506-04-2

Paperback: 978-1-965506-05-9

Dedication

To the eldest daughters who have never been naturals but
try, try, try

Also by Hallie Anne

Watford Sweethearts Series
Under Pink Skies
Sunny Skies Ahead
Through Stormy Skies

Keelbay Harbor Series
Coming in 2026

Anthologies
Love in Appalachia

Content Notes

Through Stormy Skies deals with heavy themes that might not be suitable for readers under the age of 18. There are conversations about pregnancy, pregnancy loss, grief, and narcissistic familial relationships. There are also discussions of domestic violence and spousal manipulation/verbal abuse (no graphic depictions).

This book also contains explicit sexual content, with a spice guide on the next page for those that would like to avoid—or find—the spice.

Spice Guide

When I first started writing the Watford Sweethearts series, my vision was for the series to be entirely closed door or fade to black. When I sat down to write this book, however, my intuition pulled me in a different direction.

As you'll soon find out, Cassie and Lucas's story is better for this. While this deviates from the spice levels in the first two books, I hope you feel these scenes add depth to Lucas and Cassie's story. I certainly do. That said, there are many reasons why people choose not to read open door scenes, and I will always be respectful of that.

Here's a list of spicy chapters:

- Chapter 16

- Chapter 21

- Chapter 26

- Chapter 28

All my love,
Hallie

Playlist

- Gethsemane – Sleep Token

- Midnight Rain – Taylor Swift

- Hey Jack – Priscilla Block

- Let It Happen – Gracie Abrams

- Fuck it I love you – Lana Del Rey

- 808 HYMN – Erin LeCount

- 19th Hour – Griff

- Is There Somewhere – Halsey

- illicit affairs – Taylor Swift

- Ass Back Home – Gym Class Heroes & Neon Hitch

- Provider – Sleep Token

- Sweet Fruit – Erin LeCount

- exile (feat. Bon Iver) – Taylor Swift

- Sober Sundays – The Castellows & Wyatt Flores

- The Answer – Chloe Ament

- Falling Like The Stars – James Arthur

- That's So True – Gracie Abrams

- East Side of Sorrow – Zach Bryan

- The Fate of Ophelia – Taylor Swift

Listen on Spotify

Two Months Ago

Seattle, Washington
18:30

Chapter 1
Cassie

I stared at my glass of red wine, sparkling under the house lights, trying to figure out how I'd gone from having everything I'd ever wanted to being entirely stripped of my dignity.

I watched as the man I was dating made yet another joke that had the blonde woman laughing.

I grabbed the glass and took a long sip, letting the bitter taste settle over my tongue. I wasn't typically a fan of red wine, but catching your boyfriend of two years cheating on you with the coworker he told you not to worry about warranted a tall glass of the most expensive red on the menu.

She moved closer to him, sliding along the seat until their thighs were touching. She inclined her head towards him, staring up at him with those baby-blue doe eyes, completely enraptured by his attention.

Maybe that was it.

Maybe it was my dedication to my job that pushed him away. I'd been slowly moving my way up the ranks at the law firm, working longer hours, taking more complicated cases. Helping more people.

Collin never understood why I loved law so much. Not that I'd tried all that hard to explain it to him. I'd sat there, hanging on his every word as he described his path to becoming a doctor, how much he'd wanted to help others.

But when it was my turn to talk about law, and how pivoting my career from criminal prosecution to divorce and family law had come after I'd watched my sister's life derail after her divorce, his eyes had glazed over, and he'd eagerly waved down a server and asked for the check.

The red flags had been there the entire time. I'd just been too desperate to feel like I was checking all the right boxes in life as I approached thirty.

And now, I was here, sitting in the restaurant we'd had our first date in, watching him kiss another woman. It was an hour before I was supposed to meet him here to celebrate our two-year anniversary.

Something in my gut had told me to show up early. Just to see.

I had become a master at ignoring my gut feelings. And now, I was paying the price.

"Can I get you anything else, miss?"

I turned to look at the server and gave him a small shake of my head.

"Just the check, please. I think I've had enough for tonight."

He inclined his head and scurried off again. I'd barely touched the salad, but it didn't matter: I'd already decided I'd call Lainey, my roommate, on the way home, and beg her to pick up Thai takeout from the place next door to our apartment building.

"Cassie," Collin said, eyes wide with surprise. He instinctively shoved the woman away from him. She scowled at him before turning to glare at me, and I watched with no small amount of satisfaction as the blood drained from her face.

"Hi Cassidy," I said, giving the woman I'd once called a friend a smile. "You look lovely tonight."

Cassidy at least had the sense to look guilty. She met my eyes for only a second before looking down at the table. My grandmother used to tell me to kill them with kindness, and I had every intention of doing that tonight.

I'd already given too much of my time and energy to this man-child.

"If you hadn't already guessed," I said, smoothing down the fabric of my red dress and willing my fingers not to tremble, "it's over. I'll mail back your things. I don't want to talk to you or see your face ever again. I really hope you both find what you're looking for. You deserve each other."

Collin stood to follow me out the door, but I whirled to face him.

"You disgust me," I sneered. "I gave you everything, every ounce of my attention and energy. You are despicable. It takes a special asshole to book a date with his mistress at the same restaurant that you'd booked a date to celebrate your anniversary at. *On the same night.*"

"Are you going to tell the hospital?"

The words stung like a physical slap. Of course he didn't care about me, or how all of this would make me feel. He was concerned only with his image. With the amount of dirt I had on him, the hospital would have no choice but to fire him.

"No," I said, squaring my shoulders and readjusting my dress. "You're not worth the effort."

And with that, I walked out of the restaurant with my head held high. I let myself slump forward only when the chilly Seattle air stung my lungs. I sat down on a bench outside the restaurant, taking in gulps of air to calm my racing heart.

God help me, it still hurt.

Even though I'd distanced myself in the last three months because I knew what he was doing. Even though I'd tried to wait it out, to see if eventually he'd wake up and come back to me. To see if things could go back to the way they were that first year I lived in Seattle, where everything was bright and exciting.

I'd acted like a naïve child with no life experience. I'd broken all of my own rules and trusted a man who didn't deserve a second of my time.

I pulled out my phone with shaking hands and dialed my roommate's number.

"Hey Cass, how did—"

"Are you doing anything tonight?" I said, the words tumbling out in a rush. "It's over."

I didn't need to explain the statement. Lainey let out a long sigh.

"Thank God," she muttered. "Are we going out?"

I smiled as she read my mind.

"I know you're supposed to be fasting from bar-hopping, but I think tonight calls for it."

"Hell yes, it does," Lainey said, and I heard the rustling of clothes in the background. "Meet you at Rain's in thirty?"

"I'm already on the way."

Chapter 2

Lucas

I was back in the hellhole that was Seattle, Washington, for the second time in a week.

My most closely guarded secret was that I didn't like Washington as a state. It was far too rainy and dreary for me. I'd grown up on the sunny east coast, and when I'd gotten stationed on the west coast after my unit restructured, I might have had a minor panic attack. Or twelve.

I didn't want to be here at all, much less under the circumstances. My ex-wife had tried to duck yet another legal move made by my lawyer to move the needle forward on this divorce.

It had been two years of fighting tooth and nail to separate myself from her.

Two years of having my life torn open and examined, all of my jagged edges exposed and investigated under a microscope.

I was grateful to my lawyer, Matthias, for being my rock through the process. He was trying every trick in the book, despite her best efforts to circumvent things. I'd given over every text message, email, photo, and bank statement I had to him. I had documentation of every single shitty thing she'd done to me, to where I didn't understand why there was any room for argument about who was the true victim here.

I was sitting in my favorite Seattle bar, my fingers drumming along the shiny lacquered wood as I waited for word from Matthias. Matthias was currently assembling another divorce package, attempting to satisfy her demands while also ensuring I didn't lose everything I owned or, even worse, have to pay spousal support.

The only thing I'd asked to keep was my truck. She could have the rest of it. I didn't want a damn thing from her. The only thing I wanted to do was keep the truck I'd bought with my hard-earned money, and for her to leave me the fuck alone for the rest of my life.

"Rough day?"

I looked up and smiled at the familiar face.

"Hey, Kiley," I said. "It's always a rough day when I'm in this city."

Kiley snorted and set about refilling my whiskey glass.

"Hadn't seen you in a while though," she said, sliding the fresh glass towards me. I took it gratefully, taking a small sip and relishing the familiar burn.

"I'd thought last time might be the last trip, but alas, I'm still fighting the good fight."

Kiley knew enough about my situation without many of the finer details. She and her girlfriend owned Rain's, a small corner bar tucked into one of the refurbished retail spaces that lined the Seattle streets.

Rain's had become a sort of home for me here. A place that I knew I was welcome at.

"Sorry to hear it's not better news," Kiley said, giving me a soft smile. The bell above the door chimed, signaling new patrons, and I turned my attention back to my phone. Matthias's contact finally appeared on my screen, and I eagerly swiped accept on the call.

"Hey Lucas," Matthias answered. He sounded exhausted, and my heart sank.

"Hey man," I said, taking another sip of whiskey to calm my nerves. "How did it go?"

Matthias sighed. "I sent the package off to her lawyer again, but I didn't change much. She really wants that damn spousal support. She finally stopped asking for the truck, though, so that's a step in the right direction."

I gripped the phone tighter. "She took everything from me. How can the court still be debating whether she deserves spousal support?"

"I have a theory, but speaking that theory aloud would get me fired nine ways from Sunday."

I had a sinking suspicion I knew exactly what that theory was, and I understood his hesitation.

"Okay," I said. "So we're back to waiting?"

"Unfortunately," Matthias sighed. "Last time we waited three weeks to hear a response, and I doubt she's in any rush to get back to us."

I sighed and rubbed a hand down my face. "I really appreciate your work on this."

"I'm sorry I can't speed the process up," Matthias said. "You're a good guy, Lucas. We're going to figure this out. I'm not stopping until we get you free of this woman for good."

"That means a lot," I replied, my throat tight. "Get some

rest this weekend. You've earned it."

Matthias laughed before ending the call, and I put my phone down on the table. A few seconds later, it buzzed with a new text message notification.

Kameron Miller

> When are you coming back??

> I miss you :(

Imogen Phillips

> Ignore him, he's stressed and loopy. Have fun. But not too much fun.

> Promise you'll be here on time for the presentations tomorrow?

Me

> Pinky promise.

Imogen Phillips

> <3

> I meant what I said earlier. BEHAVE.

Me

> I always do.

I looked up from my phone then, downing the rest of my whiskey in one go. It was my second of the evening, and I was already feeling the pleasant buzz of it.

I didn't drink in Watford out of respect for my two closest friends, both of whom were sober. I didn't need to drink to have a good time or even unwind, but it was nice to have a drink every once in a while.

Yet another reason I loved coming to Rain's: sure, it was technically a bar, but they had an elaborate mocktail menu, and never encouraged their patrons to drink alcohol if they didn't want to.

My gaze swept down the bar, snagging on the woman occupying the last seat.

It was her brown eyes that caught my attention first.

God, she was stunning. High cheekbones, tan brown skin, straightened black hair that rested just above her shoulders, and red lipstick that finally made me look away before she clocked me for ogling her. Red lipstick was my freaking kryptonite, and paired with that red dress she was wearing...

That was a revenge dress if I'd ever seen one.

I stopped myself, shaking my head to clear that line of thought from my head. I reminded myself that she had looked completely defeated and crestfallen in the seconds before I'd started staring at her like a damn creep. She was clearly going through something, and the last thing I needed to do was get myself entangled with someone when I wasn't in Seattle regularly.

"You're staring."

I whipped my head towards Priya, Kiley's girlfriend, who entered the bar from the backroom with a tray full of freshly washed shot glasses in hand.

"I *was* staring," I corrected. "I stopped."

"She's off limits," Priya said, waggling a finger in my face. "Her boyfriend might be an asshole, but he's still her boyfriend."

I let out a small breath. Of course, she had a boyfriend.

Though, based on the way she began angrily tapping away on her phone, my theory about the revenge dress stood.

"Do you want wings?" Priya said. "We only have enough for three more orders, so tell me now before we sell out and I have to deal with you giving me the sad puppy-dog eyes."

"Yes, please," I said, enunciating the word please. "You're my hero."

"Noted," she called over her shoulder as she strolled down the bar to speak to the mystery woman and the patron next to her. I shook my head and focused my attention on the TV screen on the other side of the bar. Two random NBA teams I didn't care about were playing, but at least it was something other than doom scrolling on my phone.

"I stand corrected," Priya said ten minutes later, sliding the basket of wings towards me. My mouth watered at the smell of buffalo sauce and crispy chicken. "They broke up. Apparently, he cheated on her."

I choked on my sip of water. "Do you normally divulge this level of personal information about your customers? Makes me wonder what you might have told people about me."

Priya rolled her eyes affectionately. "I don't enjoy seeing sad and mopey people in here."

"You own a bar. Isn't that your ideal client?"

Priya snorted and said, "Hardly. I much prefer it when people are happy and excited. They tell the interesting stories. We actually have a wall of couples who have met here over the years."

She jerked a thumb over her shoulder to point at a small corkboard full of a dozen Polaroid portraits. I smiled.

"I'd always wondered who they were," I said. "You guys have built an amazing place here, Priya."

Kiley came over and planted a kiss on Priya's cheek. "We're pretty proud of it."

My gaze lingered once more on the wall of Polaroid pictures, and I bit the inside of my cheek.

I could have fun, right? Fun was allowed.

I'd banned myself from fun after all the partying I did on active duty. I'd stopped going to bars when I started working at Winding Road, a nonprofit run by my two best friends, and put myself on the straight and narrow. I'd adjusted to civilian life as best I could, even if deep down I wasn't sure civilian life was what I wanted.

Screw it.

I picked up my steaming hot basket of wings and my half-drunk glass of whiskey, strolled down the bar, and took the unoccupied seat next to the mystery woman in red.

"Hi," I said. Already off to a great start. The woman looked at me, the wings, and then back to my face before narrowing her eyes.

"Did you hear me berate Kiley for giving away the last orders of wings without telling me?"

My eyebrows raised. Not what I had expected her to say, but I could roll with that.

"I didn't, but I guess tonight's your lucky night."

I wanted to bury myself alive.

I *needed* to get out more.

Being around happily committed men had drained my

ability to flirt successfully.

I was surprised to see a teasing gleam in her eyes when she scoffed. Maybe I wasn't as off my game as I thought.

"How do I know you're not a serial killer?"

"He's not," Priya's voice had me damn near jumping out of my skin as I turned to face the bartender, who was dipping the rim of a margarita glass into salt. "I wouldn't have let him talk to you if he was."

"You don't *let* me do anything."

"In my bar, I do."

I rolled my eyes affectionately.

"Thank you for looking out, Priya. We're fine here."

I could have sworn Priya bit the inside of her cheek to keep from smiling, but she turned away from me before I could call her out on it.

"So, you brought these over here to share?" the woman said, eyeing my basket of wings and fries.

"Have at it," I said. "I'm Lucas, by the way."

"I'm Cass," she said, reaching for a wing. She moaned as she took a bite. I averted my eyes quickly, knowing my mind was already in the gutter. I signaled to Kiley for one more round of whiskey. One more drink would get me to the buzzed, chilled-out place where I'd still be ready for my morning run after enjoying a beautiful night out.

A night out that I was suddenly hoping ended with this woman's number in my phone.

Present Day

Watford, Washington

Chapter 3
Lucas

After Imogen sold the farmhouse, we moved our weekly Wednesday night dinners to Winding Road. Connor and Abbie were still on the hunt for a little slice of Watford County to call their own, so the farmhouse was the next best place to host it.

I stood in the farmhouse kitchen, contemplating my beverage options. Finally opting for a non-alcoholic beer, I strode over to the fridge and pulled one out, cracking it open with the bottle opener Kam had installed on the side of the cabinet. It was a running joke among the three of us that we even had a bottle opener in the house, given that Kam and Connor were both sober, and I didn't drink in their presence.

I drank little at all, but if I did, I waited until I was in Seattle, or at a bar in one of the nearby towns. My best friends had been sober for years, and I would not be the asshole who drank around people who had clawed their way to sobriety.

Bass, Kameron and Imogen's dog, came bounding through the back door, dashing through his dog door like he was being chased by a wolf.

"Damn," I cursed as he ran through my legs right as I was taking a sip of my drink. "Bass, *dude*, you've got to chill out."

Kameron stepped through the back door a few seconds later, brushing his boots off before bending down to loosen the laces.

"Everything good?" I asked, leaning back against the counter. Kameron kicked his boots off and stretched his back.

"Yup," Kameron said. "Memphis is a little restless tonight."

I nodded. "Yeah. He's been more anxious than usual this week. I'm wondering if he got spooked by something in the pasture this week."

"Who knows," Kameron said, flopping down on the couch with a loud groan.

"You're young to have the full spectrum of blue collar back problems, aren't you?"

"Shut up," Kameron said. "I spent the last year of my Marine Corps career picking up your slack. That's a heavy load to carry."

I scoffed, dropping onto the couch opposite him. Kam splayed his legs wide, draped his head against the couch, and shut his eyes.

"You're funny, Miller," I said. "I could kick your ass then, and I could definitely do it now."

"I'd like to see that," Connor's voice boomed from the bottom of the farmhouse stairs. He ran a towel through his long blond hair, shaking it out as he walked towards us. Connor had grown his hair out again after cutting it to be in dress uniform regulation so he could wear his blues at his and Abbie's wedding.

"It'll be a chilly day in hell before I take this kid to the mat again," Kameron said, eyes still closed. The fucker could probably fall asleep right now if he wanted to.

"Who are you calling kid?" I said, looking over my shoulder. "I don't see any children in the vicinity."

Connor chuckled as he draped the towel over the back of the couch I was currently occupying, making a beeline for the fridge to grab a beverage of his own. He returned to the couch, and I chewed the inside of my cheek, trying to figure out how in the hell I was going to broach the subject that had been eating away at me for the last few weeks.

"What's going on?" Connor said, taking another sip of his drink.

I let out a long sigh and stood to my feet. I couldn't sit still during this conversation.

"I don't know if I'm done."

The words tumbled out before I could think better of it. I didn't expect either of them to understand. Both Kameron and Connor had established beautiful lives for themselves outside of the Marine Corps.

"What do you mean?"

"With the military," I said. "I don't know if I'm done."

"You want to re-enlist?"

I swallowed tightly. The word unsettled me. It brought too many feelings to the surface. A nausea-inducing cocktail of excitement and anxiety.

"It's on the table," I said, turning back towards the living room, where I suddenly had two pairs of curious eyes on me. I was grateful neither of them had a judgmental bone in their bodies when it came to big life decisions.

My blood family was a shitshow, and had been since my divorce, but these guys had become family without me even realizing it.

"Can I ask why?" Connor said, holding my gaze. I pressed my lips into a line.

"When I left the military, I was at my lowest point. I was exhausted by all the fighting: with my wife, with my squad leader. All I wanted was to be done with it. I wanted out."

"But you weren't done," Kameron said, and I saw the understanding in his eyes.

"The Marine Corps fucking sucks sometimes," I said, gesturing to the three of us. "We all know that. But it also gave me a sense of direction that I haven't been able to find sense. No offense to either of you. You know I love Winding Road and everything you do here. I'm certainly better off for having been part of it."

Kameron shook his head. "You don't have to justify your feelings to either of us. This is our passion; that doesn't mean it has to be yours."

"I'm fucking terrified," I said bluntly. If we were baring our feelings tonight, I might as well lay all my cards out on the table. "I'm terrified to go through the process of getting back in, only to hate it and want out again."

"Well, if you re-enlist, you'd be contractually obligated. That's the good part," Connor said. Kameron reached forward across the couch and smacked him gently on the arm. I chuckled.

"Some of us do better in that kind of environment, Harvey."

Connor rolled his eyes, but some of the tension eased

from his shoulders as he smiled at me.

"I think you've been floundering for a long time," Connor said. "Neither of us wanted to push you, but you've never been happy here. Not in the way it matters. If being back on the Marine Corps' roster will bring back that Morales spark we all know and love, then I'll want you to do it."

"In the same thread," Kameron said, looking from Connor to me, "if the only reason you're considering joining the military again is because you don't know how to navigate civilian life, you have options."

Connor nodded.

"He's right. Re-enlisting because you feel in your gut like that's where you need to be is one thing. Re-enlisting because you don't know what the hell else to do means you need to go to therapy."

I barked out a laugh and took another swig of my beer.

"I should probably clarify that I'm not planning to go back to active duty. I don't think I could stomach another four years at Camp Pendleton." A shudder crawled down my spine. "I am *not* a California boy."

Kameron laughed. "No, you are not. You've barely acclimated to life on the West Coast."

He was right. I'd grown to love the specific region of Washington State where Winding Road was located.

The rest of the West Coast could kick rocks.

In a nice, loving way.

"So, reserves?" Connor said, raising an eyebrow. I stared out the kitchen window, smiling faintly when I saw Abbie and Imogen returning from their evening walk. Abbie was cackling at something Imogen had said, and Imogen's entire body lit up at the sound. Imogen waved her hands animatedly, clearly in the middle of retelling a story that Abbie found drop-dead hilarious.

"Yeah," I said, swallowing back the emotion suddenly clogging my throat. "I want to be here as much as I can. I think I also just need something for me, you know? Because my personal life was in shambles, I left active duty, hoping for peace."

I polished off the beer and rubbed a hand down my face. I set the bottle down, turning to face my two best friends, who were both looking at me with curious expressions.

"I don't know. I haven't made any decisions yet. I have a meeting with a prior service recruiter this week, though."

Kameron nodded his head. "It never hurts to talk to them."

Connor rolled his eyes. "Spoken like someone who would have gone the recruiter route for his B billet."

Kameron playfully punched him on the shoulder. "Shut up."

Feminine giggles filtered into the living room as Imogen and Abbie stepped through the front door. Their cheeks were both tinged red, hair tousled gently around their faces from the wind. Abbie made a beeline for Connor at the same time as Imogen reached for Kam.

What did I do? I checked my damn text messages for the twentieth time that day.

It had been weeks since that night in Seattle. Weeks since I'd stayed awake until five a.m. with a woman I hadn't been able to get out of my head. I replayed moments from that night while I was doing my ranch hand work, exercising the horses, and supervising the farm machinery in the crop fields.

My mind was a dangerous place these days, because she was there.

I'd given her my number hoping she'd use it.

So far, I'd come up short.

"What board game are we playing tonight?" Abbie said, leaning back against Connor. He wrapped his arms around her waist, his hands gently caressing her baby bump. She was showing now, and I swore I'd never seen Connor wear his emotions on his sleeve as much as he had in the weeks since they'd confirmed what most of us had suspected.

I looked away. I normally didn't mind being the forever third wheel when it came to my best friends and the love they'd found.

Since Kam and Im had finally stopped dancing around the thing between them and Abbie and Connor had found out they were expecting, I was well past the point of being the third wheel.

I was just a spare, hovering awkwardly in the corner.

"Not *Catan*," Kameron jumped in. "I don't feel like having my ass handed to me tonight."

"*Risk*, then?" I offered. Every single person in the room groaned loudly.

"Absolutely not," Connor hissed. "You don't play the game right."

"What?" I said, affronted. "The whole point of the game is world domination."

"You can't just hide out in Australia and make it an impenetrable fortress," Imogen said, shaking her head. "When we get to the end, it's boring because you don't attack, and anyone who tries to invade you meets instant death."

I shrugged my shoulders. "Sounds like a personal problem."

The conversation devolved further until we finally settled on *Texas Hold Em* instead of a board game—without betting, because that was a level of stress nobody needed tonight.

I looked around the room and shoved away the pang in my chest at the thought of the childhood game nights I'd shared with my family.

Those days were long gone now. I'd made a new life for myself.

But damn if it didn't still sting.

Chapter 4
Cassie

I steeled my shoulders as I stared at the sign for Watford General.

You can do this.

I'd gone to law school, for God's sake. I passed the bar exam on the first try. I'd gotten an elite internship at one of the most renowned law firms in Seattle. I'd weathered far more harrowing storms than this.

And yet, I found myself immobilized on the sidewalk, unable to move.

Purchasing a one-way ticket to Watford and quitting my job in Seattle felt like a good idea at the time.

Several people whispered as they passed by, and I let out a long breath. I'd barely had time to pack the essentials, and changing out of my blouse and slacks had seemed like a waste of time. Unfortunately, in my haste to get the hell out, I'd neglected forethought. My outfit made me stick out like a sore thumb. In a town like Watford, business casual wasn't common attire.

After another moment of indecision, I walked in.

I was struck by how little Watford General had changed in the years since I'd left town. Exposed wooden beams and that gorgeous wooden counter that held the cash register and bags.

And then I was stunned by the image of Abbie Collins hunched over the counter, examining something on her clipboard.

She'd grown up so much. The last time I'd seen her, she was a teenager, the same age as Imogen, but now a woman stood before me.

She looked up. Her eyes went wide as she took in my suitcase and business attire.

I'd never felt more out of place in a town I'd once called my home.

"Hey, Abbie," I said awkwardly.

Off to a stellar start.

"Cassie?" Abbie said, shock still written on her face. "You're—it's so good to see you."

Abbie ran over and enveloped me in a crushing hug. I let out a sound of surprise but hugged her back. Of all the reactions I'd expected, a hug wasn't on the list.

Maybe this was why I'd come to Watford General first. Abbie was the least likely of anyone in town to react poorly to my return. My body seemed to know that before my mind did.

"I thought you lived in Seattle?"

"I do," I said, stepping out of the hug. "I'm just, uh, in between jobs at the moment. And boyfriends."

This conversation was quickly going off the rails.

Abbie raised her eyebrows. "So you're back in Watford because..."

I swallowed audibly, trying to clear the emotion from my

throat. Honesty was always the best policy, and I'd have to share a hell of a lot more in the coming weeks if I expected to put my life back together.

"Hey Abbie, I just finished inventory. I'm going to—"

My eyes snapped to the storeroom entrance, and my heart dropped into my stomach as I stared at my brother.

Kevin. My eccentric, sweet, hilarious brother.

"Hey," I said weakly.

Kevin just stared at me, the confusion clearing from his face, replaced with anger.

"I'm going to Blackbeard's to see Kyrie on her lunch break," Kevin said, looking from me to Abbie, who nodded.

"Sure," Abbie said. "I'll be here for the rest of the afternoon."

Kevin nodded, grabbed his hoodie from the hook next to the checkout counter, and walked right past me.

I closed my eyes and inhaled deeply.

I'd expected that kind of reaction from Imogen. But somewhere along the way I'd convinced myself that Kevin might come around earlier.

But the anger on his face told a very different story. I'd hurt both of my siblings in ways I was only just now wrestling with.

It was foolish of me to think either of them would respond well to my sudden reappearance in their lives.

Abbie looked at me with an unsure expression, pressing her thumb to her bottom lip as she waited for me to answer her question.

"I'm here because my life is falling apart, and I didn't know where else to go."

Abbie's features softened as if she knew exactly what I meant.

"Well, believe it or not, this is a great place to figure your life out."

I wanted to ask about Imogen. I needed to know how she was. We hadn't spoken for months. The last time we'd spoken on the phone, she'd told me she never wanted to talk to me again. Her words had cut deeper than I thought possible, and I didn't know how to approach her.

I couldn't find the words to explain to her that I had always prioritized the wrong things, and I didn't realize it until it was too late.

I'd put my energy into everything that was wrong for me, and didn't reserve a scrap of it for the things that truly mattered.

Like taking care of her and Kevin.

I was their big sister. The one person in the world who was supposed to look after them. And I abandoned them because I couldn't deal with my shit.

"I'm glad to see you, Cassie, but I have to ask: does Imogen know you're here?"

I winced.

"She doesn't," I murmured. "I'm sorry. I know this is putting you in a bad spot."

"Oh man," Abbie said, pinching the bridge of her nose. "She's going to *kill* me for this."

"For what?"

Abbie returned to her place behind the cash register, drumming her fingers along the counter. Her beautiful wedding ring sparkled in the late afternoon light trickling in through the window, and my gut twisted painfully. I hadn't been there for her wedding, even though I'd been invited. I'd been too damn excited about my new job, and too scared about the possibility of returning to Watford to show up for her.

Now, I was here, and that new job I'd been so excited about had crashed and burned.

"Do you have a place to stay tonight?"

I shook my head. "Truthfully, I hopped on a train first thing this morning and didn't look back. I'd been visiting my roommate's family on the East Coast and had recently returned to Seattle, but I just... I couldn't do it. I've had a horrendous few weeks, so I packed up what I needed, bought a ticket, and just left."

"Wow," Abbie said. "That's... not like you."

My laugh was borderline hysterical. "No, it's not like me at all."

I was drowning, and it was entirely my fault.

"I'm sensing that there's more to the story here," Abbie said, "but you can spend the night at my place."

"Abbie, I couldn't—"

"It's okay," Abbie said, waving a hand noncommittally. "Connor is at Winding Road until tomorrow afternoon finishing up their cohort, so it'll be just you and me."

I swallowed down the emotion swelling in my throat. I didn't know what Winding Road was, but if Connor and Imogen were involved, I knew it was a good place to be.

Everything Imogen touched was golden. It was her superpower in every way that mattered—something I didn't know I'd ever stop being jealous of.

"That's very generous of you."
Abbie smiled gently.
"It's good to see you, Cassie. Welcome home."
Home.
I was *home*.

Chapter 5
Cassie

Fresh coffee and frying ham greeted me the next morning. I emerged from Abbie's guest bedroom in a pair of sweatpants and my favorite college hoodie. I avoided Abbie's hallway mirror because I already knew I looked like hell. A visual reminder wasn't needed.

"Good morning," Abbie said with a yawn. "Did you sleep well?"

"Yes, thank you. I don't think I've ever slept on a mattress that soft."

Abbie's laugh made me smile, too. "Isn't it amazing? We upgraded the mattress in the guest bedroom while my father was recovering from his accident, and I'm jealous. When Connor and I got married, we decided the first upgrade we'd make when we moved into our own place was getting a mattress from the same brand."

My stomach twisted with guilt as I gave her an apologetic smile.

"I'm really sorry I couldn't make it to your wedding," I mumbled. Abbie shrugged.

"It's okay," Abbie said. "I appreciated the gift you sent."

"Did you tell Imogen?"

Abbie shot me a wry smile that told me I was veering into dangerous territory.

"I didn't tell her it was from you."

I let out a sigh of relief. The last thing I wanted was Imogen thinking I was trying to buy my way back into their lives.

"We need to talk about Imogen, though," Abbie said. "I was happy to let you hide out here after a long day of traveling, but I'm kicking you out today when Connor gets back."

I bit the inside of my cheek. "Thank you for letting me crash here last night."

"What are you doing here, Cassie?" Abbie said, handing me a steaming mug of coffee. Black with two sugars, exactly the way I liked it. I couldn't believe she'd remembered such an insignificant detail, especially when we hadn't been close by any stretch of the imagination.

"I quit my job," I said. Abbie blinked twice.

"You quit your job?" She asked, as if the two things were incongruous with each other.

"Shocking, I know."

"But you were always so... type A."

I cocked my head to the side, and Abbie let out a small laugh.

"Not that being type A is a bad thing. The Cassie we knew growing up was the straightest arrow in town. Did something happen?"

"I caught my boyfriend cheating on me with my coworker," I said. Abbie's face morphed into a shocked expression.

"It's been a couple of weeks since that night, and I tried

going back to the office, but I couldn't do it. I couldn't sit there and work on divorce cases knowing the girl who smiled and greeted me every morning while actively sleeping with my boyfriend at night was just a few cubicles down from me."

Abbie let out a low whistle. "That's screwed up."

"It is. So I told my boss I was done. She was disappointed in me, but it was for the best. I couldn't focus on my clients or their cases without being distracted. They deserve a lawyer who can focus entirely on their needs."

"That's mature of you," Abbie said.

I shrugged and took a sip of my coffee. "I'm trying to do the right thing."

It was the only defense I had at this point. I had always wanted to do the right thing. *Always.*

I just really sucked at it most of the time.

"Speaking of doing the right thing," Abbie said. "I called Imogen."

I sat up straighter, my heart lurching into my throat.

"She's coming here?"

"She'll be here in an hour," Abbie said. "You don't have to be scared of how she'll react."

"She told you what happened the last time we talked, right?"

I never want to hear from you again.

My skin crawled at the memory, and I hated myself all over again. I hadn't warned Imogen that there was a good chance our mother was going to attempt to weasel her way back into her children's good graces.

I'd been too scared of the fallout of cutting my mother off

completely to stop for five seconds and understand how deeply those wounds ran in Imogen.

It was just one more notch in the very long "Cassie is a selfish bitch" post I'd been carving my entire life.

"Yes," Abbie said. "Imogen was working through a lot of crap when she said that. It doesn't excuse her treatment of you. But trust me when I say Imogen wants a relationship with you."

"I doubt that," I said.

I wasn't naïve enough to expect my sister—the one person in life I should have protected with my life—to accept me back with open arms after I'd turned away from our mother's treatment of her.

"You'll also meet Kameron today," Abbie said.

"Who is Kameron?"

Abbie gave me a wistful smile, and my stomach flipped.

"Her boyfriend?" I guessed.

"What's the word for a boyfriend who is more like a husband but they're never going to get married because that's not what they want, but they're head over heels for each other and would do anything to see the other person smile?"

My jaw practically hit the table. Imogen had found some-one. Not that I'd ever doubted her ability to do so. I was just grateful, and so damn happy that she'd found someone who treated her right after the disaster that was her marriage to her ex-husband.

For what felt like the millionth time that day, I shoved my feelings down into the deep recesses of my heart I kept under lock and key.

"Seriously?" was the best response I had.

"Seriously," Abbie said, that lovey-dovey grin returning to her face. "They're adorable together."

"So much has changed," I said, rubbing my temples. "It feels like my head is going to explode."

"So, now is also a good time to tell you I'm pregnant?"

My eyes shot up to hers. I couldn't stop a wide smile from splitting my face.

"Oh my God," I said, my voice choked with a sudden emotion I couldn't name. "Congratulations, Abbie. That's wonderful."

Abbie's eyes welled with tears as she rubbed a hand over her belly. Something in my heart cracked at the sight.

"I'm so happy for both of you. If anyone deserves this, it's the two of you."

Abbie smiled and picked up her coffee mug again. She gestured towards me.

"Change—even unexpected change—can be a good thing. Scary. Terrifying. But good."

My stomach clenched with a fresh wave of anxiety.

"I hope you're right," I replied. "I really, really hope you're right."

Because God knows I needed a change. I'd been running my entire life. From my feelings, and my siblings. It was what I was best at.

The constant bait and switch, giving the people in my life just enough information that kept their insatiable appetites fed.

Imogen and Kevin weren't on the lists of parasites in my life. They had never been.

But it was so much easier to navigate life when they hated me. The door to my relationship to both of them had been left halfway adjacent in the years since I went to college: a door propped open far enough that someone could peek inside, but not wide enough that someone could look inside and see what was happening.

I preferred things that way. I wanted people at arm's distance.

Life was so much fucking easier without all the emotional attachment that came with family and close friends.

Unfortunately, life was also lukewarm and miserable without the said attachment.

Yet another reason I was in my current predicament.

"I'm going to run down to the store and check on Kyrie before Connor gets here," Abbie said. Her voice jarred me from my thoughts—that self-destructive spiral I knew all too well. "She's learning the ropes. If Kevin's there, I'll let him know you're here?"

She made it sound like she was asking, but I knew I couldn't ask her to keep my visit a secret. Abbie had already done more for me than I expected anyone to do upon my sudden arrival.

"Yeah, you can let him know," I said. "I'm going to hop in the shower right quick. You said they'll be here in an hour?"

"Probably closer to 45 minutes now," Abbie said after a brief glance at her watch, and I nodded.

45 minutes to get my shit together.

45 minutes until I saw my sister again.

45 minutes to figure out how in the fucking world I was going to apologize and explain things to her.

I quickly realized that even if given all the time in the world, I'd never come up with a way to apologize for how badly I had hurt my sister.

I paced in front of the couch when the door opened. Abbie reappeared from the hallway, squealing with delight when Connor came through the threshold. She practically sprinted into his arms, wrapping him in a full-body hug. I watched as he visibly relaxed the second she was back in his arms, burying his face into her neck and smiling wildly when he pulled away. Abbie grabbed his hand and excitedly pulled him towards the hallway, talking animatedly about a new idea for the nursery.

I watched them retreat, Connor briefly giving me a wave and a nod before the subtle click of a door closing had me bracing for whatever impact came next.

Imogen walked through the door next, followed closely by a tall, black-haired man with a neatly trimmed beard and a kind face.

Imogen was drop-dead gorgeous. Tan brown skin, stunning brown eyes, shoulder-length black curls. All features that mirrored mine. She had always been gorgeous, even when we were younger, but now that she was 200 pounds lighter after dropping her abusive husband, she was unstoppable.

Imogen stared at me, looking me up and down, trying to make sense of why the hell I'd suddenly reappeared. I opened my mouth to say something, *anything*, but quickly shut it when I realized I had nothing to say. Every thought had eddied from my mind.

"Hi," the man next to her said. "I'm Kameron."

He extended a hand to me, and I took it gratefully.

"I'm Cassie," I said, swallowing back the emotion forming in my throat. "It's nice to meet you."

"Likewise," Kameron said, and his smile was warm and welcoming. Genuine in a way that momentarily unnerved me. He was everything Jacob hadn't been. Whereas Imogen's ex-husband had been all harsh words and hard lines, Kameron was grounded and unwavering.

I could see why Imogen was drawn to him—and I was grateful to see she now had someone in her life who was going to care for her and cherish her the way she deserved to be.

Imogen continued to stare at me. Her brown eyes, so similar to my own, gave nothing away. Kameron turned to whisper in Imogen's ear, and her narrowed eyes didn't waver once.

I swore I heard him say, "It's rude to stare." I shifted my weight to my other foot. Imogen sighed loudly.

"Hi," she finally said. "It's good to see you."

I wanted to tell her she didn't have to lie, but I knew just how thin the ice I stood on was. If I so much as blinked at her wrong, she'd bolt, and any hope I had of salvaging the broken pieces of our relationship would be futile.

"It's good to see you too," I said, giving her a small smile. "You look beautiful. And it's so nice to meet Kameron."

She nodded at me, the motion impractical and harsh. The jerky, unpolished movement was so unlike Imogen that I felt that familiar guilt threaten to pull me under.

Stay calm.

I had to keep my wits about me. Imogen unnerved me because I knew she saw past every layer of bullshit. She could flay me on the kitchen counter with a few words.

In less than three sentences, she could undo every single one of my walls, exposing me for the sham of a big sister I was without so much as a second thought.

But she didn't do any of that.

Her eyes remained fixed on me, assessing a threat, while she leaned back into Kameron's embrace. I didn't think she realized she was doing it, and the thought of her being comfortable enough with Kameron to let her guard down on that primal level made my heart swell.

I'd fucked up so many things in our relationship. In the early hours of the morning, when my insomnia and nostalgia choked me in equal measure, I often thought of every time I'd turned away from her, and every moment I should have opened up more.

Every time she'd come to me, I'd shut her out.

"Would you like to get breakfast with us, Cassie? We didn't eat before leaving Winding Road, and I have exactly—" he flipped his wrist over to check the time on his watch "—ten minutes to get this woman some food before she becomes an entirely different person."

Imogen let out a surprised squawk and batted his arm playfully, all while maintaining her scowl. I chuckled. There was an ease between the two of them that had made my heart ache.

I'd had that ease in my life exactly one time, with a man

I'd never see again.

Life was cruel like that.

"I'd love to. Let me grab my wallet."

I retreated to the guest room and grabbed my wallet and phone from the nightstand. I wasn't surprised to see two text messages from the one person I never wanted to talk to or see again.

Collin

Please don't act like this.

It was a mistake.

I bit my bottom lip so hard I thought I might draw blood.

I should have blocked his number a long time ago, but old habits died hard. This hadn't been the first text messages from Collin following our breakup, and I was certain they wouldn't be the last. The act of formally closing that chapter by blocking him was, evidently, a step I was unwilling to take.

The night I also met someone who had consumed more of my waking thoughts—and dreams—than I cared to admit.

There was only one phone number that burned a permanent hole in my notes app.

My night out with Lucas had been the most carefree fun I'd had in the years since I'd moved to Seattle. Lucas saw *me*, in a way that was so unfamiliar to me. He cut through my bullshit and defenses so fast that I was still coming to terms with it.

I shoved those thoughts to the side as I returned to the living room. There were many reasons I hadn't reached out to him.

Lucas was figuratively one in a million. The night we'd spent together was something most people would never experience.

I'd also never see him again.

I'd make my peace with that, eventually.

Kameron and Imogen were speaking in whispered tones. I'd recognize that familiar heat in Imogen's eyes anywhere. Imogen was *angry*. She felt cornered. I know she did, because this wasn't the first time I'd seen her like this. Kameron took her hand in his and smiled back towards me.

"Lead the way," I said, squaring my shoulders back.

I prepared for war the entire walk to the diner.

Chapter 6

Lucas

I stood in the one place I hoped I'd never stand again.

The familiar, highly propagandized posters lined the walls of the office. Multiple branches had recruiters stationed here. Brighton was the central city in this stretch of mountains, so it made sense that all the armed forces would have their main recruiting efforts housed here.

"Lucas?"

I looked up to find a sergeant in the classic short-sleeved Chucks combination.

Was I really about to do this?

I was.

I didn't say a word, instead nodding my head once as I stood to follow him into his office. This wasn't a typical recruiting office that focused on finding new people to indoctrinate into military life. This guy was the prior-service recruiter for the Watford County area.

"I see here that you served six years in the Corps right out of high school," Frye said, cocking an eyebrow in my direction. "What brings you to my doorstep? Just can't stay away?"

I let out a small laugh, shaking my head. "Something like

that."

He leaned forward, clearly intrigued.

"You're less than two years out from the end of your contract. I've seen guys coming running back to the Marine Corps, but it's typically years down the line, when they're going through a quarter-life crisis and want to fall back on the one constant they've ever had in their life."

"Is this whole interrogation strictly necessary to learn more about the process?"

In a strange way, this kind of banter was comforting. I loved Kameron and Connor to the death, and I'd forever have their back through whatever I could. But they had both found their strides in civilian life in a way I simply hadn't.

I couldn't find my stride in that way because I'd left my career unfinished. Kam and Connor might have accomplished everything they set out to do when they finished active duty, but I sure as hell hadn't. I'd fucking panicked when my enlistment was up.

I panicked and begged for the first available opportunity. This was my chance to fix my screw up.

"Nah," Frye said with a smirk. "Color me curious."

"Not really your business, is it?"

Frye shrugged off my obvious annoyance. "Not unless it impacts your ability to sign a contract."

A contract. *Fuck.*

"Let's talk about that," I said around the tight ball of emotion that had wedged itself in my throat. "I'm assuming I'm still eligible for enlistment?"

"Yep," Frye said, swiveling slightly in his chair to face his monitor as he pulled up my file. "Since it's been less than two years since you left active duty, you'd be eligible to re-enlist under a special program. They wouldn't make you redo boot camp."

I barked out a surprise laugh. "How generous."

Frye continued to scroll, tapping a few keys on his keyboard before slouching back in his chair. He rubbed his chin with his hand before gesturing to me.

"You're a prime candidate for re-enlistment. Is there a specific package you're after?"

"No," I said quickly. "A re-enlistment bonus would be nice, but..."

Now it was Frye's turn to laugh. "One of us."

He turned back to the computer, clicking through a few more pages.

"Do you want to change your MOS?"

Fuck, did I? I really hadn't thought this through. I'd spent six years doing the same job day in and day out. The notion that things had changed completely in the two years since I'd been active made my skin prickle.

I knew I needed to sort out my shit. This was supposed to just be a conversation with this guy. I wasn't supposed to have all the answers.

Hell, not having all the answers was exactly how I'd found myself in this position six years ago. Broke, alone, and with extremely limited options.

"No," I said, trusting my gut on this one. If this avenue required going to an entirely new MOS school and essentially starting from scratch, I didn't think that I was something I wanted.

"Alrighty," Frye said, the keys on his desktop keyboard clacking loudly. I rubbed idly at my jaw as he worked. My thoughts drifted somewhere they really shouldn't be.

I revisited that night way more than I could ever admit out loud to another person. It felt wrong to lust after a one-night stand on the level that I did.

Far too often, when my mind finally quieted to a dull pulse after a long day of farm work, my thoughts drifted to a girl with beautiful brown eyes and luscious dark hair that had felt angelic wrapped in my fist that night.

It really wasn't healthy. It also didn't stop me from checking my phone religiously, wondering if—when—Cass would finally give in and text me.

I also didn't feel great about lying to my closest friends. I'd been so damn close to spilling the beans to Kameron and Connor about my that night. I wanted to tell them that the two of us had stayed out the early morning because neither of us wanted the night to end.

What had started with playful flirtation in the bar had ended with both of us coming up with new activities to do together.

To draw the time out as long as possible.

It was only supposed to be one night.

So why couldn't I just move the fuck on with my life?

"Are you still married?"

Frye's question pulled me from my thoughts with such quickness I felt vaguely lightheaded.

"What?"

"Are you still married?" Frye repeated. "It says here that you're married to Mall—"

"I know her name," I said, my stomach tumbling. "We're getting a divorce."

Frye hummed in acknowledgement, presumably clicking a checkbox on his screen before moving onto the next one.

Divorce was not uncommon in military circles. The Marine Corps, despite having a larger-than-life reputation, was also a relatively small group of people. When you whittled down the statistic even further, focusing solely on infantry Marines like Connor, Kameron, and I—the statistical rate of divorce shot up drastically.

Long deployments, extended training, and inconsistent work days weren't exactly conducive to a happy home life.

That was certainly how it had been for Mallory and I. I'd been far too eager to get out of the barracks, and Mallory had been far too excited to get out of her hometown.

Our story was one that had been repeated tens of thousands of times since the Marine Corps' inception.

But I'd never expected our story to end with her wiping all our accounts and concocting a fictional story that would forever taint my career.

I shoved those thoughts away. If I ended up re-enlisting in the Marine Corps, it wouldn't be because of her.

Or in spite of her.

"I'm not seeing any negative paperwork or holds on your file," Frye said. "Are you wanting to go for max time and max incentive?"

I swallowed tightly. How much of my life was I willing to sign away to the military?

This wasn't something that was often talked about where I came from. Sure, there were plenty of people who used the military as a means to an end. I'd started out that way.

But the minute I'd set foot on those yellow footprints—for the whole three seconds I'd stood there—something had changed within me.

For the first time in my life, I wanted to be better. I'd wanted to succeed at something. I didn't just want to succeed—I wanted to be one of the best.

And I fucking accomplished that.

When all the shit had gone down with Mallory, it had been at the worst possible time. Mallory's deceit had coincided with the end of what was supposed to be my final deployment. I had fully planned on getting out of the military, of making a clean break, and of moving to wherever the two of us decided to go next.

It was a laughable notion now. But looking back, I would have moved us wherever Mallory wanted. If she told me to jump, I would've only asked how high.

I loved big, and I loved hard, despite what most people saw when they looked at me. There were a few people who knew the full story—Kameron, Connor, and Imogen were among them. But I kept that shit close to my chest for many reasons.

Namely, because Mallory and I's demise was a story that had become so twisted, layered with lies and deception with roots so deep, I wasn't sure I'd ever fully be free.

"I'd like to explore the reserves, too," I said, not knowing where exactly that came from. The nice thing about the military was that there was more than one way to serve. As much as I felt like my work in the USMC wasn't done, I also wasn't particularly keen on uprooting my entire life again.

Frye chuckled as he navigated to yet another screen. "Knew it."

I spent the next ten minutes reviewing the other qualifications I had to meet to be formally certified as eligible for re-enlistment.

When Frye stood up to shake my hand with a promise to call me with more details, I swallowed tightly.

Telling Kameron and Connor I was putting in my notice to go back to the one place the two of them swear they'd never go again would be a fun adventure.

Chapter 7
Cassie

W atley's Diner hadn't changed much, but out of all the establishments in Watford, this was the one place I'd expected to stay the same.

Red and white color-blocked booths and dazzling black and white portraits of Marilyn Monroe covered the wall space in between booths. The comforting smell of breakfast food frying made my stomach growl. It had been years since I'd had one of Lonnie Watley's world-renowned waffle creations, and I was suddenly craving it.

A waitress came by to grab our drink orders before retreating behind the bar counter. I turned my attention to Kameron and Imogen. Imogen was still staring at me in that accusing way that told me she felt ambushed. I had technically ambushed her, but since she blocked my number, I didn't have another way of warning her, anyway.

"So, how did you two meet?" I asked, taking a sip of my lemonade. Kameron turned towards Imogen, and his features softened. A small smile crept onto my face. He was completely smitten with her, and seeing it made my heart swell.

"Should you tell the story, or shall I?"

Imogen rolled her eyes, but there was no heat behind the gesture as she leaned into Kameron's side.

"Technically, we met through Connor and Abbie. We're the best friends who fell in love with each other after swearing we wouldn't. I started working at Kameron's non-profit while working through selling the farmhouse last year."

Something sharp and acidic sliced through me.

"You sold the farmhouse?"

Imogen bit her bottom lip.

"Yeah. I did."

Fuck. That shouldn't have stung the way it did. It's not like I'd bothered to come back to Watford. I'd begged my grandmother to leave the house to Imogen instead. She'd wanted it to go to me, and I'd turned her down: I knew I was leaving Watford. I'd never wanted to stay here. But Imogen...

Imogen had the creative drive to turn the farmhouse into something beautiful. She could build on our Nana's legacy. And she had.

I think deep down our grandmother harbored this idea that the three of us would find our way back to each other, that somehow the farmhouse might become a beacon of hope, a center point for our reconnection despite our chaotic childhoods.

Things didn't shape up that way.

"I'm sure that was hard for you."

Imogen's jaw twitched. Kameron threw an arm over the booth behind her, feigning a stretch. It was a casual gesture, but I caught the meaning fully.

I could practically see Imogen reinforcing the walls around her mind and heart. I'd made so many damn mistakes when it came to being a big sister.

"It was the right decision," Imogen said, crossing her arms over her chest as she continued staring at me.

"I don't doubt that," I said. I was so far out of my depth with this conversation. "Sorry if that came off harsh. I'm just surprised."

"By what? The fact that things are different?" Imogen scoffed. "Jesus Christ, Cassie. You can't just waltz back into town and expect things to be the same as they were when you left. Things are different now. We're different now."

"I know," I said, wincing. "I saw Kevin—"

"Kevin wants nothing to do with you."

The words landed like a punch to the gut. My insides twisted painfully as oily shame slid through my veins. Coming back to Watford had been a colossal mistake.

None of us were ready for this. I thought maybe time and distance might soften us all somehow. I'd been wrong.

So fucking wrong.

I didn't have anywhere else to go now, though. I'd have to make my peace with that somehow.

"Imogen, I'm not expecting that things are going to be weird or awkward. They already are. But there's nothing waiting for me in Seattle anymore, and I—"

"Wait, what?" Imogen narrowed her eyes. "You quit your job?"

My cheeks heated. Imogen had never been one to pull her punches. She was like a heat-seeking missile when it came to people's insecurities sometimes: it's like she could sense when there was already blood in the water, and she pounced hard and fast.

"I might have quit my job, yes," I said, taking another sip of my drink. Kameron still sat there stone-faced. Still assessing whether the big sister was as awful as Imogen said I was.

I wouldn't blame the man for not trusting me. But no one, not even Imogen, hated me for my past actions as much as I hated myself.

I didn't know Kameron's backstory, but it was obvious he was protective over Imogen, even though he also clearly understood that she didn't need protecting.

Imogen's laugh surprised both of us. Kameron's eyebrows hit his hairline, and the heat in my cheeks reached a fever pitch.

"Im," Kameron said gently, his fingers delicately tracing a circle over her bare shoulder.

"I'm sorry," Imogen managed to get out in between gasping laughs. "I just... I thought you were always so put together. And now you, Cassandra Claire Phillips, have quit your job and moved back home to the one place you swore you'd never come back to. I don't understand it. I don't *get* it."

There was only so much of this I could take. Imogen had grown up in the years since I'd left Watford, in ways that I could never understand.

But at the heart of everything lay the scars of a sisterhood that had never fully healed. Hell, we'd never even really gotten off the ground. A relationship that failed to launch in the ways that mattered.

Imogen had always looked up to me, and somewhere along the way, I'd shattered that trust.

And now that we were meeting again as adults, she no longer took me seriously.

That, I decided, was what truly got under my skin. I'd worked too damn hard not to be taken seriously. Even though I had colossally screwed up in the last few months, and even though I was acting so far out of character my own sister didn't recognize me, I deserved to be taken seriously. I'd fucking earned that much.

Imogen didn't have to respect me. I'd have to earn her respect. I'd never expect something otherwise.

But I wanted—*needed*—her to take me seriously.

"What do you want me to say, Imogen? That I quit my job and bought a train ticket home without so much as a second glance? That I'm terrified that all I've ever done in my life is make a series of horrible fucking mistakes that have ruined all the important relationships in my life? That I'm back in Watford, the one place I swore I'd never come back to, because even after all these years and everything that happened here, it's still home? Because I'll say all of that. I'll tell you whatever you fucking want. No more lies, no more secrets. You have a question? Ask it."

The two of them sat there in shocked silence after my outburst. I no longer felt shame or embarrassment. If anything, it felt like a weight had been lifted off my chest.

"You have some nerve," Imogen said quietly. "Did you really think you'd show back up here and we'd do the happy sister thing, as if the past decade of our lives never happened?"

"No," I said, not cowering under her gaze. "I'm apologizing for not showing up for you in the way I should. I'm telling you that I *know* I've screwed up more than I will ever be able to atone for. And I want to try."

Imogen's face softened almost imperceptibly. If I didn't know her as well as I did, I would have missed the slight tilt of her head and the way the heat in her eyes dimmed slightly.

"I can't promise it will be perfect," I choked out. "Hell, I can't even really promise it will work but damn it, Imogen, I miss you. And I know it's taken too damn long for me to get to this point. To get enough courage to come home and look you in the eyes."

Imogen considered this for a long minute. Kam's fingers continued to trace circles against her skin.

"Okay," Imogen said quietly. "We can try."

Sharp relief that cut through me and left me gasping as Imogen hesitantly untangled her hands from Kameron's and reached across the table towards me. The tears I'd been barely holding back spilled over.

"You cry now?" Imogen said, surprise coloring her tone. I squeezed her hand with both of mine, holding her fingers in mine like she'd change her mind if I let her go.

"I try hard not to," I said through labored breaths. "I don't like it."

Kameron chuckled quietly. "You're sisters, alright."

Imogen squeezed my hands one last time and then withdrew, sinking back into Kameron's side like it was the most natural thing in the world for her. The ease with which the two of them operated around each other made my chest ache. The anxiety I'd held onto for years with Imogen and her romantic partners seemed to evaporate in that moment.

Kameron was it for her. I knew from the way he looked at her like every secret to the universe was written somewhere in her eyes. I knew it from the way Imogen's entire face lit up when he leaned in to press a kiss to her cheek while we ate our breakfast.

Kameron told me about Winding Road and their new event venue, the place where Abbie and Connor had gotten married, and where they'd be hosting their baby shower a few short weeks from now.

Imogen gushed about her role as the official event coordinator for the farm, and how everything they did—at both the farm and the venue—helped increase accessibility for veterans who needed help getting their lives back on track and working through their trauma.

I found myself getting teary-eyed several more times as I listened to Imogen talk animatedly about the work she was doing. She'd always been passionate about things, everything from music to books and pop culture.

Knowing that she'd not only found a job she could be passionate about, but a romantic relationship too, had my chest clenching tightly.

My sister had found herself. She'd walked through hell and come out on the other side.

We didn't talk about anything from the past. We didn't talk about our parents, or Watford, or the way we'd left things.

The door was open. There would be more conversations

in the coming days and weeks. There were things we both needed to say to each other, stories that demanded to be told. Behaviors and comments that needed not justification, but simple explanation.

And for today?

The door being open was enough.

After breakfast with Imogen and Kameron, I floundered for what the hell I was supposed to do next. I didn't have the courage to ask, but I didn't have to, because as soon as we hit the sidewalk, Kameron was turning around to face me.

"I'm not sure what your accommodations look like for the next few days, but you're welcome to come stay at Winding Road. There's a tiny house with your name on it."

"A tiny house?" I said, unable to stop the slow smile forming on my face. Imogen nodded her head eagerly.

"There's two of them now," Imogen squealed. "They're stunning. I stayed in one of them most of last summer and it's perfect."

"I wouldn't want to intrude," I said, trying to keep the emotion out of my voice. I tightened my grip on the purse strap. "Winding Road sounds like an incredible place, but it's also a working farm, and if you have a cohort—"

"It'll be another few weeks before our next cohort starts," Kameron said. "And when that happens, we'd be more than happy to set you up at the Watford campsite. Anything to help you get your bearings."

"I... thank you."

I was trying so damn hard to accept their kindness for what it was and not feel like a miserable asshole because of it. Kameron was a rare breed—kind, gentle, and open.

I was the opposite of those things, and the last thing I wanted to do was make either of them feel like I was taking advantage of their generosity.

"Is your stuff still at Abbie's place?" Imogen said. "We parked near her condo. If you want to run upstairs and grab it, you can meet us at the car."

"Sounds good," I said, thanking them both again before heading towards her street. It surprised me how easy it was to navigate my hometown. I climbed the stairs to Abbie's condo and knocked on the door, pushing the door open when I heard her call out that it was open. Abbie was lying on her couch, scrolling on her phone, and I gave her a thumbs-up. She squealed excitedly.

"I knew it was all going to work out," she said.

I didn't have the heart to tell her that Imogen not ripping my heart out of my chest and stomping on it was the bare minimum necessary for us to repair our relationship. I looked to Connor, who was standing in the kitchen stirring a mug of coffee. He gave me a small nod, and my shoulders relaxed slightly.

Connor Harvey had always been a man of very few words, but he saw and heard more than most. He could read between the lines of people's conversations and body language in the way that only someone who had walked through fire could. Abbie had been through rough times with her father too, but Connor had always been quieter. Different.

And Connor Harvey also knew more about my personal history in Watford than I wanted him to.

I didn't know how much he remembered about that day, or how much he cared. I didn't know for certain if Abbie knew, but based on the fact that Imogen clearly didn't know, I'd wager that Connor had kept my secret.

Even if I hadn't asked him to.

A shiver ran down my spine as I walked towards the guest bedroom, determined to grab my suitcase and leave Watford behind for a few days while I figured out my next steps.

My phone lay forgotten on my bed, and my eyes damn near bugged out of my head when I saw it laying there.

When was the last time I'd gone anywhere without the thing glued to my hip?

There were two unread texts from Lainey.

Lainey

Did you make it???

Okayyy, gonna assume your find my iPhone location is correct and that you're currently riding off into the sunset with a hot cowboy

I barked out a laugh and quickly tapped out a response.

Me

Yeah right.

I made it safe though. And I'm spending the night in a tiny house.

I shook my head and smiled to myself as my phone buzzed with a dozen excited all caps text messages from

Lainey. I grabbed the rest of my belongings, remade my bed, and made my way out of Abbie's apartment.

Imogen and Kam were talking to someone on the sidewalk, but my sister stepped away when she saw me coming, grabbing Kam's keys from his back pocket and unlocking the truck bed so I could slide my suitcase inside.

"Hi," I said. "I'm ready to go."

"Cassie Phillips, is that you?"

I internally groaned. I'd been three minutes away from making a quick getaway and avoiding being seen by anyone in town before I was ready.

I turned to face the person, and my heart shot into my throat when I saw Dr. Patricia Conrad standing there. She was older now—the decade of time that had passed between the last time I saw her and now had etched dark lines into her face. But her eyes remained the same. Kind and welcoming.

"I don't know if you remember—"

"I remember," I said, forcing a weak smile. "It's, uh..."

"It's good to see you," she said gently. "I've got to get back to the medical clinic. Be well, you three."

Dr. Conrad turned around and headed back down Main Street, and I stood there, hands shaking, trying to calm my racing heart.

Out of all the people I'd expected to see in Watford again, Dr. Conrad wasn't one of them.

Why had I assumed she would have retired by now?

And she'd remembered me.

Who was I fucking kidding. Of course she'd remembered me.

I was a hard one to forget.

"All good?" Kam said. I turned to face him.

"Yeah," I forced out. "I'm good. Let's go."

If Imogen noticed my trembling hands, she didn't say anything. She sat in the front with Kameron, flipping through her music library to find the album she wanted.

I sat in the backseat, watching as the quiet downtown streets of Watford faded into the Washington treeline, until there was nothing left but the valley between the mountains, and lush evergreen forests. The windows were rolled up, but the memoryof crisp pines, and the feel of the fresh afternoon rain on my skin, were visceral.

It felt like an omen of some kind. A premonition of what was to come.

I was home.

I loved Seattle and the Washington coast with every fiber of my being.

But these forests, these mountains, were what my soul longed for.

Kameron had told me at breakfast that Winding Road was a place people found themselves again.

The deeper we headed into the mountains, the more I understood exactly what he meant.

"This is the part of the evening where we typically go to our separate corners and decompress for the day," Imogen said once we were back at the Winding Road farmhouse. "It's extra quiet this evening because Lucas isn't back yet—"

"Lucas?" I said, my heart lurching into my throat. Imogen gave me a weird look before shrugging it off.

My traitorous heart fluttered.

Lucas was a fairly common name, and there was no way in hell *this* Lucas was the same Lucas from that night, but *damn.*

Just the mention of his name was enough to send me tumbling into memories of that night.

To remind me of the phone number that sat untouched and unused in my phone. His name spoken aloud in the quiet silence of the mountains felt like an accusing finger pointed straight at my damn face.

Because I was the bitch that had the best night of my life with a funny, kind, hot gentleman and then told the universe to kick rocks.

Karma was a tricky subject for me. After everything I experienced as a teenager, I wasn't sure I believed the notion that there was any kind of universal justice. That didn't stop me from pushing things.

"Oh yeah, you haven't met him yet," Imogen said, sliding a water bottle towards me. I nodded my thanks.

Imogen turned her attention back to Kam and asked, "When *is* he due back?"

"Hell if I know," Kam said, rubbing the back of his neck. "He'll definitely be back before the baby shower."

"When is that?" I asked.

"This Friday," Imogen said. "It's at the Winding Road barn, so you won't have far to go."

"Can I help with anything?" I said, eager to have something to do. "This whole 'not working a full-time job for the first time in years' thing is not doing good things for my mental health. I could really use a task. I'll do anything."

"I don't suppose you know anything about horses?" Kameron said, scratching his beard. "With Lucas being out of town, I could use a second set of hands."

"Does she ever," Imogen said, and my heart kicked up at the teasing lilt to her voice. "You're looking at the girl who would have ridden professionally if our parents hadn't been assholes."

Kameron's eyebrows hit his hairline. "Really?"

"I stopped riding when I was sixteen," I said, cheeks flushing scarlet. "And Imogen's being nice. I was never that good. It's been years since I've ridden, and even longer since I competed."

"Bullshit," Imogen exclaimed. "You were—"

"I can help with the horses," I said quickly, cutting off whatever she was going to say. I hadn't let myself think too much about what could have been. I'd made my decision to walk away from the horse world, and there was no sense in rehashing it.

It would be nice to get back in the saddle this week, if only for a few hours.

"Well, that settles it," Kameron said, sticking his hands in his pockets. "You can help me fill in the gaps with Lucas's absence this week. Can you be up at five tomorrow so I can show you the ropes?"

The smile that crept onto my face was genuine in a way that hurt my cheeks. "Yeah. I'll be up then."

Kameron nodded once and stepped forward to kiss Imogen's forehead. "I'm going to walk the grounds and make sure everything looks alright. Can you show her to the tiny houses, Im?"

"Sure," Imogen said, wrapping her arms around him and pressing a kiss to his cheek. "See you in a few."

"Love you," Kam said, blowing a kiss over his shoulder as he stepped through the front door, letting the screened door slam shut.

I stared after him.

My knees nearly buckled with relief, knowing my sister had found someone who seemed to understand her so well.

Bass rubbed against my leg again, and I leaned down to give him a scratch behind the ears.

"Ready?" Imogen said.

"Yeah," I breathed out, all too eager to step into what I hoped would be a new chapter. "I'm ready."

I woke up early the next morning and met Kameron on the front steps of the farmhouse. He showed me the path to the barn and showed me the motions of their morning routine.

I picked it up quicker than I was expecting, easily falling into the motions of caring for each horse and prepping them for the day ahead. There was a monotony in caring for animals that made me pause, reflect.

"Do you ride with them every morning?"

"It depends," Kameron said, slinging the saddle over the white palomino named Chesty. "Lucas typically rotates who gets ridden each morning. Reckless is an old man these days and prefers going straight to the pasture in the morning, but this guy—" Kameron hiked a thumb over his shoulder towards the newly saddled horse "—needs to get some energy out."

I chuckled and reached out to stroke the horse's mane.

"And you're comfortable with this? Me riding, I mean."

Kam shrugged and crossed his arms over his chest.

"Imogen showed me pictures of you at your last competition."

"Of course she did," I muttered, turning my attention to the horse in front of me.

"You looked happy," Kameron murmured.

I closed my eyes.

"I was," I choked out. "I *loved* riding."

I'd loved riding more than anything. As a teenager, I worked hard to balance school, debate, and family commitments. I did all of that, sacrificed so much of my sanity and physical energy, all for the fifteen hours a week that I got to spend in the arena.

I couldn't decipher the look on Kameron's face when I re-opened my eyes.

There was something about being here on this land, standing in the barn as the earliest rays of dawn sun filtered in through the rafters that made my mind quiet.

In Seattle, there was always a place to hide.

There was always a car honking, someone shouting or laughing or singing, the clanking of silverware on ceramic plates as you walked down the street. A constant barrage of light and noise.

I could escape into the recesses of the night without so

much as a second thought. I could find a bar to hide away in and dull my thoughts. I could bury myself in casework and wonder whether this was all my life would be.

But here in the lush mountains of the Cascades, I couldn't hide.

I'd realized last night, as I lay in bed looking up through the skylight of the tiny house, that I'd lost the ability to sit with my own thoughts. I'd spent so long outrunning this place that I never stopped to consider how hard it would be to come back here.

"Take your time," Kam said quietly while I finished tacking Chesty. "There's a riding path that will take you down past the barn and into the forest. There's signage to guide you around the property if you feel like off-roading, but if you stick to the main path, it basically makes a big loop that will bring you right back here."

I took a deep breath before I grabbed the saddle horn and put my foot in the stirrups, hoisting myself over.

I let out a long breath of relief as I adjusted my hips in the saddle, taking in the familiar stretch of my muscles.

"Feels good, doesn't it?" Kam said softly.

"Nothing else like it," I whispered. "I'll bring him back safely."

"That, I don't doubt. I'll probably be at the farmhouse or the venue. I trust you can find your way around here well enough to untack when you're done?"

I nodded, smiling as Chesty shifted beneath me.

"Have a good ride, Cassie. And you behave," Kameron said, giving Chesty a warmhearted smile. He stepped aside to allow us through.

The moment we were on the path and heading into the forest, I felt a weight lift off my chest.

And damn if my head wasn't quiet for the first time in what felt like months.

I took things slow, but Chesty seemed all too willing to let me guide him. We stayed on the main path, as Kameron suggested. There would be plenty of opportunities for exploring, but I wanted to keep things simple during my first time back in the saddle.

Instead of tuning out the world around me, I let myself feel it.

All of it.

Chapter 8
Lucas

"**I**mogen, I love you. You are one of my best friends. I've told you things I'll probably never tell another soul. But I can't do this for you."

Imogen scowled in response to my statement.

"It's my lifelong friend's baby shower today," Imogen said, cocking one hip out and pointing an accusing finger in my direction. "I need you to put aside your—"

"No," I choked out. "We can play whatever other weird-ass baby shower games you found on Pinterest, but I'm *not* sucking on a baby bottle."

"Why not?" Imogen said. Her foot tapped impatiently against the hardwood floor of the Winding Road Barn.

"Because," I said weakly, scratching the back of my neck. "I don't want to?"

"Not good enough," Imogen said, jabbing a finger into the center of my chest. "Abbie has allowed *one* cringy baby shower game, and as the event planner, this is the one that will bring the most laughs, in my professional opinion. Therefore—"

"Jesus," I said, chuckling. "And here I thought your sister was the lawyer."

Imogen winced. "About that, I actually need to tell—"

A loud crash interrupted whatever Imogen had been about to say, and we both took off sprinting toward the catering kitchen.

"Bass. *Dude*."

Connor was standing in the center of the kitchen, eyes screwed shut as he tried to regulate his breathing. I winced at the sight of vanilla frosting smeared down the front of his shirt. Imogen paled.

"Please tell me those were not the gender reveal cupcakes."

"Nope," Connor croaked out. "And there was only one."

I realized then that he looked slightly guilty. The corners of my mouth tilted up in a smile.

"Why Connor, you little—"

"Shut up," Connor muttered. "I'm stressed. I eat when I'm stressed."

Bass let out a joyful bark, and the three of us glanced down at the wiry white dog who was very much embodying the Marine he was so affectionately named after, chasing his tail at a rapid pace.

"And you, little man, should be nowhere near the barn," Imogen admonished, reaching for the dog. He happily jumped into her arms and allowed her to escort him out of the kitchen. "That was naughty, and you know it."

She turned back to the two of us.

"Can you two hold down the fort long enough for me to take this menace back to the farmhouse?"

I nodded. "We've got it."

"Don't even think about removing those baby bottles,"

Imogen hollered. "I will dump an entire bottle of Thousand Island dressing on your pillow."

I cursed under my breath. She knew how much I hated that salad dressing, and the mental image of an entire bottle soaking into my sheets was enough to make me gag.

"Has she always been like that?"

Connor huffed out a quiet laugh. "As long as I've known her, yeah. Many people have made the mistake of underestimating her over the years."

No *shit*. "I guess I'm contractually obligated to play this shower game, huh?"

"Please," Connor scoffed, reaching for the collar of his now ruined button-up and undoing the top button. "Imogen is making the three of us do it, and I'm positive you'll hand Kam and I's rear ends to us on a silver platter."

I rolled my eyes as we exited the kitchen. "I wasn't *that* much of a party boy."

Connor coughed. "Whatever helps you sleep at night, Morales."

He wasn't wrong, though. I had been a party boy in those early years. I'd stopped after Mallory and I started dating seriously; until she'd started begging me to go out more on the weekends.

Taking her to all the house parties my friends and coworkers threw was one of the dumbest things I'd ever done.

"Do you have another shirt?" I asked, gesturing towards Connor's ruined shirt, suddenly desperate to change the subject.

"You're looking at the father-to-be," Connor said, and

I didn't miss the way his eyes softened at the notion of fatherhood. "Of course I have another shirt."

He brushed past me to exit the kitchen, and I got to work cleaning up the remnants of mashed cupcake on the floor. That dog was a hellion on four legs, and we all adored him. He brought chaos and spontaneity into our little group, and Lord knew we needed that sometimes.

After Connor changed clothes, we resumed our decorating and organizing. The baby shower wasn't until this weekend, but Imogen wanted everything set up well before Saturday afternoon.

As much crap as I gave my best friend for how much of a control freak she was, I was grateful we had someone with her level of organization.

Winding Road had been an administrative disaster before she came on the payroll. I was more than happy to move the table and chairs around to be exactly how she wanted them.

After another two hours of manual labor, I desperately needed a nap and a shower before tonight's farmhouse dinner. Thankfully, Imogen was in charge of cooking, so all I had to do was show up.

"See you in a few hours?" I said, trying to decipher the look on her face. Imogen seemed to ponder whether to tell me something, but I knew better than to push her.

Imogen and I's friendship was based on a special kind of mutual respect. She would come to me when she was ready. Whatever she was holding back, she had her reasons.

"Yeah," Imogen said, giving me a smile. "Thanks for your help."

"Anytime," I called over my shoulder as I headed for the footpath that would take me back to the farmhouse. On the way up the hill from the barn, I stopped to pet Reckless and Memphis, who were grazing in the main pasture near the house. Chesty was on the far side of the pasture in his own world, which was par for the course for him.

I took a moment to breathe in deep, letting the fresh mountain air and faint scent of early autumn wildflowers flow over me.

This place was special to so many people for different reasons, but to me, this place represented a new start. Winding Road was somewhere you laid down your burdens and be seen for who you truly are, not just the mask you presented to the world.

After a quick shower and changeover, I placed my phone on the nightstand, cranked on my sound machine, and set an alarm to be downstairs on time for dinner. Imogen would have my neck if I was late.

As much as I loved Winding Road and the Washington mountains, I inexplicably fell asleep to the memories of a bustling coastal city several hundred miles away, the sound of a woman's laugh drifting over my skin, her hand just out of reach.

I took the stairs two at a time after my nap, eager to get downstairs for dinner. When the familiar smell of home-made pizza hit my nose, I let out a contented sigh. I rounded the staircase, making a beeline for the kitchen. Imogen was fishing around for something in the fridge, and I approached the stovetop, where two of the pizzas were cooling off.

"Don't even think about touching them."

I rolled my eyes but obeyed.

"Are you aware your girlfriend has eyes in the back of her head?" I called out to Kameron, who was sitting in his usual spot on the couch. He chuckled.

"Oh, I'm very aware," Kam said. "She has a talent."

"The pizzas will be ready in ten minutes. Until then, shoo."

"Shoo? Really?"

The affectionate glare Imogen sent me had me moving my ass toward the couch.

"Love you," I called as I launched myself over the back of the couch, flopping down on the waiting cushions and shooting Kam a smile. He pressed his lips together in a thin line to keep from laughing.

"You break it, you buy it," Kam warned, but there was no heat in his tone.

"Your life would be so incredibly boring without me," I replied. Kam shrugged, but the amused expression on his face gave him away.

"Where are the lovebirds?"

"On their way," Kam said. His jaw twitched. "Speaking of newcomers, there's another—"

The sound of Abbie's lilting tone filtering through the screen door alongside the familiar sound of boots stomping up the wooden staircase cut his sentence short.

"We had daisies at the wedding, but I thought it would be cute to have them at the shower too, like a sweet callback to the day we got married. Is that too much?"

"Um, I'm not sure?" a female voice said. "I think it's a cute idea, but ultimately you should do whatever you want. It's a shower in your honor after all. People are celebrating you as much as the baby."

Every nerve ending in my body lit up with awareness. I straightened immediately, my eyes going wide with surprise.

I was hearing things. I'd officially stared at my phone for long enough that I was expecting something that couldn't possibly exist.

I slowly turned my head towards the door, watching as Abbie pushed it open and gave all of us a wide smile.

"Whoa, you got started without us?" Abbie said, her smile quickly turning into a pout.

My heart pounded as I gripped the armrest of the couch.

My vision tunneled to the halo of a figure standing behind Abbie.

Imogen appeared from the kitchen, and upon seeing me white-knuckling the couch, cocked her head in my direction. I could feel Kameron's eyes on me, but I didn't care.

There was no way. There was no damn way—

"You haven't missed anything," Imogen replied, turning her attention away from me and nodding her head to the woman approaching behind Abbie. "Lucas, this is..."

Her voice faded as the ringing in my ears grew. The words didn't resonate because I already knew who the woman was.

I would recognize that voice anywhere.

It was the voice that played in my head over and over at

night when I was lonely and couldn't sleep. The voice from that night in Seattle for the Warrior's Grant presentation, where I'd thrown every rule I'd ever been told to follow out the window and focused solely on what I wanted instead.

What I'd wanted to give the woman with those stunning brown eyes I'd wanted to drown in. The woman who was hilarious and sexy and flirty—the most lethal of combinations that brought me to my damn knees.

Abbie stepped aside, and there she was.

Brown eyes, straightened black hair, tan skin—I recognized every feature all too well. Only this time, she'd traded the red dress and high heels for high-rise jeans that clung to every curve, a white mock neck tank top, and boots.

It was her.

Cass.

Dream girl.

Best night of my fucking life.

Not Cass.

Cassie.

Imogen's sister.

Fuck.

Her stunning brown eyes widened in surprise, plush red lips parting around a silent gasp.

"Cass?" I said, voice rough with something I couldn't decipher, and the sound of her name on my lips caused a shudder to run through her. I opened my mouth to say something else and came up empty.

"Fuck," she whispered, and dropped the wine bottle in her hands.

Chapter 9
Lucas

Seattle, Washington
20:30

"Wait, *wait*, you're telling me you came home from deployment and found your wife in bed with your best friend?"

"I swear on my life," I said, snatching another fry from the basket between us. "He got sent home early from deployment for a family emergency, which is rare enough as it is. When an entire unit is returning from overseas, they split the flights up because not everyone can fit on one chartered commercial flight. I ended up being on the first flight out. Thought it would be nice to surprise her."

"Oh no," Cass said, grimacing. "In your bed?"

"Yep," I said, popping the "p" for emphasis. "It was a full-frontal display, too."

Cass let out a low whistle, grabbing another fry.

"My biggest mistake was not moving all of my money out of the joint account that day," I said, sighing as I reached for my glass and downed the last bit of whiskey. "She moved every cent into her account. Completely wiped both our joint checking and savings."

Cass did a spit-take. My eyes widened as I let out a disbelieving laugh.

"Are you kidding me?" Cass shook her head. "What a bitch."

I was cutting myself off after this: firstly because I knew my limits and there was no way in hell I was going to get drunk enough to cause a scene, and secondly because Imogen would have my balls if I showed up hungover and late tomorrow.

One of the two was excusable, but both were a death sentence.

"Hence why I'm in Seattle on a semi-regular basis. The two of them live here now, and the divorce proceedings have been quite an adventure."

"Oh?" Cass said, her entire face lighting up. "Do tell."

I gave her a wry smile. "Are you a drama hog?"

"No," Cass said, matching my smile as she leaned her head on one hand, resting her weight against the bar top. "Call me curious."

It required every ounce of my mental strength not to reach forward and put my hand on her thigh. At some point during the conversation, Cass had turned towards me, crossing her legs just below the knee.

"The story of my divorce proceedings is at least a second date story."

Cass pouted, and holy shit, it had been a long time since I'd wanted to kiss someone the way I wanted to kiss her.

"I know Kiley already spoiled *my* story, but I dropped some weight tonight," Cass said, grabbing one wing and dipping it in buffalo sauce.

I smiled and crossed my arms over my chest.

"You wouldn't be prying me with a story of your own in order to placate me into giving you mine?"

Cass's eyes sparkled with amusement. "You're a clever man."

"I'll bite," I said. "Asshole boyfriend?"

"Well," she drawled, finishing her wing and wiping her fingers off with a napkin. "He took his mistress to the same restaurant where we were supposed to celebrate our anniversary tonight."

I let out a low whistle. "Damn."

"Exactly," Cass said with a long sigh. "Which is why I ended up here. My friend was supposed to join me, but she got a call from her parents on her way out the door and stayed home, the turncoat."

"What a shame."

Cass smirked at me. "A real shame indeed."

My eyes glanced towards the now empty basket of wings and fries. I didn't want this conversation to end. I racked my brain for a reason to keep it going.

"Did you know Lucas hates Seattle?" Kiley's warm voice drew my attention away from Cass's face to the other side of the bar, where Kiley was pouring me another glass of water.

Cass let out a choked gasp. "*What?*"

I glared at Kiley, who blew me a kiss as she sauntered away from the bar again.

"I'm not a city boy," I said by way of explanation. "Or a West Coaster."

"That doesn't matter," Cass spluttered. "Seattle is incredible."

"I grew up on the East Coast," I attempted again.

"That's *no excuse*," Cass said with a shake of her head. "I won't stand for this."

I rolled my lips together to keep from smiling.

"And how are you going to convince me?"

Cass drummed her fingers along the lacquered wood. Her gaze bore into mine, and I saw a million different thoughts within her eyes. I had so many questions and too few answers. The only thing I knew for certain at that moment was that I didn't want the night to end. Not without knowing more about the woman in front of me.

"Let's go."

Two words that sent my heart into overdrive.

"Where?"

"I won't be able to sleep tonight knowing there's a handsome man who hates my city only a few blocks from my apartment."

I barked out a laugh. "I'm sure there are plenty of people in Seattle who—"

"Don't say that there are thousands of people here who hate it," Cass groaned, covering her ears. "I can't bear it. Grab your phone."

I threw down several twenties on the table to cover both of our tabs and did as she asked. Priya smiled wildly at me while Cass grabbed her coat from the rack.

And when Cass grabbed my hand and pulled me towards the door, I was helpless to do anything but follow her.

We left the bar stools spinning in our absence and stepped out into the cool Washington night.

Chapter 10

Cassie

"**Y**ou two know each other?"

Fuck. *Fuck.*

My brain misfired again.

Start. Stop. Start again.

I couldn't come up with a half-decent lie to save my life.

I just stood there gaping at him, his gray t-shirt, dark wash jeans, windswept black hair, faint stubble lining his jawline.

Lucas's hands gripped the couch so tightly that the fabric bunched beneath his fingers.

I hovered in the doorway, half expecting to wake up from whatever insane dream I was having.

"Not exactly," Lucas said with a laugh that sounded fake to my ears, but seemed to appease his friends. "We've met in passing. My lawyer works at her firm."

That was a lie—I knew for a fact his lawyer didn't work at my previous employer. I had to give it to him, though. It was a damn good lie to throw out on the fly.

He'd saved my ass. *Both* of our asses.

Somehow we ended up on the same page about whether to reveal the one night we'd spent together, without even having discussed it.

"Worked," I blurted. "I quit my job."

Lucas's expression sharpened into something that looked a lot like pride.

He knew better than anyone else in the room just how bad things had gotten, how desperately I'd wanted to get the hell out of there.

"And you didn't know she was my sister?"

Based on the look Imogen was giving Lucas, with her narrowed eyes and suspicious stare, I knew she didn't believe me. Lucas rolled his eyes, feigning an indifference I was certain he didn't feel.

"I met her *in passing*. As in, we passed each other in the hallway when I was at the office for a meeting. Matthias briefly introduced us, and we went on with our days. How many lawyers are in Seattle on any given day? C'mon now."

"And you remembered her name was Cass?" Kam questioned.

"I'm good with names," Lucas said with a shrug.

He was too good at this.

Once upon a time, I was too, but evidently I locked up when coming face-to-face with the man who had turned my entire world upside down.

Not just that, my brain helpfully reminded me.

The man who lived rent-free in my fucking head, and had since the moment I'd felt his calloused hands on my skin.

"This is so weird," Imogen muttered. "How many people even live in Washington State?"

Eight point one million.

"Not really," Lucas said. "Just a coincidence."

How was he so relaxed about this when my body was on *fire*?

Visions of the night we spent together danced behind my eyelids when I blinked.

Nope. Not going there.

I didn't wait to see what Lucas said next.

I muttered, "I need some air" before I stepped out onto the back porch, needing the crisp mountain air to remind me I was still awake. That this wasn't a cruel dream.

The room was closing in on me. Seeing Imogen with Kameron, and Abbie with Connor, was like having a knife driven directly into my chest and twisted.

It was a wicked sort of punishment, to see the people you loved more than anything else in the world be so happy, while your life was falling apart.

And to have the last person who made me feel something other than fear and anger show up in the last place on Earth I would ever have expected?

That feeling made me the most selfish person in the fucking world, and somehow, that revelation only made me burrow deeper into my head.

Lucas being here tonight was not helping my ability to work through the crap I needed to in order to be on the straight and narrow again.

I gasped a shaky breath. The ground beneath my feet threatened to give way.

Or maybe it was just a toxic mix of the glass of red wine I'd downed to cut the nerves and my inability to clear my thoughts.

I couldn't fucking *focus*.

"Hey."

Lucas's voice danced over my skin, heating my body from the inside out.

It was *not* normal to have such a visceral reaction to someone's voice.

I was *unwell*.

"Hey yourself," I said, licking my lips to soothe some of the dryness there. Lucas handed me an open nonalcoholic beer, and I gave him a wry smile. Lucas didn't say a word. He just stood there, arm outstretched towards me, waiting for me to take it.

He was just as steady as I remember. Like he could see right through my bullshit excuses for not doing something.

And damn him, I accepted the peace offering for what it was.

I took a large sip, immediately wrinkling my nose at the bitter taste. I wasn't normally a beer girl, but seeing as my bottle of red was now soaking into the dirt beneath Kam and Imogen's front porch, non-alcoholic beer would have to be enough.

"This is an interesting development," Lucas murmured.

God, his voice.

I'd assumed that in the weeks since that night my memory had faded: that somewhere along the way I'd lost track of the cadence and the roughness of it.

No such luck.

"You could say that."

Lucas came to stand beside me, mirroring my position and leaning over the rail. If I moved my elbow another inch to the right, our arms would touch. The realization had me pressing my lips together in a tight line.

"So you're the third ring in this circus, huh?"

Lucas chuckled.

"Is that what you've been calling it?"

I let out a long breath.

"When Imogen mentioned you, I figured there was no way in hell it could be the same person. Lucas isn't that uncommon of a name."

Lucas hummed in acknowledgment.

"Seems we both missed the signs right in front of our faces," Lucas mumbled.

I exhaled, fingers tightening around the bottle.

Damn it.

I didn't have the words to tell him exactly how many times I'd almost called him.

There didn't seem to be a reason now that he was standing beside me, anyway.

Fuck. He was *here*. He was in *Watford*. And he was my sister's closest friend.

"Why lie to them?" I whispered. "You could have just as easily told them we'd already met in a more... official capacity. I wouldn't have blamed you."

Lucas scoffed and took another swig of his drink.

"And face that interrogation blind? No thanks. Trust me when I say Connor and Kam would have sniffed out the truth from a mile away. They're probably already suspicious."

I let those words hang heavy between us. I tried to absorb them, to make them stick in my head so I had a laundry list of reasons leaning into this man any further than a simple conversation about the past was a terrible fucking idea.

"You really didn't know Imogen and I were sisters?" I said a few minutes later. "You didn't have any idea when she told you?"

Lucas sighed and hung his head.

"I know it makes me an idiot, but no. The thought didn't cross my mind. Cass, Cassie—they're close enough, I guess. For what it's worth, I really only knew your name. I didn't know much about you other than the two of you having a rocky relationship. Imogen doesn't talk about you much."

I winced, but said nothing. I'd earned her ire.

Clarity washed over Lucas's face.

"Your presence is probably what Imogen wanted to tell me earlier. She got cut off by Bass's escapades."

I couldn't stop the small smile that appeared on my face at the mention of the insane dog that had captured all our hearts. I'd only been back in Watford a short while, but Bass was so insanely lovable.

I finished my beer with my next sip. "What a train wreck. I come back to Watford to escape all the sins of my past and try to start life over again, and I run into my most recent one night stand."

Lucas shot me a devilish grin. "I'm on the sin list?"

I rolled my eyes. "You're something."

Lucas exhaled.

"This is only weird unless we make it weird."

"You've seen me naked, Lucas. It's already weird."

His gaze heated as his eyes darted down to my lips, scanning my face for something I was trying like hell to hide.

Atta girl.

I blinked twice to clear the mental image from my mind.

"So, that's it? We're going to act like it never happened?"

If I were being honest with myself, that was the last thing I wanted. But I couldn't bring myself to say it.

"Do you have a better idea?"

"I have several ideas," Lucas murmured, a hint of a smile on his lips.

Fuck, this was bad. Catastrophic.

"Lucas, we *can't*."

There was a note of desperation in my voice I hadn't expected.

Lucas looking at me like he was remembering every single damn detail of our night together was unraveling me down to my fucking core. I couldn't do this with him.

Not here. Not now.

"Things like this don't happen, Cass."

His voice was quieter than it had been a minute before.

Fuck, did he not think I *knew* that?

"Imogen and I are not on good terms," I tried again.

Lucas looked entirely unconvinced.

I let out a frustrated huff.

"It was supposed to be *one* night."

"And?"

"You're her best friend," I said, waving my hand around like I could snap him out of whatever dreamland he was living in. "I'm her *sister*. That's asking for trouble."

"And if I tell you I've thought about you every damn day since that night at Rain's?"

He inched closer, his elbows grazing mine. The simple

press of his arm against mine sent my brain into overdrive.

"What if I told you I've been waiting every day for two months to see a call from an unknown number on my phone?"

"You shouldn't tell me that," I snapped, trying to ignore the way my heartbeat kicked up beneath his gaze.

"Now, Cass," he said, tutting gently. "You should know better than to give me orders."

If God existed, he really was trying to screw me over.

"Lucas," I whispered as he leaned in. His face was only inches from mine, and even though the feeling of his nearness was dizzying, I was all too aware of his friends eating dinner and laughing only a few feet away.

If one of them saw us out here like this, everything I was trying to build would blow up in my face before I even had the chance to work on it.

There were only six people here for dinner tonight. It was obvious that the two of us were missing. I didn't know how long we'd been out here, but I knew it was long enough to raise questions.

"You call the shots," Lucas said when he pulled back, though the tick of his jawline told me he was disappointed. "But please remember that you don't have to live life on someone else's terms."

His words were a subtle reminder of the conversation we'd had in his hotel room, where I'd shared far too much about the state of my life, my hopes and dreams for what might be different in my life, eventually.

If only he knew I'd been doing that my entire life. I didn't know how to do anything else.

I'd lived my life as the eldest daughter perfectly. I got good grades. I went to a good college. I got a good scholarship. I became everything my parents wanted me to be and more.

I'd had to give up writing when it became too much—the only passion I'd ever had outside of law—and it still hadn't been enough for them.

And one reckless decision is all it takes for every domino to fall.

This was just one more domino in a long line, and I wasn't brave enough to risk knocking them down after spending the last decade of my life building them back up.

"We don't even know each other," I whispered. It was a weak lie, even to my own ears. "You don't know anything about me."

"You're going to have to try harder than that," Lucas said. I didn't miss the way his nose crinkled around the words, as if trying not to laugh. "How long are you in Watford?"

"I don't know," I said honestly. "I really don't. And this—" I motioned a finger between our chests "—is not happening. Imogen is barely speaking to me as it is. If she found out I was sleeping with her best friend behind her back, the little progress we've made would disappear. I want her in my life. I can't do anything that will jeopardize that."

The words were true enough.

I wouldn't put Imogen in a position to get hurt by the residual effects of the shitshow that was my life. I'd hurt Imogen in so many ways over the years—most of it unintentionally, but carrying on a secret relationship with someone she loved and cared for would be an intentional betrayal.

Lucas scratched his chin, considering my words.

"It doesn't have to be a secret."

I barked out a surprised laugh.

"Good to know your arrogance is still in the room with us."

"What does it matter if they know? The only reason I lied to them earlier is because you looked like a deer in headlights. You froze up."

"This entire conversation is ridiculous," I hissed, finally turning around to face him.

He was far closer than I remembered him being, and if I leaned forward another inch, my chest would brush his.

My mouth went dry as I tilted my head up to look him in the eyes.

I'd forgotten how much he towered over me. I'd always been on the taller side, but with Lucas being over six feet and me having traded my high heels for cowgirl boots this week, the height difference was remarkable.

"We spent one night together," I said. "One night of me trying to convince you that Seattle wasn't the worst city on Earth, and things ended with the best sex of my life. But we don't *know* each other. I don't know what weird string of coincidences brought us together again, but I left your room that morning fully expecting never to see you again. It was one night. We both agreed."

I could have sworn hurt flashed in his eyes before he schooled his features into that arrogant, humorous indifference I knew all too well.

It was the same mask I'd worn throughout law school.

The same mask I wore at my first job, where I was too

scared to rock the boat with one silly comment and lose everything I'd earned up to that point.

"Best sex of your life, huh?"

I pushed past the twinge of guilt that sprang to life in my gut at the knowledge that he'd been showing me something real, and I'd forced his walls back up.

It's *better this way*, I reminded myself. This couldn't happen. It didn't matter that my body was practically screaming at me to entertain his suggestion.

I opened my mouth to make another snarky comment, but Lucas surprised me by closing the distance between us, slipping one of his thighs in between mine and pushing me back against the railing.

His arms bracketed my hips, and I had to swallow back a moan and resist the desire to push my hips forward.

My head fell back slightly, and when our eyes met, I almost caved.

I wanted him to open his mouth and say every filthy thing that was going through his head. I knew exactly what that mouth was capable of, and I craved it. I hadn't stopped craving it for a second.

His eyes refused to meet mine as he leaned down to whisper in my ear. I shivered as he lips caressed the sensitive skin there. My fingers white-knuckled the railing, even when I wanted nothing more than to shove my fingers into his hair and pull his mouth to mine.

"I'm not a little boy, Cassie. I know what I want, and I can be patient."

This arrogant, loud-mouthed, insufferably *hot* man.

Remembering all of the reasons why this was a bad idea,

I put both of my hands on his chest and shoved him backwards. Lucas's chuckle skittered down my spine. I readjusted my shirt to ensure it was still tucked into my jeans.

"That's not going to happen," I said, but the words sounded weak and breathy.

There was no sense in trying to hide the effect this man had on me.

He already knew how my body responded to his.

He hadn't whispered in my ear because he was trying to convince me.

Because he already knew he didn't need to.

Under any other circumstances—see: him not being in my sister's close friend group—I would have already climbed into the backseat of his truck and pulled him on top of me.

Lucas was a master at teasing. At drawing things out.

He'd give me just enough and wait for me to fill in the rest.

I was so beyond screwed.

Lucas simply winked and said, "I'll be here when you're done," before shoving his hands into the pockets of his jeans and heading back into the farmhouse.

I turned my gaze to the rolling hills beyond, blowing out a long, hard breath. My fingers tightened on the dusty railing, and I stepped back, my head hanging low between my arms as I tried to clear my head.

Putting my life back together just got infinitely more complicated.

Lucas had been the one thing I'd chosen for *myself* in Seattle.

The one true vice I'd allowed myself to indulge in.

Now he was here. In Watford. With me.

And I didn't know how long I'd be able to hold myself back.

Chapter 11

Lucas

I didn't sleep the night I saw Cass—Cassie—again.

Dinner went off without a hitch. I felt the weight of Kam's stare on me the entire night, but at least he had the decency not to bring it up in front of everyone else.

I was going out of my mind knowing that the girl I'd been thinking about non-stop since that one mind-blowing night was only a few hundred feet away from. She was staying in the second tiny house, built right next to the one Imogen often stayed in when she needed a break from the business of the farmhouse.

My dream girl was just down the hill from me. And I couldn't go to her.

I didn't know what I'd been thinking when I insinuated we could pick up where we left off. The empty hotel room the morning after our night of excursions spoke volumes.

I hadn't expected to see you again.

I wanted to eliminate that sentence from both of our vocabularies. I'd meant it when I told her that this felt stronger than a weird string of fate.

Three quarters of a million people lived in Seattle.

The odds of the two of us running into each other again

were astronomical. Impossible.

I tried to remind myself that she clearly had a lot going on. I did too. That was part of what had made our night out in Seattle so special. We had both laid down our heavy loads for those twelve hours. We could be ourselves.

I tried to put those thoughts out of my mind as I got ready for the baby shower. There would only be a handful of folks in attendance, but I still wanted to look good. I laid out my nicest button-down and jeans so I could do a quick outfit change after taking care of things at the barn.

Best foot forward and all that.

I made myself a to-go cup of coffee before strolling out of the farmhouse and heading off down the hill towards the barn so I could tend to the horses this morning. I damn near tripped over myself when I saw a woman already hard at work.

"Hey," I said by way of greeting. Very casual. Very calm.

"Hey yourself," Cass said, giving me a soft smile. "I didn't mean to step on your toes. Kameron has had me working with these guys in your absence, and I had trouble sleeping last night, so..."

She shifted her weight from one foot to the other, and I was amazed at how naturally she'd transitioned from corporate city to country. Her jeans hugged every curve—curves I'd tried my damndest to memorize—and the heeled boots accentuated her height.

"It's fine," I said. "More than fine. They're clearly comfortable with you. And you look comfortable here."

She didn't miss the subtle question in my statement. The corner of her mouth kicked up in a small smile.

"I used to ride."

"Yeah?" I said, heart thundering in my chest.

God, what even was this?

There was no way I was having this kind of physical reaction to a simple conversation. I was having trouble calming my heart rate enough to drink in the details of her, this woman who had consumed my waking hours for the better part of two months.

"Yeah," she said, stroking Memphis's mane. He let out a low whinny of approval and inclined his body towards hers. My chest tightened.

The three horses we had here at Winding Road were therapy horses, which meant that they interacted with humans in different ways. They were calm, trusting, allowing people to get close to them because they trusted that we as their caretakers wouldn't let any harm come to them.

It made every interaction I witnessed that much more special.

"Why'd you stop?" I asked.

I instantly wished I could take the words back when Cassie's face crumpled.

She turned her attention back to Memphis, finishing her brushing before moving towards his tail, picking out the stray pieces of grass that had lodged themselves in his hair.

I picked up my set of grooming tools from the bench and headed for Chesty. He nudged my shoulder in greeting, and I gave his nose a good rub before I started brushing him down.

"That's at least a sixth date question," Cassie murmured a few minutes later, and there went my heart, galloping away from me while I stood there trying not to gawk.

"It's a shame we never got past date four," I said, trying my luck.

To my surprise, Cassie chuckled.

"A shame indeed."

A physical ache had taken up residence in my chest. An absence I couldn't soothe.

"Reckless is already back in the pasture," Cassie said a heartbeat later. "Would you mind finishing up here? I desperately need a shower before this afternoon."

"Sure," I said, walking around Chesty so I could see her. "And thank you for working so hard."

"I'm happy to have something useful to do," Cassie said. "Seeing as I'm unemployed for the foreseeable future."

I choked on my next inhale. "You really quit?"

Cassie's eyes beamed with pride for the briefest of seconds before it winked out, extinguished by whatever external pressure had crushed that light inside her.

"I did," she said. "I met a guy who basically told me I wasn't getting any younger and that I needed to spend more time doing something for myself instead of following someone else's rules."

"I don't remember saying that."

"In so many words," she amended, with that wry smile I craved still on her face.

This woman. *Fuck.*

"See you later?" Cassie said, putting her tub of brushes on the bench. I swallowed the lump in my throat.

"Yeah," I said, still dumbstruck by the notion that she was here. In the Winding Road barn.

Looking like she'd walked out of my wildest dream.

"See you later."

As soon as Chesty and Memphis were back in the pasture, I made a beeline for the farmhouse. I was under strict orders from Kameron not to stress his girlfriend out, which meant I needed to be on time.

On my way back to the farmhouse, my phone rang. My heart thumped in my chest before I even pulled my phone out.

"Hey Morales," the recruiter said. "How are things?"

"They're going," I said. "You have an update?"

"You're good to go," Frye replied, and I could hear the smile in his voice. Recruiting was a tough job, and in a small county like Watford, I'm sure he had his work cut out for him. "Can you be in my office on Wednesday to sign paperwork?"

He then rattled off a list of things that would need to happen before I'd get any information about my reserve unit—namely a physical exam, running a PFT, and swearing in.

Thinking about swearing in again had emotion swirling in my chest.

I was a kid who grew up wanting to serve my country. I always thirsted to be part of something bigger than myself. And my parents had supported me every step of the way. Even my father, who had served and almost given his life, stood next to me at my bootcamp graduation.

I finalized the details for what time I'd be at the station and what I needed to bring and then slipped my phone back in my pocket. I absentmindedly rubbed at my chest, as if that would somehow ease the ache forming there.

My relationship with my family was strained these days, but growing up, we'd been incredibly close.

But divorce was a hard line for most Catholics to cross, and that meant my relationship with my parents looked different.

I talked to them when I had big news to share, but gone were the days where I'd call up my dad to tell him about the dumb stuff that happened that week, or when I'd text my mom to ask her to please send me a recipe for the thousandth time because I never remembered to save them.

My relationship with my sister, Adriana, had disintegrated beyond repair following my separation. She'd believed my soon-to-be-ex wife's version of events without ever stopping to ask me the truth.

If any of them knew I'd been entertaining the idea of a romantic relationship while still technically married—or that I'd slept with Cassie—they would probably disown me entirely.

It didn't matter that Mallory had cheated on me back when I was fully and completely committed to her.

It didn't matter that she had drained me of every penny I'd earned during my first enlistment to help her start life anew on the Washington coast.

It didn't matter that I'd spent the last six years painstakingly putting every part of my life back together, re-knitting the very fabric of my soul into something that wasn't heartbreak.

Divorce was a sin in the eyes of the Catholic church, and I was doubling down on that transgression by keeping the door to a second chance between Mallory and me firmly shut.

I clenched and unclenched my fists as I walked up the staircase to my room, eager to get in the shower and let the hot water wash away some of the shame that still permeated my skin when I thought about my relationship with my family.

My decision to divorce Mallory had been the right one, for both of us.

We hadn't been happy in a long time, and when she got in bed with someone I once considered a friend, it became very clear that only one of us was willing to work to save the marriage.

A marriage takes two people. So I left.

When I got out of the shower, I glanced at the time on my phone and swore loudly.

I quickly dressed and ran down the farmhouse stairs, heading for the barn, but abruptly stopped as I glanced down the hill to where the two tiny houses sat side by side, just past the chicken coop.

I bit the inside of my cheek. I knew who occupied the second house, and there was a chance Cass hadn't made it to the barn for the baby shower yet either.

After our run-in at the stables this morning, I was desperate to see her again.

Decision made, I took off down the hill, knocking twice before stepping back from the door.

A whole minute passed, and I sighed, resigned to my fate, when the door finally swung open.

"Lucas?" Cassie's eyes widened in surprise. "Sorry, I had my headphones in and didn't hear you knock. I'm almost ready."

"Walk with me?" I asked.

She hesitated, fingers drumming along the doorframe, and for a second, I thought she might actually turn me down.

"Alright," Cassie replied. "Just let me grab my shoes. You can come in, if you want."

My brain short-circuited, and in the heartbeat it took her words to sink in, her cheeks flushed as she realized the gravity of her words.

"I didn't mean—"

"I know," I said, voice rough. "I can wait here."

Cassie's shoulders relaxed, and as soon as she disappeared back into the tiny house, I turned away.

I pinched the bridge of my nose and let out a long breath, willing the primal part of my brain to chill the hell out because she *wasn't* mine.

No matter what delusions I entertained at night while trying to sleep.

She re-appeared in a new pair of boots, black leather with matching stitching. Her sleeveless white linen blouse boasted a respectful scoop neckline, revealing tan skin and *many* memories of tracing that exact spot on her collarbone with my tongue.

The sight of Cassie Phillips in jeans was enough to take me out, and I was suddenly questioning what in the hell had possessed me to come here in the first place.

"These are my going-out boots," she offered.

"Right," I said, trying to tear my eyes away from her thighs. "You look..."

Stunning. Incredible. Like I forgot my damn name when I looked at her.

"You're staring," Cassie teased.

I didn't have the heart to deny it.

I also didn't miss the hitch in her breathing when I extended a hand towards her, offering her a hand down.

It was a ridiculous notion, considering there were only two small stairs between the two of us, but to my eternal surprise, Cassie took it.

One touch.

That was all it took for the memories of that night to invade my headspace, suffocating every thought that had nothing to do with her. She still had the same effect on me as she had that night—she made the noise in my head go quiet.

When I was with Cassie, I felt like I could take on the damn world. There was no divorce, no re-enlistment, no stress about what was coming next.

As soon as she descended the steps and we were on equal footing, I pulled her closer, daring to rub my thumb over the back of her hand. I raised my free hand to tuck a stray piece of her black hair behind her ear. I watched her throat work as she swallowed.

"There," I said, voice lower than usual. "Had a flyaway."

"What a gentleman," Cassie whispered.

"Only for you."

Cassie's answering gasp had my control slipping. I reached out to brush my fingertips against the slender curve of her jaw and her eyes widened.

"Cass, I—"

"Hey!" Imogen's voice rang out from the top of the hill, and I let go of Cassie's hand like it was on fire. "You're supposed to be at the barn in ten minutes!"

"We're coming," I shouted back. "Don't freak out."

"Ten minutes, Morales!" came Imogen's shrill response.

I rolled my eyes.

Imogen's anxiety manifested itself in many ways, but the most prominent of them was her need to control the outcome of every event she planned. Not only was event coordinator her paid role at Winding Road, but she took great pride in her ability to plan events for her friends.

"Some things never change," Cassie said, starting up the hill. I quickly matched her pace and caught up with her so could walk side by side, because there was no way in hell I was surviving staring at the round curve of her ass the entire way to the barn.

Cassie didn't reach for me again, and I didn't dare reach for her this close to prying eyes.

But I felt her drift closer to me as we walked, without even realizing it, and somehow, that felt more like an acknowledgement than words could express.

"Chug, chug, chug!"

The words echoed in my skull like a dare. I sucked harder

on the silicone nipple, putting every ounce of my willpower into getting the apple juice through the tiny opening.

There was no damn way I was about to let a *baby bottle* beat me.

Not in front of my best friends, and certainly not in front of a woman I wanted to impress.

"Oh crap, it's between Lucas and Connor," Abbie said.

"Yeah, babe, I love you, but you're done," Imogen agreed. "You can safely drop out now."

Kameron let out an indignant sigh as he slammed the bottle down on the table. I didn't dare break my concentration. I chose one rafter and stared at it, putting all of my mental and physical energy into sucking.

Connor let out a frustrated grunt. A few seconds later, I hazarded a glance at my bottle. One or two more good sucks, and it would be over.

"Screw this," Connor muttered and slammed his bottle down on the table in front of us. "There's no competing with him. He's a machine."

Not one to win by default simply because the other guys dropped out, I finished the task and slammed my bottle down on the table, a victorious grin spreading across my face.

"There he is," Kameron said, clapping his hands and whooping with amusement. "That's the Morales I know and love."

I turned to look at Imogen and blew her a kiss. "Happy?"

She wiped a stray tear from her eyes as her shoulders shook with laughter.

"Like you wouldn't believe," Imogen managed through

gasping breaths.

"I can't," Abbie wheezed. "You were so into it."

"I don't like losing," I said, pointing an accusing finger at Connor, who was shaking his head, a silly grin on his face. "Don't taunt me if you don't want the smoke."

Connor held up his hands in mock surrender.

My gaze finally landed on Cassie, who was staring at me with a mixture of confusion and awe, like she couldn't figure out what the hell was going on inside my head.

And truthfully, I didn't know either. I couldn't think properly when she was around.

"Okay, gender reveal time," Imogen said, clapping her hands together. "And before anyone asks, Abbie and Connor decided they wanted to do this at their baby shower. Nobody pressured them."

I raised an eyebrow. "No external pressure? None?"

"It's true," Abbie said, cheeks flushed pink, her hand resting gently over her baby bump. "As fun as a surprise would have been, I've been too anxious not knowing. Imogen has had the results letter for forever, but we're finally letting her use it."

Imogen beamed in triumph.

"We've got two cupcakes, one for each of the parents to be. There's colored icing in the middle."

"Wait," I interjected. "You know?"

"Duh," Imogen said, a smile on her face. "Someone had to order the cupcakes from Blackbeard's."

"Okay, last guesses," Kam said, jumping in like an eager golden retriever who was seconds away from being allowed to swim in the lake. "I say boy."

"Girl," I said. I didn't know why, but when I looked at Abbie and Connor, that was what felt right. Everyone turned to Cassie, who tucked that same stray piece of hair behind her ear and shrugged.

"I think it's a girl," Cassie said softly.

"And I'm not guessing because then I'd spoil the surprise," Imogen said. "Dig in."

Abbie and Connor both grinned at each other before they tore into their cupcakes. The joy that radiated from Abbie's face when Connor pulled back with a mouthful of pink icing had my chest tightening. She let out a surprised gasp. Connor was grinning from ear to ear.

"Yes!" Kam hollered, fist pumping the air. "Baby girl Harvey."

Connor leaned forward to hug Abbie, whispering something in her ear that made her fingers tighten in his shirt. If there were ever two people who deserved this kind of fairytale happy ending, it was the two of them.

The energy in the room was infectious. Abbie and Imogen dived into a conversation about the future nursery, while Kam and Connor struck up a conversation about how things were going with finding a plot of land to call their own. It sounded like they were keeping Abbie's condo for the next little while, wanting to be close to Watford and Abbie's father, and with the housing market the way it was, it was probably in their best interest to wait.

Finally, my eyes landed on Cassie.

There was an emotion on her face I couldn't place. A mix of wistfulness and joy that I didn't think I'd ever seen before.

Before I was even fully aware of what I was doing, I stood

up and walked over to her, occupying the empty seat next to her.

"I feel like I've seen this movie before," Cassie said, gesturing to me sliding into the seat next to her.

"Did you like the ending?"

Cassie's eyes crinkled in amusement.

"Did you just make a Taylor Swift joke?"

"That depends on whether you're a fan."

"Of course I'm a fan," Cassie said, affronted. "You should know that."

I grinned. "I do know that. I remember things."

"Yeah?" Cassie said, inclining her head towards me. "What things?"

"Everything," I admitted. "I remember everything."

Chapter 12
Cassie

Seattle, Washington
21:30

"N o."

"No what?" I said, gesturing to the beautiful bookshop in front of us.

"There's no way I'm going in there. I'll get lost and die forgotten in the stacks."

I rolled my eyes. "It's big, but they have signs. You *can* read, right?"

"I don't read," he said.

When my eyes widened in horror, he quickly backtracked and explained, "I don't read *often*."

"Tell you what," I said, turning to face him. "How about we pick out books for each other?"

Lucas's nose scrunched in the most adorable way. The way this man oscillated between hot and cute was a talent that needed to be studied.

"Do we know each other well enough for that?"

I considered this for a moment. "You're right. I'm changing our itinerary."

I grabbed his hand again, linking our fingers together and dragging him down the sidewalk, away from the world's largest bookstore and back into the heart of the city.

"I would ask where we're going, but something tells me it's another surprise."

"The entire purpose of this excursion is to help you fall in love with Seattle," I said.

We brushed past another couple, and when I pressed closer to Lucas to avoid a full-on collision, he folded my body into his like it was the most natural thing on the planet.

The feral part of my brain very nearly lost it.

"Thank you," I murmured, reveling in the warmth of his body, the sheer closeness of him.

Lucas was objectively handsome. Tan skin, black hair, clean-shaven but still rugged around the edges. I was not a short woman, especially in heels, but he still had at least two inches on me.

The difference made my heart flutter.

We resumed our stroll. I grabbed his arm, trying not to gawk at the feel of hard muscle beneath my hands.

"This is Batter Up," I said, throwing my arms out in my best ta-da motion. "The best cookie shop in Seattle."

"Now this is what I'm talking about," Lucas said, eyes lighting up with glee. "Those cookies look like they're the size of my head."

"Yes," I squealed. "And they're fucking delicious."

"You know the way to a man's heart," Lucas said, a laugh rumbling in his chest. The sound sent a skitter down my spine. He pulled the door open for us, and we stepped inside. There was a massive line at this time of night, given that Batter Up was one of the more popular late-night places to get a late night sweet treat in this block of town.

"So, what's the best flavor?" Lucas asked, sensing that we'd be waiting in line for a minute.

"Any of them," I said honestly. "Though I'm partial to the chocolate brookie or white chocolate macadamia nut."

Lucas let out a low whistle.

"I did *not* peg you for a macadamia nut kind of gal."

"It's the most underrated flavor," I said with a shrug. "Constantly overshadowed by its more popular siblings. I'm still waiting for it to have its viral moment on social media, but until then, I'll be waiting patiently. Probably here."

I didn't know where this was coming from. I rambled about my love affair with white chocolate macadamia nut cookies because I feared the conversation would end if I stopped talking.

"Good to know," Lucas said, bumping my shoulder with his. And it wasn't a friendly bro bump either. It was more of an 'I'm tucking this new piece of information away for later' bump, and I *really* didn't know how to handle that.

As the line crept forward and we approached the display counter, Lucas slid his hand onto the small of my back.

Just like his touch on the street, the move was natural. Practiced.

As if we'd been dating for years and were simply out on a

date night.

We ended up ordering half a dozen cookies. Lucas, being a cookie aficionado, wanted to try the daily flavor—orange crème—in addition to their usual run-of-the-mill flavors like chocolate chip and snickerdoodle. I won the wallet race at the checkout, slamming my smartwatch over the tap-to-pay button before Lucas could. We even snagged a booth after a family vacated it right as we were walking past.

"Lucky break," I said as we sat down opposite each other. "It's usually impossible to find a seat in-house on a week-night. It's not too loud for you, right?"

"Nah," Lucas said, waving a hand dismissively. He set the cookie box down in the middle. "I work on a farm. I'm used to the background noise."

"A farm, huh?" I said. "Now that explains your dislike of the city."

"The city is… growing on me."

I beamed so wide my cheeks hurt.

"We've barely scratched the surface of what Seattle offers."

"Call it a hunch," Lucas said, smirking. "I have an excellent tour guide."

I pressed my lips together in what was probably a very unattractive trying-not-to-smile facial twist. Conversing with Lucas was *easy*. There were no masks to wear. No agenda to go through. No pressure to be anything other than who I was.

There was a layer of anonymity that comforted me. I could be myself because there was little chance of this extending past one night. I was fresh off the heels of a breakup, and Lucas deviated from my typical, easily segmented life.

"Okay," I said, clapping my hands together. "Let's dig in. You first."

Lucas opened the box, revealing the thick, perfectly baked cookies.

"We're supposed to be interviewing each other before our book-finding mission," Lucas said. "How about I take a bite for each question you answer?"

"You have a deal," I said, all too eager to keep the night going as long as possible. It was strange, this feeling of not wanting something to end. I realized with a start that I couldn't remember the last time I'd felt it.

"Favorite animal?"

"Giraffe."

Lucas chuckled.

"What's funny?"

"I guessed right," Lucas said. I narrowed my eyes at him.

"You're not using your masculine wiles on me, right? Lying about getting the answer right just to impress me?"

"Ha ha," Lucas deadpanned. "I'll have you know that guessing people's favorite animals is one of my talents."

"Of which I'm sure you have many."

Lucas's jaw ticked in amusement as he reached for the snickerdoodle cookie.

"I'm good at reading people," Lucas said. "As for the other talents, we'll have to make it to our third date to find out."

I let out a surprised laugh. "Is this our second date?"

"Sure is," Lucas replied. "Rain's was our first. Batter Up is our second."

My face was sore from how wildly I'd been smiling the entire time.

"And our third date?" I said, out of breath.

"I guess we'll find out."

I shivered, and not because the air conditioning suddenly cranked on.

"Favorite Disney princess?" Lucas asked, giving me a thumbs up as he finished his half of the cookie. I sat back in the booth and pursed my lips together in contemplation.

"In terms of relatability or aspiration?"

Lucas pondered this for a second.

"Both."

I finished my bite of snickerdoodle and considered this.

"I guess I relate to Tiana the most. I'm a workaholic and a perfectionist. When I'm focused on something, it takes up all my mental energy. That kind of ambition doesn't always lend itself to romantic relationships." I winced. "As is evident from the fact that I caught my boyfriend cheating with my coworker tonight. I can only assume she was more emotionally available than I was."

Lucas's eyes darkened and his fingers flexed, an involuntary reaction to the mention of Collin that sent a thrill through me.

I was certain that Collin had never been in an actual fight in his life. He had a doctor's hands: pristine and unblemished. Steady in a clinical way.

Lucas, on the other hand? His hands were just as steady, but his calluses made it clear that he knew the meaning of manual labor.

I got the sense that he'd been on the receiving end of a few punches and had thrown a few of his own.

A thought that shouldn't have been as attractive as it was.

"And for aspiration?"

I sighed wistfully.

"I'll answer honestly, but you can't make fun of me."

"I won't," Lucas said, swearing across his chest.

"Cinderella," I admitted. To Lucas's credit, he didn't balk. He simply gestured for me to explain.

"There's something about the fantasy of love at first sight that's always intrigued me. What do you mean this handsome fairytale prince knew from one dance that this was the woman he wanted to marry? The idea that two people could share such a brief, intimate connection that then consumed them until they reunited is comical. And yet there's this part of me that thinks *yes*. That's the kind of love I want one day."

Lucas's expression was full of something I couldn't name, his features softening.

"Sorry," I choked out, suddenly embarrassed. The fruity cocktail I had at Rain's was catching up with me. "You did *not* ask for that."

"I did," Lucas murmured. "That's one of the realest, most honest things a woman has ever said to me on a date."

I reached for the plastic knife we were using to cut the cookies.

"That's probably the most honest thing I've said to someone in a long time," I admitted quietly.

So much for anonymity.

Lucas reached for my hand. Just like at the bar, my entire

arm lit up with awareness, sparks traveling where our fingertips met all the way to my chest, which flushed hot at the contact.

"I like you honest," he murmured.

Normally, I would make a quip about how guys like their women honest until it's too much.

Men respected honesty until it overshadowed them. Guys wanted the truth until it painted them in an unpleasant light.

Somehow I got the sense that Lucas wasn't like that. In the three hours since he first struck up a conversation with me at Rain's, he'd never given me a reason to doubt him.

"What's the verdict?" I asked half an hour later when most of the cookies were gone. We'd swapped questions in between bites. Everything from his favorite Disney princess—Ariel—to what cruise we'd go on if money was no object. To my eternal surprise, we both said the Balkans, because we loved the ocean but were sick of the Pacific and Atlantic.

"Damn," was all Lucas said as he crossed his arms and leaned back against the booth.

"Rendered speechless," I said, delighted by his reaction. "Told you they were good."

"I never doubted you for a second," Lucas said, sighing and patting his stomach. "But now you've put me in such a sugar coma that I don't think Powell's is a good idea."

I considered this for a moment, jerking forward as an idea struck me.

"Let's go for a walk," I said. "It'll be good for both of us. Work some of the sugar rush off."

Lucas's smile was blinding.

Stepping onto the Seattle sidewalk felt different this time. Charged with something I was scared to name and wanted desperately to grab hold of.

My body was a live wire as Lucas took my hand in his again. This time, he didn't just hold my hand. He linked our fingers together and pulled me in close to his side as we walked.

"You know, this place is growing on me," Lucas said, and something warm and heady filled my chest.

"I've done my job well then," I said.

"And the night's not over yet," Lucas remarked as I steered him towards Kerry Park. It would be a longer walk from the city, but well worth it for the view of the city and the quality time spent with this man.

"Yeah," I said, squeezing his hand as we walked. "The night's not over yet."

Chapter 13
Lucas

A week after the baby shower, the five of us had settled into a strange rhythm. Cassie and I took care of the horses in the morning before heading to the fields to check on the crops and orchard, while Kam, Connor, and Imogen typically spent the mornings going over event and cohort logistics.

Abbie spent most of her time house hunting and thinking about the nursery, and I was damn glad she was taking time to rest and enjoy her time. Her father had maintained his sobriety in the last year and was now working closely with Kevin, Imogen and Cassie's younger brother, to take back over operations at the general store the Collins family owned.

This morning, however, had been awkward.

Imogen and Cassie had spent all of yesterday in Watford. Doing what, I didn't exactly know, but I assumed it had been a lot of sightseeing and reconnecting, given that it had been well over a decade since Cassie had been back in Watford.

When Imogen and Kameron descended the stairs to join Connor, Abbie and me at the breakfast table, Imogen's gaze was stormy. Kameron's thumb made a silent slicing motion beneath his chin, and I heard his message loud and clear. Imogen was on the warpath this morning. I had a feeling Cassie wouldn't be joining us for breakfast.

"This house is too fucking crowded," Imogen muttered as she made her coffee. "It's making me claustrophobic."

"I can stay in the other tiny house," I offered. "Abbie and Connor are heading back to Watford today since it's getting harder for Abbie to sit in the car for that long. You two can have the farmhouse to yourselves."

Abbie shot me a grateful smile, clearly not wanting to rock the boat too much.

Imogen nodded, leaning into Kam when he came to stand beside her in the kitchen.

"*Please.*"

"Consider it done," I said. I made a mental note to myself to pack a bag later.

Our setup at Winding Road needed adjusting now that Imogen lived here with Kam full time. The farmhouse had transitioned from a bachelor pad into a central hub for everyone's coming and goings.

I didn't blame Imogen for being overwhelmed, and selfishly, I was happy to have an excuse to be near Cassie. Even if she didn't want to talk to me beyond basic pleasantries and the occasional string of flirting that went nowhere meaningful.

We still hadn't really talked about Seattle. Not since the first night when we were both too blindsided by being in each other's presence again.

I wanted to ask her about it, but every time I got close, Cassie evaded the question or completely changed the subject.

"I'm going to the barn to work this morning," Imogen said. "I need some damn *space*."

I nodded. "Text me if you need anything."

Kam mouthed "thank you" as he followed her out the front door of the farmhouse, letting the screen door slam shut behind him.

Abbie's stare brought me up short as I turned back to my plate of eggs.

"Um, is everything okay?"

"I'm on to you," Abbie said, narrowing her eyes at me. Connor took a long sip of his coffee while Abbie stirred her tea, her eyes never leaving mine. It was unsettling when Abbie stared at people for this long, like she had x-ray vision that could see through even the sturdiest defenses.

"I don't know what that means," I said carefully, keeping my tone as neutral as possible before shoveling a bite of eggs in my mouth.

"*Something* weird is going on. Every time you and Ca—"

"Abs," Connor said, nudging her leg with his. "Don't push."

"I'm not pushing," Abbie said, eyes bright with amusement. "I'm just letting you know. I'll figure it out. I always do."

I rolled my eyes affectionately.

"Never change, Abbie Collins."

"Don't plan to," she said sweetly, sitting back in her chair.

"How are you feeling?" I said, eager to change the subject. Her features softened as she rubbed a hand over her belly.

"Still good," Abbie said. "I keep waiting for things to take a turn and to be miserable until she's born, but pregnancy has treated me well so far."

"I'll say," Connor murmured. I let out a choked laugh as Abbie blushed and playfully punched his arm.

"I'm heading to the stables," I said, stretching my arms above my head.

"We'll see you in a week," Abbie replied. "Hopefully."

"Drive safe," I said, clapping Connor on the shoulder as I stood up.

"We always do," Connor said, squeezing Abbie's thigh affectionately. Something in my chest tightened whenever I observed the two of them. There was an ease in their relationship that I envied.

There had been only one time in my life that I'd felt that kind of intimacy with another person.

And she was the only person at Winding Road that wanted nothing to do with me.

When I entered the stables, it was immediately apparent that Imogen was not the only Phillips child not having a good day.

Cassie normally kept the stable impressively organized, always putting tools and tack back in their proper places, but today the place was in disarray.

My relationship with my sister had been strained in the last few years, but I remembered how the two of us would walk on eggshells around each other when we had bad days.

"Today is not a good day," Cassie said when she saw me.

I did a double take at the sight of her in jeans—again—and threw my hands up in mock surrender. "Don't push me."

"I wasn't planning on it," I said as calmly as I could manage. Cassie was a firecracker when her emotions got the best of her.

"Good," she quipped, reaching for the hoof pick hanging against the barn wall. She gripped it firmly in her hand and headed for Chesty's stall. I blinked in surprise when I realized he was the only horse in the stable.

"How long have you been here?"

"Long enough," she muttered as she entered Chesty's stall, giving his neck a rub before lifting his leg up and picking the dirt and clay out of his hoof.

I pressed my lips together, fighting off my annoyance.

"What do you want from me, Lucas?" Cassie said, exasperated.

"I want you to talk to me," I said, gritting my teeth together.

I could handle Cassie's big emotions. I wasn't scared of her, or the way she lashed out when she felt cornered.

I also knew she would try like hell to hide from me.

And I wasn't having that.

"I want you to stop the hot and cold act."

"Hot and cold act?" Cassie scoffed, moving to Chesty's other leg. "God, this is such a nightmare."

"I don't understand how we went from that night in Seattle to here. You were an open book, Cass. You told me things I'm sure you've never told another soul. But ever since we saw each other at dinner, it's been different. You're fine with my presence one day, and give me the cold shoulder the next day," I said, the words tumbling from me.

I ran a hand through my hair, trying to rein in my own temper. Cassie could rile me in a way no one else could. I wasn't as unflappable as Kam or as stoic as Connor. Of the three of us, I was the one most likely to fly off the handle. But I'd worked damn hard the last few years to be better.

Cassie though? She got under my skin.

"I'm so sorry to shatter the illusion that some people aren't happy-go-lucky every damn day," Cassie snapped. I was so taken aback by her tone that I stood there, counting backwards from a hundred while she finished cleaning Chesty's hooves. She placed the lead around his neck and led him from the stall. I followed her to the pasture, fists clenching and unclenching at my sides.

I was a persistent bastard, but it still stung every time she kicked the metaphorical door in my face when I tried to be there for her.

"That wasn't what I meant, and you know it," I said as she released Chesty back into the pasture.

Cass turned back to me, eyes filled with a fire I hadn't seen before.

"What do you want me to say?" She asked, curling the lead around her hand as she stormed past me, heading back to the stable.

"I want you to tell me what happened yesterday that has you and your sister so upset," I said. "I want you to be honest with me."

"Why do you care?" Cass spat.

I couldn't help it; I snorted.

Her eyes simmered with anger. A muscle in my jaw

twitched, and I crossed my arms over my chest as I took a step closer to her. She adjusted her feet, widening her stance as if she were preparing for a standoff.

Something flared in my chest at the realization that I got under her skin the same way she did to me.

"Why is it so hard for you to accept that I care about your wellbeing, Cass?"

She sucked in a sharp breath; she didn't have a snappy comeback for that one. Cass let out a groan of frustration and fisted her hair with both hands as she turned away from me.

"I don't know!" she finally shouted, pressing the heels of her palms against her eyes. The sound echoed off the rafters of the stable, her desperation reverberating in my bones.

"*Fuck*, Lucas, I don't *know*. And repeating the same question isn't helping me figure it out."

That was a fair criticism, but she was still dodging the heart of the problem.

I wasn't Imogen. And there was no way in hell I was going to let her turn away from me.

"Then talk to me," I said, pleading. "Let me help you."

Cassie swore loudly, taking another step away from me and refusing to meet my eyes.

I stood there, arms crossed over my chest, listening in the silence. I would stay here for hours waiting if she needed me to.

I'd wait her out.

She could throw whatever she had at me, and I would still be there, ready for her with open arms.

"I went to Watford with Imogen yesterday," she finally whispered. "And it was fucking awful."

"What happened?" I murmured.

She flinched. It was an almost imperceptible twitch of her shoulder that made my heart sink.

"Whatever you're carrying, Cass, I can hold it."

Cassie finally dared to look at me, and the pain and devastation on her face was enough to crush me.

"I think there's too much between us," Cassie choked out. Her sniffle was the only signal that she was on the verge of crying. "Imogen and I—there's too much hurt. There are too many things I can't explain, things I can't justify. She needs answers from me, and I *can't* give them to her."

I realized then that there was panic lining her features. Cassie's hands trembled when she wiped them on the front of her jeans. I knew Cassie, Kevin, and Imogen didn't have good relationships with their parents. I didn't know everything, but I knew enough.

I knew Imogen had a hard time trusting people after her piece of shit ex broke her down mentally and physically.

And Cass...

She had experienced something life-altering in Watford. I didn't know what it was, and I didn't want to speculate. It wasn't my place.

But seeing her broken and falling apart was breaking *me*.

"She'll wait for you," I said, trying to close the distance between us. I wanted to hold her hand, to make her look at me and remember that it *would* be okay. "I promise you she will."

Cassie's laugh was harsh, the sound so different from the

laugh I knew.

It wasn't the loud snort that took her by surprise, the one she couldn't stop when she was so fully in the moment she forgot to tamper with the sound, to make it more palatable for others. It wasn't even the fake chuckle she threw out as a party favor.

"I want to believe you," Cassie whispered, kicking a stray piece of straw on the floor. "I think coming here was a mistake." She let out a shaky breath. "And I don't know what the fuck to do about that, considering I no longer have a job to go back to. Everything I told myself I wanted, everything I worked for... I burned it all to the ground."

"You'll figure it out," I said. "You always have."

"Yeah," Cassie muttered, wiping her nose before putting her hands on her hips. "I guess I'm just really fucking tired of it."

"Of figuring it out?"

Cassie let out a long sigh, tipping her face to the ceiling. "Of all of it, Lucas."

Chapter 14
Cassie

When I pushed past Lucas to walk back to my tiny house, I prayed he wouldn't follow.

Lucas disarmed me in a way I couldn't handle on a day like today. I'd worked too damn hard over the years to keep everything tucked away in a neat little box.

Watford was in a box. Imogen was in a box. I'd shoved my career and Collin into boxes.

Lucas had never fit into a box.

I'd never even tried to put him in one.

That night played on a loop in my mind on the bad days. The conversations we had, the truths we shared, the memory of his skin against mine—there wasn't a box in the universe big enough to hold all of my feelings about that night and Lucas's presence in it.

I'd been okay with that until I saw him in person again.

There would be no drinking at the Roadhouse. First, because it would be a slap in the face to Abbie, Imogen, and the rest of their friend group who had chosen sobriety. Second, because my desire to get messy-drunk might impact my ability to make good choices.

I wanted it to. And if there's one thing I knew about

Watford, it was that there weren't many options for poor decisions.

And God did I want to make a poor decision.

Even as I waited on the front steps of the farmhouse for the Uber that would take me to Brighton so I could drown my sorrows, I knew this is what it was like to spiral out of control.

I was a textbook warning sign of a problem. I'd lost my job, lost my relationship, and then had a one-night stand with a man I couldn't stop thinking about.

A man who was best friends with my younger sister and was now trying to help me work through my shit.

Did I mention I was also trying to mend said relationship with my sister, after years of turning a blind eye to her pain because I couldn't manage my own?

It was a shitshow.

When my Uber driver finally arrived, I did the bare minimum and verified the license plate matched before climbing in the backseat.

I pulled out my phone to scroll, immediately regretting my decision when the first post on my Instagram feed was Collin and Cassidy.

They were at the top of the Needle, Collin's face pressing a gentle kiss to her jaw. It was so *casual*, so intimate, like the two of us hadn't been on the verge of celebrating an anniversary less than six months ago. Like he hadn't texted me multiple times in the same timeframe.

He'd taken me on the same date last year. I'd thought it was so special, the way he'd meticulously planned every detail of the excursion. He'd said all the right words, made the ticket reservations for the perfect time so we got the best view of the city.

But it wasn't just that he was taking his new girlfriend on the same date he'd taken me on that brought my thoughts to a screeching halt.

It was the girl's wide smile and her outstretched left hand, which now boasted a rock that I knew damn well cost Collin every dime he had.

Betrayal coiled deep in my stomach.

The knowledge that their affair had gone on for months unraveled the last thread of my sanity. I would probably never know exactly how long the two of them were running around behind my back.

And for him to have texted me just days ago saying it was a mistake?

That poor girl had no idea what realm of insanity she'd just entered.

"Bastard," I seethed. "You absolute *bastard.*"

My driver glanced up as I finally blocked the asshole's number, turned my phone face down, and shoved it between my legs.

The audacity of this man not only to throw away whatever connection we once had, but to flaunt it on social media. I knew I should have deleted the Instagram app months ago. I knew I should have formally laid that chapter of my life to rest. I had no one but myself to blame.

Ignorance was bliss, and I'd shattered the illusion I'd been hiding behind for the last month.

I stared out the window for the rest of the ride. When we passed the sign for Brighton, I gestured to the neon bar sign on the right side of the main street. Unlike Watford, there were several bars and restaurants in Brighton. The world was my oyster for the next few hours.

"That one works," I said. "Thank you."

The driver muttered something unintelligible. I added a tip as I stepped onto the sidewalk, all too eager to get inside.

I stood outside my bar of choice and snapped a picture of the green neon sign that read "Jaded Lady." This was definitely the place I needed to be tonight.

The place reminded me of Rain's, with one pool table shoved towards the back wall and a mismatched collection of chairs and barstools that only added to the ambience of the dimly lit space.

To my relief, the bar wasn't completely packed, but there were still a dozen people milling about. That meant more anonymity and less small talk for me, and that was what I wanted from my evening. I didn't want to think about Watford or Imogen or the conversation we'd had yesterday.

"Whiskey, please. Neat," I asked the bartender after sliding onto a stool towards the end of the bar. He nodded and grabbed a shot glass.

"Bad day?" the man asked as he slid the amber liquid towards me.

I shrugged and downed the drink in one go, signaling for another one. The bartender didn't so much as shrug as he poured me another, sliding it over to me.

"Family problems."

He let out a hum of acknowledgment. "Explains the whiskey straight off the bat."

"Anything to take the edge off," I muttered.

"Boy problems too, or just family problems?"

I laughed in slight disbelief.

"It's a little early for assumptions, isn't it?"

"Color me curious," the man said. "I'm Jared, by the way."

"Jared," I repeated, sticking my hand out for him to shake. "I'm Cassie."

He quirked his eyebrows in amusement but took my hand.

"Are you from around here, Cassie?" Jared asked as he picked up the rag lying on the counter and threw it over his shoulder.

I bit the inside of my cheek.

To lie, or not to lie.

"I'm from Watford, actually."

"No shit," Jared said. "We used to have a regular from there. He was in here damn near every Sunday night. Haven't seen him in a while though."

A faint smile graced my lips.

"Malcolm?" I offered.

Jared snapped his fingers as his eyes lit up with recognition. "That's the guy."

"He got sober," I said.

"And he's doing well?"

I nodded.

"Good," Jared said, and something like relief settled over his features. "Glad to hear he made it out okay."

I toyed with the shot glass in my hand, a million thoughts flitting through my mind. I had too many fucking thoughts these days and no way to distill them into something manageable.

Uprooting my life in Seattle threw more than just my career off kilter.

I was on a different trajectory now—floating aimlessly in the void of life.

I slid the glass back to him and nodded, not meeting his eyes. Jared didn't push, but I got the sense he would watch me closely tonight.

If he knew Malcolm, he knew Abbie—and Lord only knows who else he knew.

Fine by me.

I had no fucks left to give.

I was pretty convinced I could fly if given the opportunity.

For the first time in weeks, I let my hair down, a mixed drink in my right hand. The bar got crowded after eight, people pairing off in groups or couples and swaying to the music with increasing vigor as the drinks kept flowing. The speakers blasted a pop artist I didn't recognize, and I realized that the most beautiful aspect of music was that it was a universal language.

I didn't need to know the words or artist. I just had to dance.

As I swayed to the beat, my eyes briefly scanned the crowd. It had been over a decade since I'd been back in Watford County, even longer since I'd been on the Brighton strip, but I needed one night where I wasn't worrying about impressing someone. My eyes snagged on the door as a tall, dark-haired, glowering man entered the bar.

I swore under my breath when I realized who it was.

I stalked towards the bar, eager to intercept him before Jared told Lucas more than he needed to hear.

No such luck. Lucas clocked me as soon as I exited the throng of sweaty bodies, making a beeline straight for me.

"Who told you I was here?" I exclaimed when he was within arm's reach. "I came all the way out here so—"

"No one would come after you?" Lucas said, crossing his arms over his chest as he stared down at me.

People continued to dance around us, but they gave us a wide berth when they saw Lucas staring down at me, clearly annoyed.

"Tough luck. I was the one doing rounds tonight, and imagine my surprise when I knocked on the door of your tiny house to ask if you needed anything, only to find all the lights off and you nowhere in sight."

Oh, hell.

"I called your phone," Lucas said before hiking a thumb over his shoulder in Jared's direction. "He picked up, confirmed you were here, and gave me the address."

"You answered my *phone*?" I yelled accusingly at Jared, but the sound barely carried over the bass thumping around us.

Jared didn't look the least bit sorry that he'd taken my phone an hour earlier, citing that I should be free to enjoy the dance floor unhindered. That conniving little bastard.

"You should really get a passcode on that thing," Jared commented helpfully.

I sighed, looking up towards the ceiling. Big mistake,

considering the room nearly spun out from underneath me.

I flailed unceremoniously.

Warm hands grabbed my waist to steady me. My eyes flew open, and *damn.*

Lucas looked beautiful when he was vaguely pissed off. I didn't know if it was the alcohol clouding my vision or the fact that I was clearly near my ovulatory phase, but he looked more incredible in the dim light of the bar than my memory had given justice to.

"I need to pay my tab," I said, trying to shove past him.

"It's taken care of," Lucas murmured against my ear, placing his hand in the small of my back. Every nerve ending in my body lit up with full awareness of how big his palm was against me.

Did I have a hand kink? Was that a thing?

Did I have a size kink because there were very few men in the world who were taller than me *and* commanded a presence?

Or was it just a Lucas kink?

My head spun with the possibilities when I closed my eyes briefly, and I quickly decided that I could not close my eyes without risking a broken neck.

"Let's go," Lucas mumbled, clearly exasperated by this turn of events for his evening.

Tough shit. I didn't ask him to come save me.

"Oh, here's her purse-clutch-thing," Jared said, thrusting my personal effects towards Lucas. "I don't know what we're supposed to call it these days."

"Thanks," Lucas muttered, grabbing the small black bag

from his outstretched hand. I frowned at Jared, the turn-coat.

"Not a problem," Jared replied. "It was nice to meet you, Cassie. You two have a good night."

I could have sworn there was a smirk on Jared's face as Lucas guided me through the throng of people crowding the entrance, all too eager to get inside and join the party. I pouted when I realized my night of fun was done.

"Jared was nice to me," I said, words slurring as I clung to Lucas's side. "He even cut me off after my last drink and said I was done." I hiccuped. "What a *gentleman*."

"I'm glad," Lucas said, but his voice was tight. I frowned as we approached his truck, whirling around to face him.

I spun too fast, nearly losing my balance until Lucas wrapped his arms around my waist, steadying me.

My eyes darted up to his face, and I watched as he swallowed, a muscle ticking in his jaw like he wanted to say something, *do* something, and was barely holding himself back.

"I want you," I blurted. I was driving this steam train of an evening straight off the tracks and I was helpless to stop it, the alcohol in my veins blurring the lines. "I can't stop thinking about what you said—"

"Don't finish that sentence," Lucas said quietly, his voice choked.

His fingers tightened around my hips, and I squeezed my eyes shut, remembering how good it had felt to have him naked underneath me.

"I am trying really hard to do the honorable thing here, but you're..."

"I remember," I confessed, pulling back to look him in the eyes. My arms wrapped around his neck, and he shivered—honest to God *shivered* —when my nails grazed his nape. "I remember all of it."

"*Cassie*," Lucas whispered, my name a plea on his lips. "You know how badly I want you. I already told you. And if you want me back in your bed, I will come willingly and eagerly. But not when you're drunk and an hour away from home."

A noise escaped my mouth that sounded suspiciously like a whine.

"Fuck me," Lucas muttered, rubbing a hand over his face. "Please get in the truck."

"Kiss me," I pleaded. "Please."

Lucas swore again, the sound barely audible. He cupped my jaw with both hands, tilting my face up towards his. Yes, *God yes*—

He pressed a chaste kiss to my lips before taking a step back.

Cool air rushed between us, and I gasped at the loss of contact. I wanted to reach for him, drag his body back to mine, but the pained expression on his face made me pause.

"Get in the truck," Lucas said, wiping a hand down his face. "*Please*, Cass. I'm begging you."

The whole time I'd been thinking about me and my messed up life, and I hadn't taken a step back to look at him. The twist of his facial features, the internal war he was fighting, the heat in his eyes.

I'd basically called him here. Not physically. But Lucas

was a good man.

There wasn't a snowflake's chance in hell that he wouldn't drag himself out of bed in the middle of the night to come pick me up after I willingly made a series of horrible choices.

"Okay," I whispered, turning my back towards Lucas and opening the car door with shaky fingers.

Lucas stopped at the driver's side door, putting both of his hands out to grip the top of his truck. I could see his chest rising and falling with deep breaths, his biceps flexing with the restraint he clung to. I swallowed tightly and squeezed my eyes shut, trying to block out the tidal wave of memory that washed over me. I knew exactly what he liked, how he *felt*—

He finally opened the door and climbed inside, slamming the door shut as both of his hands rested on the steering wheel.

"I'm—"

Lucas quickly silenced my apology with a kiss.

One minute his hands were on the wheel, and the next they were on me, hot and demanding, putting me exactly where he wanted me. One hand was curled around the back of my neck, tilting my face up towards his.

His other palm rested gently on the column of my throat, his thumb running a line across the sensitive skin beneath.

I reached out for him, my hands cupping his stubbled jaw, deepening the kiss, licking into his mouth like I had the right to.

This was what I'd needed. What I'd craved every day since Seattle.

When he pulled away, he looked completely windswept, his black hair disheveled from my roaming hands and his eyes dark with desire.

His palm was still on my throat, and even when he pulled his hand away entirely, I felt its presence there, like a brand I wanted to keep.

"Why did you wait?" I said, breathless and slightly dizzy from the feel of him this close to me. Lucas pulled back entirely.

"Because if I have to drive, I have to stop kissing you," Lucas said, clicking his seatbelt into place. "And if you'd stayed pressed up against my truck like that, asking me, *begging* me—I don't think I would have been able to stop."

Heat flared low in my stomach at his words. I swallowed tightly, leaning my head against the cool windowpane.

"I'm sorry," I whispered.

"You don't have to apologize," Lucas said, voice rough with something I couldn't name. "But we're not doing this when you're drunk. When you say yes, you'll be sober. You'll feel everything. Just like you did the first time."

I shivered, and not just from the cool blast of the air conditioning against my damp skin.

We were ten minutes into the drive before I realized he'd said when, not if.

As if he knew we were inevitable, and he was just waiting for me to catch up.

I clung to Lucas as we stumbled down the dirt path towards

the tiny house.

I opened my mouth to make a joke about the last time we took a late-night stroll, but thought better of it at the last second.

Lucas had set a firm boundary in place. As much as I enjoyed pushing his buttons that night, he'd already given me too much tonight by driving an hour to come break me out of my self-destructive spiral.

Anything more, and I'd be in debt to the man.

We approached the tiny house, and I fumbled in my purse for my keys. Lucas quickly took over when it became apparent that I was not capable, removing the key ring and handing it to me.

"Can you make it inside?"

"Yup."

"You sure?"

"Yup."

"Then why aren't you moving?"

"Good question."

Lucas sighed and took my hand in his, leading me up the stairs.

"You have nice hands."

Lucas's chuckle skittered down my spine and bloomed low in my belly.

"That's not the first time I've heard that."

I narrowed my eyes. Lucas tugged me towards the bedroom, tossing my purse onto the couch. I was suddenly thankful that this tiny house was all one story, so there was no ladder to climb to get to the bed.

"Who else has been near enough to your hands to compliment them?"

Lucas snorted as I sat down on the edge of the bed. "Jealous?"

He stood in the doorway, watching as I removed my boots and socks. I sighed.

"This sucks," I muttered, kicking over one of my shoes like a petulant toddler.

I'd sobered significantly in the car, and the gray clouds of shame were creeping across the edges of my vision.

"You'll feel better when you wake up," Lucas murmured. "A situation never looks as difficult in the light of day."

"Spoken like someone who's been there."

"You know I have."

My breath hitched in my throat. I reached for the halter of my shirt and paused, shooting Lucas a dry grin.

"You should probably leave now, given that I'm about to take my clothes off."

Lucas's hands tightened around the door frame, and my pulse kicked up a notch.

It was impossible to tell what was alcohol-induced recklessness and the want that had embedded itself in my bones during the night we spent in Seattle.

"I should," Lucas sighed. He took a step closer to me, and for a moment, I thought he might actually go back on his word. I'd never wanted someone to throw caution to the wind and make a terrible choice with me as much as I did right now.

He stood in front of me, his fingers brushing my cheekbone. His finger slid beneath my chin to lift my gaze to him, and time seemed to halt around us.

Could it really be this easy? For so long, I'd chalked up that night to one magical manic episode, a mutual outlet for both of us to work through the things that troubled us. Was this game we were playing just based on my fear?

I had valid reasons to hesitate. Reasons I couldn't yet give voice to. But maybe I was the problem.

"You are so fucking beautiful, you know that?"

I stopped breathing.

"You are too," I whispered and then blinked twice when I realized what I'd said.

Lucas didn't make fun of me, though. He simply stared at me, drinking me in like he couldn't believe I was really here with him.

"I feel it too, you know," Lucas murmured a few moments later.

An acknowledgement of the thread that tied us together.

My eyes fluttered shut when the rough pad of my thumb brushed over my bottom lip. His hand moved to cup my jaw, cradling my face. He leaned down to press a kiss to my forehead.

My eyes flew open.

"Goodnight, Cass."

He turned and left the room, cold air rushing into the space where his body had just been.

I stared at his retreating form, heart in my throat as my fingers brushed over my bottom lip.

Remembering. Wanting.

Chapter 15

Lucas

I woke before my alarm the next morning. I was used to waking up early in the morning to start farm chores, but this morning's three a.m. wake-up call was for an entirely different reason.

I was going back to the Marine Corps. I was going back to the place where it all began.

I opened my closet door, and my heart kicked up a notch when I saw my cammies hanging there, front and center. I'd dug them out of the trunk where I'd stashed all of my uniforms after leaving active duty.

When I'd run into Imogen in the laundry room yesterday afternoon, she'd simply smiled and given me a nod. Like she of all people knew how meaningful this next chapter was to me.

Because I was going back on *my* terms.

There was no Mallory, no family pressure, no existential dread. I was making the choice to go back and finish what I'd started a decade ago.

I wasn't typically that sentimental of a person, but something about putting on my cammies again—seeing the name *Morales* and *U.S. Marines* across my chest—filled me with a sense of pride I hadn't felt for years.

I grabbed the overnight bag I'd packed yesterday and my folio of important documents before descending the staircase as quietly as I could. To my surprise, Kameron was already in the kitchen, leaning against the dishwasher with a notebook and pen laid out on the counter next to him.

"You're up early," I said, fighting off a yawn as I headed for the kitchen.

"Looking for coffee?" Kam said, extending a to-go cup to me. I took it gratefully.

"Thanks," I replied. "You didn't wake up this early just to say goodbye, did you?"

Kam gave me a wry smile.

"It's your first drill. I wanted to make sure you felt set up for success."

Something tweaked in my chest.

"I do," I said honestly. "Never been more glad I kept my cammies from my active duty stint than when I went to the MCX website and got the worst case of sticker shock I've had in my life. Has that shit always been so expensive?"

Kam barked out a laugh and said, "There's a reason people pay money to get those things patched instead of buying new."

"Jeez," I muttered.

A comfortable silence settled over the kitchen. My fingers drummed nervously along the countertop.

Everything was already set in motion. My contract was signed. I'd held up my right hand and sworn to defend the United States Constitution against all enemies, foreign and domestic. The incentive for my reenlistment was already on its way to my bank account.

All I had to do was show up.

"Anxious?"

"Excited," I admitted. "It just feels different this time."

"Why?"

I considered this for a long minute.

"Honestly? I have nothing to prove this time. When I joined straight out of high school, I was a slightly overweight, anxious, acne-riddled teenager who was scrambling for anything that might give me direction. I'm going back because serving in the military feels like my life's purpose. Even though my service looks different, it's what I'm passionate about. And God knows we need guys that actually give a shit within the Marine Corps' ranks with the insanity that's happening in the world right now."

"You can say that again," Kameron muttered. "It's fucking scary."

"It is. And choosing to go back is something I can control."

Kam smiled, as if he understood everything I would have said if I'd found the words for it.

"Love you, man," Kam said, grabbing my shoulder. "I'm proud of you."

"Don't go getting all mushy on me now," I muttered, turning away from him to refill my coffee mug and grab a granola bar from the basket.

"I am, though. And it's important to me that you know there's always a place for you here."

"Can't get rid of me that easy, Miller."

"God, you're going to be insufferable after this weekend," Kam groaned.

I flashed him a grin and clapped him on the shoulder as I headed for the front door, snagging my keys off the hook on my way out.

"You have no idea, big guy."

There weren't any reserve stations in Watford County—not surprising, considering the Marine Corps was small to begin with. Instead, I'd be making the drive to Spokane once a month for the next three years. Because I'd received a small enlistment bonus for coming back to service after leaving, I had to show up any time they needed me.

It felt damn good to be back in uniform.

I hopped out of my truck, giving a brief nod to two men having a conversation a few cars down from me. All the anxiety I had been feeling earlier with Kam had dissipated.

That was one of the nice things about being in the military: once I got where I was going, my anxiety typically faded, because I knew what would be expected of me.

The Marine Corps was infamous for bad last-minute decisions, but at least I knew how I was expected to interact with the people around me, even with those curveballs.

I pinned my chevrons to my collar, ensured my nametapes were straight, and reached for my phone to text the group chat.

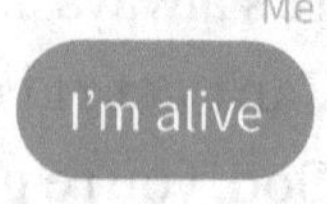

Connor Harvey

Rah

Kameron Miller

Rgr

Me

You're both the worst

Kameron Miller

Love you too

I snorted and went to slide my phone in my cargo pocket when another message thread caught my eye.

Two texts from an unknown number.

My heart damn near jumped out of my chest as I read them.

Unknown Number

Thank you for coming last night.

And sorry about ambushing you.

My jaw nearly hit the fucking floor. I rushed to hit the call button, not before saving her in my contacts, because there was no way in hell I was risking losing her number now that I had it.

"Are you serious?" I laughed disbelievingly when she picked up the phone with a quiet, *"This is Cassie."*

"I know," Cassie said quickly. "That was the lamest first text ever. I didn't know what else to say."

I turned away from the field of Marines gathering for morning formation so they wouldn't see me grinning like a goddamn idiot into my phone.

It had been *months*. Months of waiting to see that unknown phone number in my notifications. And when I finally did, she was just thanking me for having basic human decency in helping her get home safe.

"Well, I guess that makes sense, considering how much you said last night."

Cassie groaned in embarrassment, and the noise shot through me like a lightning strike.

"Don't remind me," she muttered. "Thank you for the water and ibuprofen, by the way. Very kind of you."

"Always happy to help."

A heartbeat of silence filled the space between our phones.

"Thank you for being a gentleman."

"I meant what I said," I lowered my voice and leaned back against my truck, propping one leg behind me. "Ask me again when I get home and you haven't had anything to drink, and I'll give you anything you want, Cass."

She sucked in a breath.

"I have to get to formation," I murmured.

"Right," Cassie said, slightly out of breath. "Of course."

"Get some rest today, yeah?"

"I'll try," she murmured.

I swallowed tightly. "Text me about your day. I might not respond until later tonight, but it would be... nice to talk to you."

"Really?"

The brightness in Cassie's voice had me running a hand down my face, trying to keep the grin off my face. Showing up at a new unit was always an interesting adventure, but

I'd been out of military circles for going on three years. I was showing up on highly unequal footing compared to the rest of the guys.

"Yeah," I said, clearing my throat and pushing past the sudden bout of anxiety and restlessness that swept over me. "Talk to you later."

"Talk later," Cassie repeated, her tone soft, the edges of sleep still curling around her voice. I gripped the phone tightly in my hand as I ended the call, pinching the bridge of my nose.

I was so beyond fucked.

My day was boring in the best way. I knew the novelty of being back in the Marine Corps and doing nothing but administrative work, running, and lifting heavy shit would wear off eventually, but right now, I was riding high. It felt damn good to fall back seamlessly into a life I knew so well. The reserves differed from the active duty life I was used to, but I was still grateful to be back and doing something I genuinely gave a shit about.

I was also way too excited to get in my car, charge my phone, and text Cassie that I was ready to call.

To my surprise, Cassie had already texted me.

Cass

call me whenever!

> if you still want to talk

> It's also okay if you're busy

She'd sent all three texts in the same minute. A detail that didn't escape me, because that meant she was just as eager to talk to me as I was to talk to her.

"Hey, dream girl."

I pulled the phone away from my ear right as her phone went crashing to the floor.

"Sorry," she squeaked when she picked up the phone again. "That caught me way off guard."

"Good."

"Someone's feeling cocky," Cassie said. I could hear the smile in her voice, and my chest warmed.

"I had a good day today," I said, leaning back in the driver's seat. "How was yours?"

"It was alright," Cassie said. "I finished my book. Called my roommate and caught up with her for a few minutes. Went on LinkedIn and did some job searching. Just another day."

The warmth in my chest evaporated at the mention of job searching.

"You just left Seattle, and you're already itching to go back, huh?"

Cassie blew out a sharp breath.

Fabric rustled in the background, and the mental image of her curled up on the couch in her tiny house, the blanket pulled up to her chin the way she liked, sent my pulse ratcheting up another notch.

"I don't know," Cassie said honestly. "I'm a creature of habit, I guess."

"That's so unlike the Cass I know."

"Your Cass was a different person that night," she murmured.

Those two words together had me sitting up straight in my seat, leaning one arm over the steering wheel as I fought to keep my voice even.

"My Cass, huh?"

Another long exhale, this one breathier than the last.

"You know what I meant, Lucas."

"Do I?" I said, voice low.

I didn't know if it was the physical distance or the high I was riding from my first day back in the Marine Corps, but I felt bolder than I had in a long time.

"How long are we going to do this, Cass? What happened to not playing games with me?"

"*Lucas*," she whispered.

"Tell me what you want," I murmured. "Fuck, Cass, tell me what you want and I'll scorch the earth to give it to you. You want me on my knees? I'm already there."

"When do you come home?"

That was Cassie's version of a yes. It was as close to an answer as she could give me without acknowledging how bad she wanted this thing between us.

"Tomorrow morning," I said. "I really need a good night's sleep, but I'll be there tomorrow morning."

"Come to the tiny house?"

"Don't fuck with me right now," I said. "I'm a desperate man, Cass. I need you to be certain."

"I am. Come to the tiny house tomorrow morning, before everyone else is awake."

"Okay," I said. "I'll be there bright and early."

"I'll be waiting," Cassie whispered, and in her voice, I heard the glimmer of the woman I knew that night in Seattle.

The woman who wasn't afraid to ask for what she wanted. The woman who reached for me all damn night and wasn't afraid of the consequences.

The woman who made me fall in love with a city I hated in less than four hours.

"I'll be there."

I needed sleep desperately, but I knew it would be a long while before I'd calmed down enough to get it.

Chapter 16
Cassie

I woke to my phone buzzing on the side table next to the couch. I answered the call with bleary eyes.

"I'm home."

Two words that sent a bolt of lightning straight through me.

I smashed the end call button and threw back the blanket, my heart lurching into my chest. I'd fallen asleep on the couch somewhere around two in the morning. Lucas and I's conversation had made me too keyed up to sleep.

Selfishly, I'd wanted to be close to the door for when he got home. I hadn't bothered changing out of my shorts and tank last night. I'd been having an introvert recovery day and, based on the desperation in Lucas's voice last night, I knew he wouldn't care what I was wearing.

He'd have me naked in five minutes flat.

"Oh," I choked as I opened the front door. Lucas was standing in front of me, looking like a man starved. He'd changed out of his uniform at some point on the way home—a small mercy, considering I'd probably lose my shit if he came within six feet of me wearing it.

"Can I come in?" Lucas murmured, both of his arms

braced against the door frame.

I couldn't do anything but nod, taking a step back into the tiny house, my eyes never leaving his.

The moment snapped, and I was suddenly in his arms with his lips crashing against mine.

I moaned into his mouth, an instant response to how good he felt.

The tension leeched from my shoulders as his hands wrapped around my waist, urging me into his arms. My legs locked around his waist. He lifted me effortlessly, pressing me against the far wall.

"Miss me?" I panted against his mouth when he finally broke the kiss.

He looked at me, his pupils wide, and drank in the tank top that had ridden up, exposing the tan planes of my stomach.

"Should've known," Lucas murmured. His palms splayed wide against my hips, traveling across my sides, knuckles grazing the waistband of my shorts.

"What?" I asked breathily, bucking my hips towards his touch. I was still worn out from the sleepless night, but now I was lost in the feeling of him.

Lucas's touch was painfully familiar: something I'd revisited in my mind time and time again.

And now he was *here*.

"Should've known you'd run your fucking mouth."

A low moan punched out of me as Lucas slipped his hand inside my shorts, long, thick fingers tracing the outline of my panties and stroking the most sensitive part of me.

I barely bit back the needy sound in my throat, not wanting to appear desperate.

The minute his lips tilted into a smirk, I knew my efforts were futile.

"Been thinking about this all night like I have?" Lucas murmured. He dragged his knuckles against my clit, and my eyes fluttered shut.

It was longer than one night. So much fucking longer. But I couldn't tell him that.

So I settled for, "Now who's running their mouth?"

The comeback was weak even to my own ears, but Lucas didn't miss a beat.

His lips grazed my jaw, a barely there presence that had my core tightening in anticipation.

This was what I wanted. A damn good orgasm with someone I didn't have to coach. Someone who already knew my body. Someone who—

Lucas nipped my bottom lip, forcing my eyes back to his. My hips bucked forward of their own volition when I saw the heat in his eyes.

Somehow I knew he'd been thinking about this for a lot longer than one night, even without the words leaving his lips.

Lucas kissed like every one might be his last: savoring every taste and still reaching for more.

Like he couldn't get enough of it. Like he couldn't get enough of *me*.

"Sit on the couch," I panted as rational thought threatened to take over. I slammed every mental door shut, trying desperately to stay in the moment. "Put me down and sit on the damn couch."

Lucas pulled away, allowing me to stand on my own two feet. Being barefoot, I could see just how much he towered over me. I was taller than most women I knew, standing five foot seven without shoes, but with Lucas being over six feet tall, he had to look down to take me in. Under his gaze, my core throbbed with the familiar want that only he'd been able to stoke in me.

Lucas stripped his shirt off over his head and hovered near the couch. I quickly scurried to the kitchen and pulled all the blinds shut. I did the same in the living room, dimming the reading lamp next to the tan couch.

Lucas watched me intently, crossing both of his arms over his chest and jerking his head in the direction of the couch.

"You lay down."

My cheeks flushed. "You don't have to—"

"You know I want to," he said. He stepped towards me, curling his hand through my hair and forcing my head up towards his. "Or have you forgotten exactly how much I love eating your pussy?"

"You're going to kill me," I muttered, the words quickly dying on my lips as Lucas smirked.

He released me long enough to shove the couch pillows to the floor. I stripped my tank top off over my head, shivering as the cool morning air pebbled my skin. He groaned as my breasts spilled free, tan skin on full display. I did as he asked, lying back against the couch.

He kneeled in front of me, palms splayed wide over my thighs. His stare was so much more intense than I was used to—a combination of lust and something deeper.

Something that felt close to awe. Reverence, even. Like I was truly the only thing on his mind.

"We need rules," I said, grabbing his shoulders as he hooked his fingers in the waistband of my shorts. "Before this goes farther."

"Rules?" Lucas said. He shook his head gently, as if trying to clear his thoughts long enough for us to have a level-headed conversation. The sight of him kneeling between my legs, shirtless and ravenous, was enough to take me out.

"This is just sex."

Lucas stilled, his eyes fixed on me.

"Just sex," he repeated in a monotone.

"That's all this can be."

For a moment, I expected Lucas to shove me away. I expected him to tell me he wasn't up for it.

Instead, Lucas gripped my hips, leaning over me so that he could seal the deal with another kiss. His tongue swiped against my lips, and he pulled away right as my lips parted for him, desperate to feel his tongue against mine.

"I'll take whatever you give me," Lucas murmured against my lips. He returned to his position between my thighs, legs splayed wide as his cock strained against his jeans.

The mental image of this man laid out before me didn't hold a candle to what it felt like to have his weight over me.

"I mean it," I said. I looked towards the ceiling, gulping in a breath. There was never enough oxygen in the room when Lucas looked at me like that. "Just sex."

"My hearing isn't that bad," Lucas scoffed. He pinched the inside of my thigh, and I squirmed.

"I agree to your terms, Cassie Phillips. Now, are you going

to stop talking and let me eat this pretty cunt?"

I nodded. He tugged my shorts and panties down my legs, and then he was on me. My moan was undignified and desperate. I wound my hands through his hair, needing an anchor. Lucas groaned against me, his hips bucking forward as his eyes darkened.

"Fuck," I whispered, writhing beneath him.

My lips parted on a sharp inhale when he dragged two fingers through my slit, thumb circling my clit slowly, teasing me with the prospect of more.

"Are you going to be a good girl?"

I threw my head back against the couch and squeezed my eyes shut.

Fuck. We really were just falling right back where we'd left off.

I nodded.

"Good."

And then he pressed two fingers into me, curling them in a way that had me seeing stars. I moaned again, fingers tightening in his hair as he worked me open.

"*Cassie,*" Lucas groaned when he pulled away to admire his handiwork. Long, thick fingers dragging through my slick heat. My thighs shook with the force of the pleasure building deep in my core. "Fucking dream girl."

His praise lit me up from the inside.

I didn't think I had a praise kink before Lucas, but with how vocal he was about what he loved, what he wanted more of, it was impossible not to preen beneath his hazy gaze. He slipped another finger inside me, and I shivered, completely lost to how perfect it was.

He reached up with his free hand and roughly grabbed my chin, tilting my head down so I could watch.

He ran his thumb over my flushed cheek, then tugged on my bottom lip. The way he drank in my ruined body was enough to send me over the edge.

The hand still working me pressed deeper, his palm dragging over my clit, and I let out a desperate moan, pushing my hips towards him as pleasure coiled at the base of my spine.

And then he said, "So fucking pretty. I can't wait to fuck you like this. Been thinking about it for months. How good you felt wrapped around my cock. How wet and tight—"

My thighs squeezed together, and I threw my head back as I came. Lucas groaned, working me through the height of it, until I was shaking and pushing him away.

My eyes fluttered shut, a raspy "yes" falling from my lips.

I loved being watched by him. He'd learned that in Seattle. I could get off just on his attention: that palpable desire.

Unraveling that restraint he clung to, piece by piece, made me dizzy with yearning.

"I told you last night I'm a desperate man, Cassie," he murmured, pressing a kiss to the inside of my thigh. He refocused his attention on my face, and I bit my bottom lip in anticipation of what other filthy words would follow. "And you drive me fucking mad."

He stood briefly—long enough to shove his pants and underwear off and sit on the couch next to me. He grabbed my waist and heaved me onto his lap.

"Are you going to fuck me?" I gasped, dragging my center over his cock. "Please tell me you're going to—"

"There's a condom in my wallet," Lucas said, nipping my bottom lip. Through hazy eyes, I reached towards the side table, grabbing the foil packet out of his wallet and ripping it open. I handed the condom to him, willing my pulse to slow. I wanted to remember this, just in case.

"Fuck," I gasped, throwing my head back as he stretched me just seconds later. My nails dug into his shoulders as I ground my hips down, taking all of him. Lucas groaned into my neck, gripping my waist like his life depended on it.

"I missed this," I panted, pressing closer to him. "Fuck, I missed this."

Lucas's dark chuckle sent a skitter down my spine. His grip on my hips was bruising.

"Admit it," he murmured, thrusting into me in a way that made me cry out. "You missed *me*."

"I—"

The words were lost in a torrent of sensation as his cock slid deeper. Whatever argument my mind had been forming quickly drowned in the spike of pleasure that seared through me as his thumb flicked my clit quickly. His fingers traced a slow, teasing circle, our hips setting a brutal pace.

Neither of us could get enough.

Everything I gave him, he threw right back at me. His hips thrust into me, and I pushed back, dragging him closer, keeping him there.

Lucas's fist wound into my hair, pulling my head back to expose my throat.

"I'll say it even if you won't," Lucas whispered, punctuating his words with another thrust. My eyes closed, the combined pressure of his cock inside me and the lack of air proving to be too much. "Such a good fucking girl. You know exactly what you want."

"Yes," I gasped, inhaling deeply as he released my hair, instead pulling my hips towards his.

"Look at me when you come," Lucas demanded, grabbing my chin and tilting my face towards his. "I want to fucking see it, just like before."

My lips parted around shaky breaths as his fingers deftly stroked my clit. His thrusts never faltered, maintaining a brutal pace. "Lucas—"

"That's it," Lucas murmured. "I'm there with you, Cassie. But you're going over first."

The guttural syllables of my name on his lips sent me tumbling over the edge. Every part of me shattered.

My lips parted over what might have been a scream. Lucas's hands gripped my hips, bringing me against him again and again until he came with another loud groan of my name.

Somewhere in the recesses of my mind, I knew I'd collapsed on top of him, my panting exhales expelled against his collarbone. He gathered me in his arms, his lips pressing a feather-light kiss to my sweaty temple as he slid out of me.

"Fuck," I whispered, unable to keep the awe from my voice. Lucas's gaze mirrored my own. "I don't think I can stand."

"Don't be dramatic," Lucas panted, the rapid rise and fall of his chest giving away just how affected he'd been by this.

I rolled my eyes, earning a sharp smack on the ass for the brattiness. I shoved back against him, just to tease, and the mischievous glint in Lucas's eyes warned me to behave.

"That was one hell of a wake-up call," I murmured. "I'm mad at myself for not giving in before."

"Would it have been as good?" Lucas said, shooting me a sly grin as he pulled the condom away, tying it off and tossing it toward the kitchen trash can.

"Probably not," I sighed in defeat. Lucas moved me off him. I laid back against the couch, completely naked.

The usual trepidation I felt about being completely naked in front of a partner seemed to fade in Lucas's presence.

One more bullet point on a long list of things I chalked up to our unusual beginning.

There was no reason to be nervous in front of Lucas because there had never been any walls there to begin with.

"Damn," he muttered. My limbs went limp against the couch, my swollen sex on full display. He drank my body in greedily. "You have no idea what you do to me."

Was this what it felt like to be wanted?

For months, I'd turned over our one-night stand in my mind, determined to craft a different reality. I'd told myself that Lucas had never wanted me that badly. That it had all been a fever dream.

A mutual manic episode that resulted in the most mind-blowing sex of my life and ended with a number in my notes app that I'd been too scared to use.

"Yeah?" I murmured, slipping my fingers between my thighs. I gasped when my fingers brushed over my sensitive clit, hips bucking forward of their own volition. Lucas's eyes darkened, his cock twitching against his thighs. "Tell me about what I do to you."

And he did. With his fingers and tongue.

He didn't mention the promises we'd made to each other an hour earlier.

Some things were better left unsaid for now.

Chapter 17
Cassie

Lucas slipped out of my tiny house and back to his a few hours later. I was thoroughly boneless by the time he was through with me. I took a quick shower because there was no way in hell I was showing up at the farmhouse reeking of sex. I splashed cold water on my face to lower the redness in my cheeks, but quickly gave up. The "freshly fucked" cheeks would have to stay.

I'd just have to pray no one called me on it.

I walked past Lucas's tiny house, unsurprised to find that he'd already started his workday. Lucas was all too eager to have a task to accomplish. His love of a good to-do list was yet another reason he and Imogen had become close friends.

Imogen.

My sister's name flitting through my morning train of thought was enough for reality to slap me across the face. I'd just fucked her best friend. Repeatedly. In a tiny house that her life partner had built on their property.

So much for coming back to my hometown to repair things. From the outside, it would appear I was hellbent on making things more complicated than ever.

"Good morning," I mumbled. Imogen looked at me with a guarded expression on her face.

"We made omelets this morning," Kam called from the kitchen. "There are plenty of eggs if you want one."

"Thank you," I said. I bypassed Imogen entirely. She was clearly in a bad mood.

Truth be told, she scared me.

Of all the people in this house, she was the biggest wild card.

Abbie extended as much grace as she could in my direction. Connor followed Abbie's lead at every turn. Kameron would always been in Imogen's corner before anyone else's, but he also wanted to keep the peace as much as he could.

I didn't want to think of Lucas taking a side.

I had a sinking feeling I knew exactly how that conversation would go, and I wasn't ready for him to push me away.

I was too selfish to be okay with removing myself from his life when I'd just gotten him back.

I pulled my hair back with a claw clip as I set about making myself some eggs. Leave it to Imogen to have every filling imaginable: green veggies, cheese, and multiple meats.

Against my better judgement, I sat down at the kitchen table. Imogen hunched over her iPad, most likely working on the Winding Road Barn logo re-design. My sister had a frugal side to her that always made me smile. It was Imogen, her font collection, and Canva against the world.

"What's the deal?" she said.

I winced.

"Come on, Cassie," Imogen said, exasperated. "None of this is like you. You never would have quit your job and moved back to a place you hate. I haven't pushed you since our trip to Watford because I kept expecting you to offer me some kind of explanation, and you never have."

I swallowed down a bit of eggs, even though my appetite had all but vanished.

"What explanation do you want, Im?"

"See, that's the crap I'm talking about," Imogen said, slamming the case of her tablet shut and returning to her stare down. "You keep asking me what I want. You want me to lay out exactly what I want from you so you can give it to me. Right?"

I blinked back my shock, determined not to let her know she had just knocked me completely off kilter.

"I'm not following."

"Yeah, you are," Imogen muttered. "You're doing the eldest daughter thing."

"You kind of are," Kameron piped in from the living room. He didn't look up from his book, simply flipped to the next page before returning his arm to its position behind his head.

"The eldest daughter thing?"

"You keep looking to everyone for what they need. What can I do or say to make Imogen feel better? How can I help Kameron out on the farm? How can I do this thing to avoid thinking about my own feelings?"

"I get it," I snapped. "Loud and clear. Heard."

Imogen's eyes narrowed. "Did you get enough sleep last night?"

I choked on my sip of coffee.

"I slept fine."

Imogen shrugged. "Whatever. You were always extra grumpy on the nights you didn't get enough sleep when we were younger."

"I'm fine," I repeated, grinding my molars together to keep the edge from my tone.

"Try again," came Kam's singsong voice from the couch. I groaned. Imogen beamed.

"You're outnumbered."

"Kam is obviously going to take your side."

"You don't know him at all," Imogen and Kam said simultaneously.

"That is so creepy," I muttered, turning my attention back to my heaping pile of eggs and vegetables.

"I need you to tell me one thing," Imogen said quietly. I didn't look up from my food, but nodded for her to continue.

"You shut down," Imogen murmured. "When we passed the clinic, you completely shut down."

My fork clattered onto my plate as my eyes snapped to hers.

"What?"

I saw the flicker in her eyes before she schooled her features.

Careful, Cassie.

"When we passed the medical center, you—"

Too late.

"Don't," I snapped, the panic welling in my chest. "Please don't."

"What happened, Cassie?" Imogen tried again. She reached for me. "Whatever happened, please tell me. I promise I can—"

The panic swelled to a crescendo.

I stood suddenly from the table, the wooden chair screeching across the floor.

"I said no," I shouted, my voice far louder than I intended.

Imogen flinched.

It was an almost imperceptible movement, but it was enough.

Horror flooded me as Kam stepped into the room, face stern. In less than two heartbeats, he was between the two of us.

"Too far," Kam barked. His back was still to Imogen, and even though his chest rose and fell in equal beats, I knew I'd crossed a line I couldn't take back. "Both of you take a breath."

I stumbled backwards, completely horrified by my actions. When had been the last time I'd yelled at another human being like that? Much less my sister. My sister, who had survived an abusive marriage.

My stomach lurched.

Kam crossed his arms over his chest. I caught the message loud and clear.

"I'm so sorry," I whispered.

"Whatever," Imogen muttered. She passed Kam, giving his forearm a reassuring squeeze. Kam continued eyeing me as he returned to his spot on the couch. "Now feels like a good time to tell you that the only reason you're still here is because Lucas vouched for you."

Nervous energy flooded my veins as I stared at my sister. "What?"

"After our disastrous trip to Watford, where you shut me out just like you always had, I came home and told Kameron I wanted you out. Lucas was in the living room, and he was the one who talked me off the ledge."

My ears rang.

"What did he say?"

Imogen gave me a mocking smile.

"It sucks when people keep things from you, doesn't it?"

"Im," Kam murmured.

"No," Imogen cut him off, shaking her head. "I told you months ago that I wasn't doing this shit with you anymore, Cassie. We all have trauma. We all have baggage. But no one can help you if you don't want it. And if you keep slamming the door in people's faces, one day, they'll just stop asking entirely."

"I'm sorry," I murmured. "I'm *sorry*, Imogen."

"Sorry isn't good enough."

The words stung, even though there was no heat behind them. There was just defeat and sadness. Imogen had always been the one to hold out her hand, and it was always me who couldn't do it.

It shouldn't have been that way. I was the older sister. I was supposed to protect her. In some ways, I had.

But in other ways, I caused more harm than good. For a long time, I believed that pushing Imogen away would protect her from my feelings; especially the ones I could never wrangle into submission.

"Ask me anything else," I pleaded. I'd do anything to make this right. "Ask me about anything outside of the clinic and I'll answer honestly."

"Why did you stop riding?"

I closed my eyes, gripping the back of the dining chair like it was a lifeline. Imogen came to play hardball. She was always whip-smart in school. No one had ever denied that. But she had a talent for seeing right through my bullshit. After clawing through hell and carving a life for herself, she'd stopped pulling her punches.

I was damn proud of her. Even if the thought of answering her questions with nothing other than brutal honesty made that red-hot panic flare to life in my belly.

"Mom and Dad made me."

Imogen's eyes narrowed. "Why?"

"Because I no longer met their standards. It was a punishment for letting my priorities slip."

It was the only truth I could give her.

"Sounds like Carmen," Imogen huffed as she slouched back in her chair. "You were what, fifteen?"

"Sixteen," I whispered.

"Same year you shut me out completely."

Imogen was never one to pull her punches, and I was feeling the full weight of those blows for the first time in a long time.

"I had to focus," I said, fighting to keep my voice even. "Carmen threatened to pull their financial support for college. I was scared at the prospect of doing it on my own. I'd enjoyed their financial support throughout my entire life. I didn't know to function without it. In retrospect, I know I would have been fine. But I was scared then. I was overwhelmed and scared."

When Imogen was silent, I dared to look up. She was

staring at me with a soft smile on her face. Confusion darkened my features.

"That might just be the most honest you've been with me in a decade."

I let out a long exhale.

"I promised you I would try. We all have something we don't—*can't*—talk about."

Recognition flickered in Imogen's eyes. I slid into the chair and reached across the table to take her hand. She stiffened, but didn't pull away.

I thought of the conversation I had with Lucas after my self-destructive spiral at the Jaded Lady; about how tough situations never seemed as complicated in the light of day.

Ten points to him for being right about something else. Again.

"I will get there one day," I murmured. "I'll tell you why I can't walk past the clinic without having a panic attack. But I need more time."

"Okay," Imogen said. "I believe you."

"For what it's worth: whatever you're carrying, whatever happened—I want you to know that it won't change the fact that I love you. I know I'm doing the Jekyll and Hyde thing right now because I'm trying to work through my crap, but I love you, Cassie. You're my sister. You piss me off and you've hurt me, but it's important to me that you know I love you."

"Okay," I choked out. God, I'd cried more in the last three weeks than I had in months. "I love you too, Imogen. So much. I want to work things out with you."

We drank the rest of our coffee in silence. When Kameron came to sit in the chair beside Imogen, I took that as my cue to head to the barn.

"Cassie?"

I turned around to face Imogen, who gave me a small smile.

"There's a place for you here, if you want it."

"Is this where I make a 'you can't afford my retainer' joke in poor taste?"

Kam chuckled. "It's a 'when you work with family, you get to do things differently' reminder."

"There wasn't an event coordinator position when I started," Imogen pointed out.

"And you two would be okay with hiring someone who is clearly unstable?"

"Call it a hunch," Kam said. "Helping people work through their problems is kind of our thing."

I couldn't argue with that logic.

"How did we go from you telling me you wanted to kick me out a few weeks ago to a job offer?"

Imogen's smile was deadly.

"Had to get your attention somehow."

I let out a cackle, the sound surprising all three of us.

"Last thing," Kam said. You don't have to talk to us. If you're more comfortable with Connor or Lucas—"

I damn near tripped over myself as I bent down to pull my boots on.

"Knew it," Kam muttered.

"What?" Imogen said, clearly confused. My cheeks heated.

"She's crushing," Kam said, smirking.

"Oh," Imogen said, clarity smoothing her features. "Wait,

ew, *no.*"

Kill me.

"Okay, I'm leaving now," I muttered. My heart beat wildly in my chest.

"Is that why Lucas has been all weird?" Imogen said pensively.

"My sweet summer child," Kam sighed as I stepped out the door and stomped down the path to the stables.

A crush, my ass.

I didn't have the words to tell Imogen that my feelings for Lucas couldn't be wrapped up in one pretty syllable

"Hey."

I'd been at the barn for an hour, preparing Chesty for his morning ride. Being around horses again had been good for my soul. Someone who had never connected with horses in that way couldn't easily understand the healing nature of sharing space with them. Luckily, at a place like Winding Road, these three horses were here because the people here knew exactly how powerful those bonds could be.

Connor's voice was the last one I expected to hear this early in the morning. I turned to face him, giving him a nod of acknowledgement as I walked past him to re-rack the saddle.

"What's up?"

"Just wanted to check in. Talk."

I raised my eyebrows in his direction. "You've never been one for polite conversation, Harvey."

Connor crossed his arms over his chest and leaned against the post, giving me a shrug. I grabbed the basket of grooming supplies and gave Chesty's neck a good rub before I began brushing him down.

Connor was silent for a few more minutes as I continued grooming Chesty. The horse looked like he was going to fall asleep any moment. He'd had a busy day, and we'd had a damn good ride.

"Why are you here?" I finally asked. A Connor Harvey stare down wasn't on my bingo card for today."

"I wanted to see how you were," Connor said, tone earnest. "I feel like everyone around you right now has some level of interest in your mental wellbeing and your plans, and I just... wanted to talk to you. Make sure you were settling in okay."

"Are you not also interested?" I said. "Not in an arrogant way, but just—"

Connor chuckled. "I'm the *least* interested of everyone in the farmhouse, let's put it that way."

"Ouch," I muttered. "I'm fine."

"Being back in Watford doesn't bring up anything for you?"

I scoffed.

"Of course it does, Connor. What the hell kind of question is that?"

Of everyone in the farmhouse, he understood that returning to the place that broke you was complicated.

"You should talk to someone."

"I don't want—"

I stopped short, whirling around to face him.

I'd been so focused on keeping my hands busy I hadn't bothered to look at Connor's face for the last five minutes.

And there it was.

The truth I was trying so hard to run from.

The question I hadn't dared ask him in the weeks since my return. His tentative expression gave it away.

"Do you remember?" I whispered when Connor remained silent. I didn't dare look away from him. "That day at the medical center."

Connor's gaze seared into me, and I pressed my lips together to hold back the tears. I willed myself to stay steady, even as I dreaded his answer.

"I remember," Connor said quietly.

My pulse roared in my ears.

"Does she know?" I whispered. "Abbie."

Connor shook his head once.

"No one else knows, Cassie. That was never my story to tell. And I didn't—" Connor swallowed audibly. "I never knew the details. And I knew from how you—"

Connor looked genuinely pained.

I quickly glanced away. I'd been beyond hysterical that day. I'd never felt *anything* like I'd felt that day.

"I knew I would never ask. Not unless there was a time when you wanted me to know. We hardly knew each other. We were essentially strangers passing each other in a hospital waiting room. I never told a soul, and truthfully, I put it out of my mind. We were both there for reasons we couldn't talk about."

The relief that flooded my veins threatened to bring me to my knees.

"You should tell her," Connor murmured. "You should tell both of them."

"How?" I said, my voice cracking. "How am I supposed to look Imogen in the eyes and tell her that I..."

"I don't know," Connor said honestly. "I don't have the words for that conversation. But I can tell you from experience that the secrets you hold in your chest will rot there until you rip them out yourself. The only way to kill the guilt is to let the truth out."

"I just got her back," I choked out, gently tangling my fingers in Chesty's mane as I fought to steady myself.

Chesty leaned further into me, a silent answer to a question I hadn't realized I'd asked. I let out a garbled sob at the movement, allowing him to support more of my weight.

"I can't lose her again. I *can't*."

"You won't," Connor said, taking a step towards me. "You won't lose her, Cassie."

I sobbed harder. Chesty was unwavering beneath me, his gentle snorts like a comforting balm for my soul.

I let the tears come, and Connor didn't say a word.

He just stood there, a grounding presence that reminded me I was still alive.

That I would somehow navigate this with Imogen.

"You are the last person I expected to have this conversation with," I croaked out. I stepped away from Chesty, using a dry patch of my shirt to wipe away as many tears as possible. "I didn't even realize it was you that day at the hospital until they said your last name."

Connor shrugged.

"We all need someone, Cassie. And while we're not best

friends, I fully expect that you will be a big part of our lives going forward. Especially with Abbie's due date just around the corner."

I couldn't find the right words to respond. The silence stretched between us. A gentle breeze rustled a stray strand of my hair, and I tucked it back behind my ear.

"It will be okay," Connor said a few moments later. "I know the weight of that day haunts you. And I will be the first one to tell you that letting other people lift some of that weight for you will change your life."

Connor gave Chesty a good neck rub and whispered something in his ear that I couldn't decipher before leaving the barn.

I stood there and watched him leave, rubbing my hand up and down my arm to comfort myself.

Tell him.

I had to tell him.

I had to tell *her.*

I didn't know how to. I'd carried that day alone for over a decade.

And yet, I knew Connor was right. I had to kill the guilt. I couldn't remember the last time I'd sat down and actually thought about that day with any level of detail.

I'd shut it down. Locked it away with all the other parts of myself I never wanted exposed to daylight.

Until him.

Chapter 18

Lucas

Seattle, Washington
23:00

"Holy shit."

"You can say that again," Cassie murmured.

"I am so glad you didn't take me to the Space Needle," I said, dumbfounded by the sight in front of me. We'd woven our way through the crowded late night streets of downtown and ended at a massive park.

Cassie's chuckle sent a shiver down my spine. It had been four hours of sightseeing with her, and it hadn't been enough.

"I wouldn't have taken you to a tourist hellscape," Cassie said. "My goal is to make you fall in love with Seattle, not hate it."

"I don't think it's possible for me to hate this city anymore," I said.

Looking out over downtown Seattle, lit up like a crown jewel, I meant every damn word.

"I guess I didn't realize that there was still plenty of green space here."

"Mhm," Cassie teased, clearly pleased with herself. If she smirked at me like that one more time, the small string of self-control I was clinging to would snap. "Seattle's a pretty green city, all things considered."

"So I'm learning."

Cassie turned away from me, leaning against the metal railing.

A gentle breeze tossed her hair over one shoulder, exposing tan skin that made me lose my train of thought.

She shivered.

"Can I confess something to you, Cass?"

"I'm listening," she murmured, looking back at me over her now bare shoulder.

"I'm running out of excuses for why I shouldn't kiss you."

She turned towards me fully then, pressing her back against the metal railing, arms outstretched.

A better man would have paused before taking the invitation, but I wasn't a better man.

I took a step towards her. Our chests were only inches away from one another.

If I tilted my head towards her, our noses would brush. She smelled sweet, like a flower I didn't know the name of but desperately wanted to keep.

"It's funny," Cass murmured, voice low. "I haven't been able to come up with a single one."

"Cass, are you playing games with me?" I asked, brushing

my lips over her forehead. The slight tilt of her head against the movement, and the imperceptible shift of her body into mine sent me overboard.

"I'll confess something back to you," she said, her voice barely a breathy whisper. "I'm finding it really hard to play any kind of game with you, Lucas."

"Fuck," I muttered, and finally sealed my lips over hers.

The city lights of downtown Seattle faded to a white blur as every sense honed in on the woman in my arms.

I found I didn't care at all that we were risking public indecency with our bodies pressed together against the railing.

Cass let out a surprised whimper as my tongue slid against her lips, and the knowledge that she felt whatever this thing between us was just like I did was enough to make me wrap my hands around her hips and pull her even closer.

Cass snaked her arms around my shoulders, leaning into me fully. I welcomed all of it, letting her take control of the kiss. Her nails dragged against the nape of my neck, and I groaned.

"Wow," Cass murmured when we finally broke apart for air.

Her fingers danced over her swollen lips, no doubt still tingling from the length of the kiss.

"Yeah," I said like a complete dumbass. "That was... fuck."

"Speechless, I see." Cass smiled. "It's okay. Words are hard."

"I'm sorry, Ms. J.D., I'm but a lowly—"

Cass's shoulders shook with the force of her laugh.

The sound of her laugh, her *genuine* laugh—not a polite giggle or fake chuckle—was enough to send me straight over the edge.

I was not giving up this night until she asked me to leave.

"Shut *up*," Cass wheezed, clutching her chest as she forced the words out in between laughs.

"Afraid it's not in my nature."

Cass shook her head, as if she couldn't believe this was her life. I couldn't really believe it either.

"I'm at a hotel," I blurted, and immediately wished I could take it back as Cass's jaw hinged open. "Okay, that made me sound like a serial killer, but—"

"It's okay," Cass said. She choked on an unexpected laugh that escaped her, and the warmth that had been floating in my chest before returned. "Priya and Kiley have already vouched for you, remember?"

"Right," I said.

Could I claim temporary insanity for the rest of this conversation?

I suddenly wished Kameron or Connor were here to knock me over the head with the shovel I was digging my grave with.

My train of thought abruptly derailed as Cassie's fingers trailed down my arm, leaving goosebumps in their wake. She linked her fingers with mine, and a shudder racked my spine. I wanted to pull her closer. Keep her next to me.

Physical touch wasn't something I craved. Not like this. The newness of this entire experience, the eagerness of it, had me tumbling even more off-kilter.

"You really want this?" Cass said. "It feels..."

"Borderline insane, yes," I said. "I've been there since Batter Up. Been waiting for you to catch up."

Cass let out a surprised laugh, staring at me with awe-filled eyes that stirred something in me I'd honestly thought had died off a long time ago.

"So I'm not crazy, then?"

If this connection went further than tonight—and God help me, I'd never wanted something so bad in my life—I'd press her about Collin and the other assholes in her life who had made her feel crazy or out of control for wanting something for herself.

"No," I rasped. I tugged her closer, taking my hand from hers only long enough to cup her jaw and tilt her face towards mine. That familiar warmth spread through my chest again when she leaned into me. "You're not crazy. I want to kiss you again. Here."

I traced my finger down her jaw. Her eyes didn't leave mine as my finger traveled lower, tracing the delicate column of her throat. I wanted to replace my finger with my tongue, preferably while my other fingers were—

"Christ, Lucas, please take me to bed," Cass said as my finger brushed over her collarbone. She shivered.

"Since you asked so nicely," I murmured, pressing an arguably chaste kiss to her lips before sliding my arm around her waist. "What about our book-finding mission?"

"Screw the books," Cass murmured.

"Shall we take the scenic route?"

Cass's shoulders shook with silent laughter.

"You're an ass."

"So I've been told," I replied, tipping my non-existent hat.

Cass rolled her eyes, but there was no heat behind it.

"Are we going to remember this as a mutual manic episode?"

I swallowed back the ball of emotion lodged in my throat.

"I think we'll remember this as a hell of a lot more than that."

Cass's lips parted, and I couldn't resist the urge to capture her mouth with mine again.

This kiss was slower: more promise and less exploration. I decided then and there that every kiss with Cassie would be a chance to learn something new. To kiss her a little better next time. To promise her something and then fucking deliver.

For tonight, I'd make good on every single word.

Chapter 19
Lucas

My mind was a war zone.

Between thoughts about Cassie and that morning in the tiny house, the text my lawyer sent me twelve hours ago occupied my mind.

Matthias

Call me when you can. I have good news.

There was only one piece of good news within his power to grant.

An official divorce decree, signed and sealed by the state of Washington. The only thing I'd been chasing for years.

Between court visits, document hunting, and character statements, I'd grown distant from the emotional part of the divorce proceedings. I'd somehow numbed myself to the pain of Mallory's betrayal.

I'd shared my bed, my life, my finances, with someone who was living a double life.

My wife had been willing to throw away everything we'd built together for something shinier, newer, and easier.

I'd never fully gotten over that.

I looked down at my phone, but my sight was hazy. Distant. Like I was floating above my body and looking down at a broken version of myself.

Was this really it? Had she finally conceded to the very reasonable demand that we both walk away with whatever we came in with, and that the rest of it—even the lies she spread about me after we separated—could be water under the bridge?

My thumb hovered over Matthias's number, and I swallowed down my urge to puke as the dial tone rang. I had half a mind to hang up the phone, even though I knew in my gut that this would be the phone call I'd been waiting to have for over two years.

"Hey, big man," Matthias said when he picked up on the second ring. "You sitting down?"

I couldn't open my mouth to speak. Matthias either inferred why I was so choked up or took pity on me.

"It's over," Matthias said.

My knees buckled.

"You're free."

I sank down onto the porch steps, gripping the phone in my hands like it was my lifeline.

"You're not fucking with me?"

"No," Matthias said. I could hear the smile in his voice. "She signed the papers. It's over. You're a free man."

"Thank you," I choked out. "I don't—I don't know what to say."

"You don't have to say anything," Matthias said. "I'll send you an email with all the paperwork, and we'll touch base later. Congratulations, Lucas. Talk soon."

Matthias hung up the phone. Mine clunked onto the

wooden boards of the porch as I stared blankly at the ground in front of me.

I don't know how long I sat there. My mind spun through the last two years at warp speed.

Finding Mallory in bed with the man I'd considered one of my closest friends. Getting in my truck to leave. Her calling my family to tell them I'd—

"Lucas?"

I snapped my head up to find Kam standing a few feet away from me. There was a tool belt strapped around his waist.

"Hey," I croaked. "Didn't hear you come up, sorry."

"There was a small leak in the kitchen sink in Cassie's tiny house. Needed Connor's help to hold the flashlight," Kam said, gesturing to the porch just down the hill. Connor stood on the porch and gave me a nod of acknowledgement.

"Everything alright?" Kam said, voice full of concern.

"It's over," I said, still unable to wrap my head around the words. "I'm free."

Kam's head snapped towards mine at the same moment as Connor's eyebrows shot towards his hairline. Immediately, Connor bounded up the hill towards us, with an uncharacteristically wild smile on his face as he did so.

"You're divorced?" Kam spluttered.

I nodded, unable to force words past the lump in my throat.

"We have to tell Imogen," Kam said, offering his hand to me. "She's going to flip out."

Imogen. The woman who'd been with me through some

of the lowest points of the last two years. Of all the people at Winding Road, she was the one who'd most understand just how meaningful this was to me. Kameron bolted up the stairs into the tiny house and returned moments later with Imogen.

Abbie appeared behind her seconds later, looking to Connor. A slow smile spread over her face at Connor's uncharacteristically wide smile.

"Say it," Imogen said, standing in front of me with wide eyes. "I can't believe it until you say it."

"I'm a divorced man," I said, blinking rapidly to stave off the emotion gathering in my chest.

Imogen let out a whoop of sheer delight and launched herself towards me, wrapping me in the biggest hug. I picked her up and spun her around once before setting her back down.

"It's over," she repeated, gripping my shoulders and giving me a shake. And somehow, hearing the words from someone else's lips made it even more real. "You're free, Lucas."

The words slammed into me again, the force of them nearly taking me to the ground. That they came from Imogen only added to my excitement.

I was *free*.

The nightmare I'd been living for the past three years was finally over. Mallory had signed the papers. I could finally slam the book shut on this chapter of my life and walk freely into a new future.

My ex-wife—finally, I could use the term with no qualifiers or explanations—was a thing of the past.

"Congratulations, Lucas," Connor said, clapping my shoulder. "You did it."

"We have to celebrate," Abbie exclaimed. "Do you want to go out?"

"No," I said, surprising myself. "I actually... I need to call my sister. Give her the news."

It was almost comical, the way everyone's jaws collectively dropped at my mention of my family. It was no secret to anyone in the farmhouse that I didn't enjoy talking about my family.

Knowing I was officially divorced had flayed me wide open, exposing all the raw nerve endings I'd worked so hard to cover up. The pain of my separation had ripped through everything in my life.

Nowhere was that more obvious than with my family.

"We're here if you need us," Connor said. He jerked his head toward Cass's tiny house, a silent encouragement for Kam to follow.

"I'll be alright," I said, even though I didn't believe it.

I pulled my phone out and navigated to my contacts list. My thumb hovered over my sister's name. I hadn't spoken to her for months. I didn't think she'd even pick up if I called.

And then I thought of Cass. Cass, who was somewhere on the farm, was navigating through all of her shit. Learning to open up, even when it was hard.

She made me want to be better.

So I hit call, and to my surprise, Adriana actually picked up.

"Lucas?"

"Hey, sis."

"I, um," Adri stuttered nervously. "Is everything okay?"

"My divorce is finalized."

"Oh," Adri said, and there was something close to relief in her voice. "When?"

"Today."

There was a long pause, and I fought the urge to fill the silence with something.

"Congratulations," she finally said. "It's been a long journey."

"Yeah," I said, my voice rough with the emotion clogging my throat. "I wanted you to know.

"Thank you," Adri said. "I'll tell Mom and Dad."

My stomach churned.

"You probably shouldn't."

"They'll want to know, Lucas."

"I don't give a shit," I muttered, grinding my teeth together.

I could already feel my emotions spinning out. I'd gotten damn good at reining them back in with everything but my family.

"Give me a good reason not to," Adri said. "If you want to tell them yourself, that's one thing, but—"

"Because they believed her without ever stopping to ask," I shouted. "For fuck's sake, Mom and Dad *never* asked for my side of the story. When Mallory came to them and said I'd—"

I took a deep breath, my fingers clenching into a tight fist. I pressed my hand into the siding, focusing on the dig of the wood against my skin so I didn't completely lose control.

"I don't want to tell them about the divorce because I suspect that they'll find another way to weaponize it against me. Fuck, Adri, you were *there* the night everything blew up. Mom wouldn't even look at me."

"Lucas—"

"I would never force myself on anyone. Ever," I said through gritted teeth. "And I know Mallory is damn convincing. Everyone seems to forget that I was the one married to her. I *know* how good of an actress she is. After our marriage blew up, she went into damage-control mode. She painted the man she cheated on me with as the man who saved her from a suffocating marriage. I was an irredeemable villain. And our parents believed her."

"Lucas," Adri whispered.

"No, I need to say this," I cut her off. "I need you to hear this from me. *Every* single thing I said about her was true. I *did* find her in bed with the man I considered my best friend while I was thousands of miles away. She *did* wipe every cent from our bank accounts and hide it from me. She *did* go to my chain of command and try to get me thrown out for domestic abuse.

"You want to know why I left the military? Because I didn't want to deal with it anymore. The looks. The whispers. The stares. The fucking pity for the guy that married true crazy. But what hurts more is that I could have dealt with my chain of command. If it had just been the military meddling in my life, I could have handled it. But what killed me was how you—my *family*—were all too willing to throw me under the bus for crimes I didn't commit."

"They were worried, Lucas," Adri said quietly. "You weren't very... I'm not doing a good job of explaining."

I sighed in frustration.

"I know I wasn't always the most communicative person when I was on active duty. I should have called home more. And despite what she said, I know Mom is still upset about the courthouse wedding, and that she didn't meet Mallory in person before. Trust and believe that I have already beaten myself up over and over again because I know that you and Mom would have sniffed out her bullshit while I was still love-struck. None of that excuses their never asking the question. And let's not forget that you went along with this too. For months, you didn't talk to me."

"You know why I couldn't," Adri whispered.

"I know," I said. Desperation crept into my voice as I continued, "That's why she came to *you* with that awful story. She's a narcissistic liar, Adri. She knew what happened to you."

I barreled past Adri's sharp intake of breath. I knew she didn't want to hash that period of her life out with me, and I didn't want to force her to unearth it again.

"I didn't want to drag this out any longer, and that's why I didn't talk about everything she did. But trust me when I say that Mallory is a compulsive liar. She would do anything to paint herself in a better light. Including lying to my family about why we separated. She cheated on me with my best friend, Adri. A man I trusted and respected. Rather than work through our marriage, she jumped ship, and then tried to sink my entire fucking life."

Adri was silent for a long time.

"I'm sorry, Lucas."

The words punched through me in a way I hadn't expected.

"I can't do this right now," I muttered. My grip on the phone tightened to a painful degree. "I thought the divorce being official would ease things, but I need more time."

"Okay," Adri whispered, clearly defeated. "I'm sorry you're hurting, Lucas. And I'm sorry for the role I played in this."

"I love you, Adri. That will never change. But it's going to take me a long time to work past the way you were so willing to cut me out of your life over something that wasn't true. You're my family." I choked on the word. "You were supposed to ask me for the truth. You were supposed to at least *consider* it."

"You're right," Adri said, and I knew even without seeing her face that she was crying.

"I've gotta go," I muttered. "And Adri?"

"It was good to hear your voice."

"You too."

The phone line went dead.

"Fuck," I roared, and chucked my phone onto the gravel path in front of me. "*Fuck.*"

"Lucas?"

Cass's voice was like a bucket of ice water dumped over my nervous system.

"Shit, I'm sorry," I said, running my hands through my hair.

"It's okay," Cassie said. She pulled her cardigan over her shoulders. "With Kam and Connor working on the tiny house, I was reading on the hammock. I heard your conversation getting a little, uh... animated. And I wanted to ask you if you need to talk?"

I stared blankly at her.

"Nah, I'm okay."

A ghost of a smile graced Cassie's features.

"Are you sure about that?"

I nodded.

"Alright," Cassie murmured. She turned to head back to the hammock.

Fuck it.

With one brief glance towards the occupied tiny house fifty feet down the hill, and another towards the chicken coop to make sure none of the others had slipped out of the farmhouse, I tugged Cassie behind the house, pressing her back into the siding. She looked up at me with a knowing smirk.

"How did you deal with being estranged from your family?" I said as my fingers trailed up and down her sides. "Because I feel like I'm going fucking crazy."

Cassie paused.

"I didn't," she whispered. My knuckles grazed her hips. "I buried it next to all the other shit in my life I didn't care to examine too closely."

I rubbed a hand over my face.

"I don't know how to move past this," I admitted. "I don't know how to let this chapter of my life close."

To my surprise, Cass looped her arms around my neck. I accepted her invitation without hesitation, leaning down to graze my mouth over hers.

"I'm not the person to give life advice right now," Cass murmured. "But I can help in other ways."

Her nails dug gently into my neck, urging me forward.

I pressed my lips to hers and kissed her slowly, languidly, savoring the way she softened against me. I was seconds away from grabbing her hips and wrapping those gorgeous thighs around my waist when someone cleared their throat, and I jumped back. Cass slid her cardigan back over her shoulder again, but her mouth dropped open in horror when she realized the reason for the abrupt ending had been an audience. She quickly recovered, pressing a hand over her mouth.

"Your sink is fixed," Connor told her in a monotone.

"T-thank you," she stuttered. With one more helpless glance in my direction, Cassie turned and flew towards the back door of the farmhouse, book and hammock long forgotten. Connor turned his stormy expression on me.

"What was that?" Connor said, and, fuck, he was *pissed*.

"I can explain."

"You'd better do it fast," Connor said. "And you better thank whatever god you believe in that it was me that found you two and not Imogen. Against the side of the farmhouse where anyone could see is brazen, even for you."

"We know each other," I blurted, ignoring the barb. He hadn't said anything that wasn't true. "From before. We met in Seattle."

Connor's expression turned weary.

"Are you screwing with me right now?"

"No," I said, throwing my hands up defensively even as Connor's cursing caught me off guard. "I swear to God. I went out the night Winding Road was in Seattle for the Warrior's Grant presentations. I went to a bar close to the hotel, and we met there."

"And you what, talked all night?"

I shot him an unamused glare.

"Yeah, Connor. We *talked* all night."

Connor didn't answer.

He just stood there, assessing me as if I were a threat he didn't know how to handle.

"Christ," Connor muttered, rubbing a hand over his face. "Please tell me you've thought this through."

Not *even a little bit.*

"It's new," I said. "I know it looks like we're running around behind—"

"That's exactly what you're doing," Connor said exasperatedly. He was more flustered than I was used to seeing him, and that threw me. Connor was normally the unmovable one: always stoic, collected even when faced with something that made him unsure.

"I need to ask you—"

"Don't ask me to keep this from Abbie," Connor cut me off. "You already know the answer."

"Not Abbie," I said, internally wincing. "I'm asking you not to tell Imogen."

Connor grimaced. "*Lucas.*"

"Please," I said through gritted teeth. "I've never asked you for something like this, Connor, but I'm asking now. I need to be the one to tell her. But she and Cass are working through their problems, and I'm not going to be the thing that fractures their new relationship down the middle."

"Lucas, you're not stupid, but you're sure acting like it."

I opened my mouth to argue, but Connor cut me off, lowering his voice when he realized we'd been talking too loudly.

"This has the potential to blow up in your face. If Abbie asks me, I won't lie to her. I'm not omitting information or circumventing the question either. And I won't tell her not to tell Imogen. That's her best friend."

"I know," I growled. "Fuck, Connor, I *know.*"

"Then why?"

I put my hands on my hips, looked up at the sky, and blew out a long breath before returning my focus to Connor. He crossed his arms over his chest.

"Because most people don't get second chances," I said.

Connor's expression morphed into one of understanding.

"You can't stay away from her," Connor said. It wasn't a question, but I nodded anyway.

"I really, really can't."

"I can't believe I'm doing this," Connor muttered. "What is it with people and their damn secrets around here?"

"You just cursed. I'm proud of myself."

Connor gave me a withering glare.

"Don't start. I'm not happy about this."

I'm not either, I wanted to say.

Cass's words flitted through my mind.

Just sex. That's all this can be.

Words that haunted me.

"You need to tell Imogen. Soon. This kind of betrayal will break her heart, Lucas. You know that better than anyone."

Leave it to Connor Harvey to twist the guilt knife in deeper.

"Alright."

Connor let out one final sigh before he trudged up the gravel driveway.

My eyes landed on the phone lying discarded in the gravel.

So much for a relaxing, peaceful afternoon.

Chapter 20
Cassie

I'd spent the entire afternoon hiding in the tiny house. I couldn't bear the thought of running into Connor in the farmhouse, or worse, Abbie. Because if Connor knew, Abbie would know by day's end.

Which meant it was only a matter of time before Imogen did.

Because that's how things worked around here.

I was the outcast who didn't have anyone on my side.

I'd already started planning my return to Seattle.

Somehow, I'd be able to put this insane chapter of my life to rest. I'd find a box in my mind big enough to shove Lucas into and go back to being the person I was before.

I'd go work for a big corporate law firm, where I'd spend my long work days hiding from the reality—

A knock at the door derailed my thoughts. I opened the door to find Lucas on my doorstep. He looked more unsettled than usual.

"Hey," he said.

"Hi," I murmured, leaning against the door frame. "You probably shouldn't be here."

"I know I shouldn't."

I sucked my bottom lip between my teeth.

"What do you want to do?" I asked, dreading the answer.

"He's not going to tell," Lucas murmured.

My heart pounded against my ribcage.

"You can't be sure of that."

"No," Lucas agreed. "But I think Connor of all people can respect that people have to work certain things out at their own pace."

"That's not enough."

"It has to be for now."

I gaped at him, searching for something else to say. I was exhausted.

"This is going to end poorly."

"Probably."

I was helpless to do anything but stare at him. That same freshly cut dark hair and handsome brown eyes that had captured my attention all those nights ago.

Lucas was a thunderstorm that had rolled into my life and thrown everything completely off kilter.

"Good night, Lucas," I finally whispered.

One of us had to turn away first, and I was already used to it being me.

Lucas tucked a stray strand of hair behind my ear. I tilted my head to the side in anticipation of a kiss, but instead, he pressed his lips to my forehead before stepping away.

"Night, Cass. Sweet dreams."

I watched him walk up the driveway to his house, my skin still tingling from where his lips had touched it.

"I'm going to die."

I smiled behind my phone as Abbie flopped onto the couch, groaning loudly.

We were back in Watford proper for a girl's day. Abbie was deep in the nesting phase, and she'd wrangled Imogen and I into her de-tagging crew after a week of online shopping. Imogen sat cross-legged on the couch, scissors in hand, with a small metal trashcan beneath her feet.

There were piles of baby clothes and muslin blankets strewn across her couch, waiting for their turn in the washing machine. Her living room was now painted in muted pastels and every variation of beige imaginable.

"This girl is trying to kill me," Abbie muttered, readjusting in her seat. "Dr. Conrad tried to warn me about the leg pain, but I don't think anything could have prepared me for this."

"Can you take anything for it?" I asked. I rolled my shoulders back and stretched my arms above my head.

In desperate need of a movement break after sitting on the couch taking tags off clothes for an hour, I headed over to the kettle so I could heat water for tea.

Abbie had whittled her caffeine habit down to one small cup of coffee in the morning. Something about her internalized anxiety over her caffeine intake while pregnant.

The three of us—Abbie, Imogen, and I—had actually gotten along well over the last few days. After Imogen and I's disastrous excursion to Watford a few weeks ago, Abbie had hopped in to be a buffer.

I didn't understand how a place could bring up so many emotions for me until I'd tried to walk down main street pretending like I hadn't had some of the best and worst days of my life within the same ten miles.

That was the nature of trauma, I supposed. I'd overheard plenty of conversations between Lainey and her therapist over the last few years.

Lainey and I had trauma bonded over the love/hate relationships we had with our hometowns. Lainey had grown up in Keelbay Harbor, a small coastal town in Maine, where most high school graduates took one of two paths: get out of town and go to college, or pursue a trade that kept you in Keelbay for another generation.

"I could, but relief is short-lived," Abbie said with a long sigh. "There's not much anybody can do for me until after this girl evicts herself."

I chuckled. "The plight of womanhood."

Abbie grunted in response.

Just then, Imogen reappeared from the hallway. "What's the plan today, ladies?"

"Ugh, I should go for a walk," Abbie said. "Sitting and lying down for too long aggravates the sciatica."

"What about a trip to Forest Grove?" Imogen suggested.

The kettle whistled, signaling that the hot water was ready. I got out three tea bags and put one in each mug for the three of us.

"That place is still around?" I asked.

Imogen and Abbie both looked aghast.

"Of course, Mari is still around," Abbie said.

My cheeks flushed a deep scarlet.

"I didn't mean it like that," I said nervously. "I just meant the bookstore itself. Obviously, I hope that Mari never dies. She's an icon around here."

"She's still going strong," Abbie said, taking the mug from my hands gratefully. "Doing what she does best."

My next sip of tea went down the wrong way.

Abbie drew in a long breath and settled back onto the couch, wincing as the soccer player she was currently carrying on her front kicked her square in the ribs.

"I swear my ribs are her favorite place to hang out," Abbie said. "She's gonna be athletic like her daddy."

"God save us all," Imogen muttered, and Abbie playfully nudged her thigh with hers.

"I'd love to go to the bookstore, though," I said honestly. "I can't remember the last time I set foot in there."

Abbie and Imogen exchanged a knowing glance.

"Well, let's just say that the two of us have definitely been in there recently."

I smiled. "Is Mari still trying to play matchmaker?"

Imogen chuckled. "She's always played matchmaker. It's one of the things we love most about her."

"True," I said, remembering fondly all the times that I wound up at Forest Grove Books as a kid.

Mari was one of those people who knew a little about everything.

As a kid, she was one of the few people in Watford that I felt like knew the answers to everything, and even if she didn't have the answer, she could point me to a book that did. We might not have a library in Watford, but we had Mari, and that was more than enough.

"Well, how about we drink some tea, finish that Netflix documentary we were watching, and head that way?" Abbie said.

"Sounds good to me," I replied, taking up the free spot at the end of the couch. Imogen reached for the remote.

"I wonder what the guys are doing," Abbie mused.

"They'd better be checking things off the list I gave them," Imogen muttered.

I smiled behind my coffee mug.

"You gave them a task list while we're here today?"

"Of course I did," Imogen shot me a wry smile. "Have you met those three? They can't be left to their own devices."

Something strange and foreign that felt too close to affection for my comfort swirled in my gut at the thought.

Imogen had worked so hard for so long to carve out this part of life just for her, the small section of friends and land and opportunity that wasn't afforded to her when we were younger.

I felt like I was constantly riding the line between overstepping and desperately wanting to be part of it—whatever that looked like.

When Abbie invited the two of us here today, I realized I hadn't been invited to do something solely with the women in my life for years.

Lainey was my best friend and as roommates, we naturally did a lot of things together, but there was something about another woman inviting you into their circle, opening that door and encouraging you to step through it, that I'd been missing more than I realized.

Forest Grove Books stood exactly as I remembered it: a small storefront tucked at the end of the long row of brick buildings that lined Watford's main street. Nestled next to Blackbeard's Coffee and across the street from the Roadhouse, Forest Grove was a Watford institution in more ways than one.

The bell above the door chimed as the three of us entered, and Mari's smiling face greeted us from behind the checkout counter.

"My word," Mari gasped as she took in my frame. "Cassandra Phillips, is that you?"

I blushed slightly at the use of my full name and shrugged to dispel some of the awkwardness seeping into my bones.

"Hi Mari. It's good to—"

The older woman stepped down from the slightly raised platform and enveloped me in a crushing hug, cutting off my words. I let out a surprised laugh and hugged her back.

Mari's energy was infectious. It was impossible not to match it.

"You're looking as gorgeous as ever," Mari said, squeezing my shoulders before stepping back to give me some breathing room.

"That's very kind of you."

I looked around and let out a small chuckle.

"I like what you've done with the place."

"Still a smart ass, I see," Mari said, tsking under her breath, but there was no heat behind it.

"Comes with the territory," I said, waving a hand dismissively. "Divorce law and all that."

Mari's eyebrows quirked up. "Wouldn't have slated you for divorce law. The girl I knew—"

"Wouldn't have wanted that," I cut in. "I know."

Mari simply stared at me.

"I'll take that as my cue to head for the romance section," Imogen said quietly. She linked arms with Abbie and dragged her away from the scene of whatever crime was about to occur.

"Why are you back in town?"

"That's a complicated question," I muttered, running my fingers along the worn bookshelf, stacked high with books both old and new. Forest Grove was a beautiful mosaic of history. When I was a kid, I was sure the books on these shelves held all the answers.

"I thought lawyers were professionals at asking loaded questions."

That got a laugh out of me. I shot her a wry smile.

"Touché."

"That's not an answer."

"Did you go to law school, Mari? You sure are good at cornering folks."

"My interests are varied."

That was true. Mari also had time on her side.

I knew from experience that she would happily stare at me until I finally gave her an answer.

I exhaled and squared my shoulders before pulling a random book off the shelf, turning it over in my hand and pretending to read the back blurb.

"I quit my job."

Mari let out a low whistle.

"Not the big fancy lawyer job you'd always wanted, surely."

"The very one."

"Now, why in the world would you do that?"

"Beats me."

My back was to Mari now, but I could practically hear the shake of her head.

"Of the three of you, you were always the toughest nut to crack."

"I'll take that as a compliment," I muttered.

"It is," Mari mused. "Somewhat."

"You really should have gone to law school," I said. "You would have excoriated whoever was standing on the other side."

Mari chuckled. "Maybe in another life."

"Yeah," I said, sliding the book back on the shelf. "Maybe in another life."

"So you're hanging out in your hometown for a while. Where are you headed next?"

"Haven't thought that far ahead."

"Who are you, and what have you done with Cassandra Phillips?"

I rolled my eyes. Mari was the only person who could push me like this and have my blood pressure remain steady.

"I suppose I'm realizing that the person I was when I left Watford isn't the person I want to be forever."

"Ah," Mari said, voice soft. "There she is."

"Do you remember the conversation we had?" I asked quietly. "That day I came in here and hid because I didn't want to talk to my dad."

"Which day are we referring to?"

I snorted. "Low blow. There were a lot of those my senior year."

And hundreds more before that.

Forest Grove was the only place my grandmother would let me come to alone when we were in town. My parents didn't like to stay in Watford longer than strictly necessary, and my poor Nana had her hands full with Imogen and Kevin.

I snuck away whenever I could.

"I remember every piece of advice I've ever given," Mari replied. I choked out a laugh, grateful for the burst of humor in what would otherwise be an intense conversation.

"I'm sorry to say I didn't take your advice about talking to a therapist."

"I knew you wouldn't," Mari said. "You were never one for talking about your feelings. Not that I'd blame you, of course. It's not like you had good parental examples of how to work through conflict in yourself, much less with others."

I blew out a long breath, finally turning to face her. I crossed my arms over my chest and leaned against the bookshelf.

"I met someone," I admitted.

Mari's face lit up as if someone had just handed her the winning lottery numbers.

"And you want to be better for this someone?"

"Better at communicating," I said. "I've spent the last few years of my life arguing with people, and I think I'm just tired of it."

"You don't want to argue with this person?"

"No. I really don't."

"Interesting."

"Is this your way of telling me I'm an argumentative person?"

Mari snorted, and the sound brought a smile to my face.

"Between you, Imogen, and Abbie, you were the one I spent the most time with. You've always been special to me, Cass. When you want something, you want it fiercely—and there is nothing on earth that can stand in the way of your getting it. You wanted to get out of Watford, and you did. You wanted to become a lawyer so you could help people, and you did. You've done so much more than you give yourself credit for. So yes, you are an argumentative person, but that's not a bad thing, honey. It never was. You just had people in your life tell you it was a less desirable trait. That you needed to be more palatable to the people around you. But you don't."

I swallowed the ball of emotion that lodged in my throat at the fierce confidence with which she spoke.

"And something tells me this someone you're talking about loves that about you."

My head jerked up at the casual L-word mention.

"Oh, don't act like that now now," Mari said with a chuckle. "It's not an unreasonable leap to make. You don't do casual, Cass. Your heart loves too fiercely for that."

Too close.

Too *fucking close.*

"Okay, I think that's enough feelings for one day," I said, pushing away from the bookshelf and heading down the aisle Abbie and Imogen had disappeared behind just minutes earlier.

"You might have loved those horses a little too much when you were young. You certainly spook like one," Mari called once my back was turned.

I couldn't stop a smile from forming.

"You haven't changed at all, Mari."

"And you haven't changed as much as you think you have, Cass. You're just more confident in what you want now."

What I want.

What the fuck did I want?

I paused in the middle of the long aisle. Imogen and Abbie stood together, huddled over a gorgeous hardback book with dragon sprayed edges, giggling amongst themselves. Instead of rushing past the question like I wanted to, I paused and leaned in.

I wanted to feel like I did in Seattle.

Like I could leave the world behind and just... live.

I reached a hand out to steady myself against the bookshelf. My fingertips brushed against one book. I tore my gaze from Abbie and Imogen to inspect the paperback. It was practically disintegrating, weathered by time and the hands that had touched it over the years.

My eyes widened, and I let out a breathless laugh as I stared at the faded cover. I'd recognize the little girl in a red coat and hat standing against a thick wall of ivy and foliage anywhere.

The Secret Garden.

The exact copy that I'd donated to Forest Grove when I moved out for college.

I flipped open the cover, already knowing what I'd find.

Mari's delicate, swooping handwriting forming the words: *for Cass.*

But it wasn't just the memory of reading this exact book cover to cover a thousand times, wishing I could step inside the pages like Mary sought the illustrious walled garden, that snagged my attention. It was the name Mari had written.

Cass.

Not Cassie.

Few people knew me as Cass first instead of Cassie. It was a silly difference, inconsequential in most of my day-to-day interactions.

But the list of people who *preferred* to call me Cass instead of Cassie was short.

In truth, there were only two people in the world who called me Cass most of the time.

Mari was one. Lucas was the other.

Past and present.

The universe had a sense of humor after all.

Chapter 21

Lucas

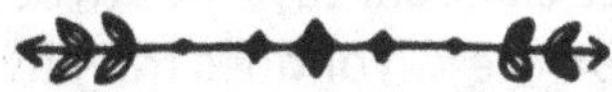

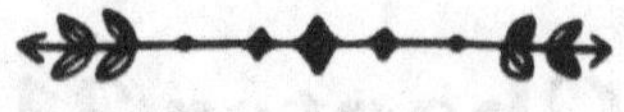

Me

Had a long day but I saw this crazy ass tree and it reminded me of that statue we made fun of in Seattle lol.

Me

Sorry to text so early in the morning, but this is the one time I'll have my phone. Hope everything's going good in Watford.

Give the horses an extra apple as a treat from me please, papa misses them

Cass

When are you heading back to Winding Road?

The farmhouse calendar says the 7th but are you driving back on the 7th or does training end on the 7th

Me

I'm driving back on the 7th.

Miss me?

No.

Maybe a little.

Disclaimer that I am slightly inebriated but I'm safe in the tiny house, I promise

It's just me and my smutty little book and my vibrator

Did I mention I'm in your bed?

Because I am

You're going to kill me, woman.

Are you going to block my number if I ask for pictures?

I drove through the night to get back to Winding Road as quickly as I could at the conclusion of annual training. After two weeks away from home, I was way too excited at the prospect of a hot shower and Cassie being in my arms again. When I finally pulled into the driveway at Winding Road, I practically sprinted to my tiny house for a shower. I pulled on a fresh set of clothes while brushing my teeth—jeans and a dark gray t-shirt—and took off toward the other tiny house.

Cassie opened the door seconds before I knocked, and I grinned at her blushing cheeks.

"Well, hello to you too."

"Shut up," she muttered. She grabbed the collar of my shirt and pulled me down for a kiss. I went eagerly, cupping her face to deepen the kiss. The low, content sound she made in the back of her throat shot through me like a lightning bolt.

"Do you want to go for a ride with me?" I asked when we finally broke apart. I propped my arm against the doorway and leaned towards her.

"Is that an innuendo?" She countered, tearing her eyes away from my biceps. I gave her a knowing smirk just to watch her blush again.

Pretty. She was always so damn pretty.

"No," I said before clearing my throat. "I missed you while I was at AT. I want to spend time with you."

Cass's face morphed into something shy and girlish.

The expression was so unlike the Cass who kept her emotions behind lock and key. My heart damn near ran away from me.

"Lucas Morales, you keep surprising me."

I stood there, silent and useless, waiting for her to finish the internal debate I knew was raging.

"Give me five minutes."

The door to the tiny house closed, and I blew out a long breath. Cass returned wearing jeans, a white tank with a tan button-up for a jacket, and her favorite pair of brown boots. I let out a low whistle, and I could have sworn she blushed under the weight of my stare.

"You and denim are my favorite combination."

"Quit inflating my ego or we're not making it to the barn," Cass teased.

She hopped down the stairs to meet me, and we walked up the driveway side by side in companionable silence. I struggled to wrap my head around how comfortable I was around this woman. Seattle had been comfortable, but there hadn't been any pressure that night. We were two strangers who were all too eager to escape reality together for a few hours.

I was still waiting for the awkwardness to kick in. I was waiting for the day to come when the heat in Cassie's gaze when she looked at me disappeared.

But the connection between us just strengthened.

The two of us made quick work of tacking Chesty and Memphis for the ride.

"Where are we going?" Cass said as she swung her leg over the saddle, adjusting herself so she was comfortable. I followed suit, letting Memphis steady himself underneath me before leading him out of the barn towards the treeline.

"Call it a nature walk," I called back to Cassie as I set off down the trail. "There's somewhere I want to show you."

I felt like one of the luckiest men alive to have access to such a beautiful, untamed, abundant backyard.

Even though most of Winding Road's operations occurred on the first ten acres, what most people didn't realize was that it was a sprawling property, stretching dozens of acres back into the Washington mountains. The path I led Cass down was more recreational, meaning we rarely used it for our recovery cohorts at Winding Road.

Namely, because it ended at the most beautiful waterfall. A sprawling cascade emptied into a beautiful, crystal clear pool near the base of the mountain peak.

"Holy shit," Cassie whispered as she regarded the clearing. "This is gorgeous."

"I come here a lot when I need a break from the farm," I told her. "I enjoy coming here to think. There's something about a cold plunge that clears the senses."

Cass snorted, but didn't poke fun at me. I showed her a place where we could hang both Chesty and Memphis's leads before we turned our attention to the waterfall in front of us.

"Wait a second."

Cass whirled around to face me, pointing an accusing finger right to my chest.

"You little shit."

I grinned. "Just now realizing?"

To my surprise, Cass lit up with that same joy I'd seen earlier at the tiny house.

"Admit it. You just wanted to get me naked again."

"I always want to get you naked," I said honestly. "But also, this is a nice place to skinny dip."

"Is this you admitting that you've come here by yourself to swim naked, smoke a cigar, and think about the military-industrial complex?"

An unexpected laugh burst out of my chest, and I fought the urge to tug her towards me.

The need to touch Cassie every time we were together was quickly spiraling out of control.

She didn't seem to mind it, though.

"I plead the Fifth."

Cass rolled her eyes. "Classic."

"I'll have you know that the Fifth Amendment was originally—"

"Good grief," Cass muttered. "I went to law school. And passed the bar on the first try. I know what the Fifth Amendment is. I could give you a history lesson on it."

"I'd enjoy that. A lot, actually."

"You're a menace. Now get naked."

I wasn't capable of denying the woman in front of me. Not when she was already kicking her boots off and unbuttoning her jeans, sliding the dark blue denim off the luscious thighs that kept me up at night.

"Do we jump?"

"It's the only way, unfortunately," I said, feigning a grimace. Cass laughed and pulled the claw clip from her hair, letting her curls fall freely. She'd stopped straightening it a few weeks ago, a detail that wasn't lost on me.

She stared down at the water, letting out a long sigh before muttering, "Fuck it."

And then she jumped. She let out a squeal of delight on the way down. She emerged with a loud gasp.

"Fuck Lucas, you *asshole*, you didn't tell me it was cold!"

My chest shook with the force of my uncontrollable laughter.

"It's the Washington Mountains, Cass," I called down. "That was a given."

"Get down here and warm me up."

She swam further away from the cliffside to give me a clear berth to jump myself. Not needing to be told twice, I ripped my shirt over my head and tossed it in the collective pile of clothes forming off to the side. I silently apologized to both Chesty and Memphis for everything they'd see today before jumping in after Cassie.

"Jesus," I said when I emerged from the jump. "It really is fucking cold."

"I told you," Cass squealed, swimming towards me. The second she reached me, I was pulling her into my arms. I walked us back towards the cliff's edge, where I could stand comfortably, and she wrapped her legs around me like we'd done this a thousand times before.

"Hi," she murmured.

"Hey."

"You missed me, huh?"

"I always miss you."

It wasn't a question she needed to ask. My answer seemed to soothe an anxious part of her, though, because she relaxed against me. Her nails grazed the sensitive part of my neck, and she smiled.

"We always seem to end up here," she said, gesturing to the beautiful image of her in my lap.

"This *is* how things started," I replied.

"I seem to remember things starting at Rain's."

Any retort I had died at the mention of the place where we'd met. In all the conversations we'd had in the months since Seattle, never had Cassie directly addressed the night we'd met.

And goddamn, I didn't know just how badly I needed her to open that door, because I waltzed right through it.

"I meant what I said that night. And all the other nights. You took my fucking breath away, Cass."

"Imogen was right. You are a flirt."

The familiar twinge of discomfort at being reduced to the flirty party boy flared to life in my chest. I quickly locked it away.

"Flirts play games," I murmured.

I would know, because the stories didn't lie. I had been a party boy once upon a time.

But I wasn't that person anymore.

That subtle jab revealed a deeper truth, one that I was all too nervous about seeing the light of day.

"I've never played games with you, Cass."

The words tumbled out of me before I could hold them back. Where I should have expected regret, was only a realization: that was the God's honest truth. Somewhere deep in my chest, I still harbored that resentment. The realization that I was handing Cassie the same blade I'd handed Mallory all those years ago should have scared me.

The woman in my arms had the power to destroy me. I should run for the fucking hills.

And yet I didn't. I pulled her closer. Pressed my face into her neck like she was the most precious thing in the world to me.

I wasn't ready to admit to myself—and I damn sure wasn't ready to tell her—that she already was.

"Lucas."

My name was a frustrated plea on her lips. It frustrated

her that she couldn't pin me down. A better man would have fessed up about the nature of his feelings. I would have told her that this arrangement was more complicated than I could justify.

That I was no longer capable of *not* feeling something for her.

"Tell me what you need," I said roughly, pushing all thoughts of brutal honesty away. Her legs tightened around me.

"I need you to kiss me," she whispered.

"Why?"

I watched her throat bob as she swallowed. But I wanted her to hear her say it.

I *needed* to hear her say it.

"Because I missed you," she admitted. Her voice was barely above a whisper. I gripped her hips and brought her body flush against mine. I wanted to capture the small gasp that slipped past her lips, replay it on a loop in my head.

"Atta girl."

And then I kissed her. Just like she'd asked for.

I held her against me, letting her take what she needed. Her arms snaked around my neck, hands dragging down my back, sending a delicious ache down my spine.

"I brought a blanket," I said when she finally pulled her mouth from mine, both of us gasping for breath.

Cass huffed out a laugh. "You're such a boy scout."

"Always be prepared," I muttered. I finally let her go, the two of us finally parting so we could both climb out of the pool on shaky legs. I'd never been more grateful for my over-preparedness than when I laid out the plaid blanket on the softest spot of dirt I could find. Cass shook her head like a dog, water droplets flying from her hair. A surprised laugh punched out of my chest as I laid down on the blanket, reaching for her.

My laugh quickly turned into a groan when she dropped in my lap, my hard length twitching as she rubbed her pussy over it.

"Not so funny now, huh?"

"You were the one making jokes," I pointed out, any further conversation quickly dying as she ground against me once more. "Fuck, Cass, could you come like this?"

"Anything's possible with you."

The words shot through me like a jolt of electricity. She didn't realize the power her words held over me. There was a lawyer joke layered in there somewhere, but I was beyond cracking jokes.

Not when Cass was bucking her hips like she couldn't think about anything else other than my body beneath hers.

Reality crashed into me when she pushed me back towards the blanket. I groaned in frustration.

"I didn't bring my wallet."

So much for being prepared.

She stilled above me, kiss-bitten lips red and swollen, her cheeks flushed with the heat of her arousal. She sucked her bottom lip between her teeth, and I decided I could die a happy man with that visual forever sealed in my brain.

"I got tested after I found out about Collin," she murmured, pulling me closer. Her hands burned like a brand on my skin, a mark I desperately wanted to keep. "And I haven't been with anyone else but you. I'm okay if you are."

Her eyes shone with vulnerability, and I held her face, thumb caressing her cheekbone. My heart hammered against my ribcage. I felt like I was standing on the precipice of something I'd never felt, but had somehow dreamed about my entire damn life.

"I haven't either," I said quietly. "It's just you, Cass. It's always just you."

Cassie sucked in a sharp breath.

She reached down to guide me inside her and I shuddered as I entered her, barely holding back a groan.

Ruined. I was fucking ruined over her.

"Don't turn into a gentleman now," she panted, rolling her hips against mine. "You weren't before."

I snarled and snapped my hips forward, forcing a loud moan from her lips.

"Oh," she choked out, throwing her head back, eyes fluttering closed as I moved inside her. "You feel—"

"I know, baby," I said, leaning down to kiss her again. I clung to whatever shred of sanity I had left, willing myself not to come too fast, to savor every moment with her. "Feels too damn good."

I sat back, gripping her hips and moving her with me. I wanted to feel her on top of me, to thrust into her until she was coming all over me, gasping for air.

Cass met everything I gave her and gave in equal measure. Her nails dug into my skin, and I prayed she'd leave marks. I reached for her bare tits, squeezing them in my hands, rolling her nipple between my fingers as I fucked up into her, hips snapping. Cassie met every thrust, her head tipped back towards the sky.

"You know I need to see you, Cass."

Her eyes met mine, and I almost lost it at the desperation in her gaze. Her eyes were glassy, and a steady stream of "yes yes yes" fell from her lips as I kept the same rhythm.

"Dream girl," I murmured when my fingers drifted over her clit. "My dream girl."

She fell apart with that gasping moan that drove me fucking crazy. Her nails dug into my shoulders as her lips parted with a cry as the full weight of her orgasm rolled through her. Her body shook, thighs tightening, pussy clenching in a way that had me slowing my pace.

"Where do you want me?" I said, slowing the roll of my hips.

"Inside," she moaned.

"Are you—"

Cassie put both hands on my chest and shoved me backwards, slamming her hips into mine as she chased the last of her pleasure.

"Please come inside me," she whined, and I realized in that moment that I was well and truly fucked.

I had never been capable of denying Cassie Phillips anything.

And when she moaned, "I want to feel you. All of you," I had a second realization: that there was no way in hell I was denying my dream girl anything.

With one more bounce of her ass, my release swept through me. I gripped her hips hard enough to hurt, grinding her into me. I wanted her to feel how much I wanted her. How much I fucking needed her. How fucking crazy she made me. I pressed my face into her collarbone and bit the sensitive skin there, unable to stop myself from claiming her.

We'd never left marks on each other. Another line we'd never crossed. Not since that first night. But in that moment I didn't give a fuck where the lines were.

And based on the way Cass whined and wound her fingers through my hair, keeping my teeth against her skin, she needed it just like I did. Her hips slowed, but her thighs tightened around me.

I smoothed my tongue over the mark before pulling away from her skin, meeting her eyes. Her chest rose and fell in quick breaths, her thighs still trembling with the aftershocks of her orgasm. I inhaled deeply as she slid off me; her nails digging into my arms like I was the thing still anchoring her to the earth.

"Fuck," Cassie panted when she dropped onto the blanket beside me. "*Fuck*, Lucas."

"I know," I murmured, pulling her against me. I needed to feel her skin against mine. "I know."

She curled into my side, throwing an arm over my chest. I felt her eyes on me as I stared at the sky, still trying to catch my breath.

"Is now a good time to say I told you so?"

"Shut up," she muttered. She reached for my hand, tracing the lines on my palm. I closed my eyes, savoring her nearness and the quiet sounds of the forest.

"Can I admit something that's probably not something men want to hear after sex?"

"Most definitely."

"I didn't expect it to be that good a second time," she

admitted. I let out a disbelieving laugh.

"Now that's just offensive, Cass."

"I know," she sighed. "But I've spent the last four months replaying every part of that night. The conversation. The energy I felt between us. How you made me feel. I guess I'd convinced myself it wasn't real. And then the night in the tiny house we fell right back into step, and just now... it's always the same. It's always good."

"Can I admit something back?"

Cassie inclined her head towards me, resting her cheek against my shoulder. I brought my free hand up to her hair to toy with the silky strands.

"I never doubted it was real."

Her breath caught. I expected her to pull away, but she linked our fingers together, resting our joined hands on my stomach.

"Yeah?"

"Yeah," I replied, clearing my throat.

"Are you saying..."

Her voice trailed off, and I hoped she couldn't hear the way my heart was about to race out of my chest.

"I'm saying I want you, Cassie. I haven't stopped wanting you since the first time I fucking saw you. And I don't see that stopping anytime soon."

"Okay," she whispered, her lips against my collarbone. "I want you, too. So much it actually scares me."

"I told you weeks ago that I'll give you whatever you want," I whispered. I shifted onto my side so I could look her in the eye. My throat bobbed as my eyes snagged on the blooming mark on her skin. I wondered if it meant more to her than just a reminder of a good fuck.

Wondered if she knew the reason I put it there was because I was physically incapable of letting her walk around without a reminder of me after she let me fuck her bare.

"I only ask for one thing in return."

"What's that?"

"Whatever truth you can give me," I rasped. "You have your reasons for building your walls up. I won't push you. But I'm asking you, as someone who cares about you, who wants you—give me *something*."

To my eternal surprise, Cassie didn't look away. She held my gaze, fingertips trailing over my face like she was trying to memorize my features. I knew the feeling all too well.

"I have a bad habit of sabotaging things," she whispered. "It's a character flaw. If someone gets too close or something feels too good, I shove them away and kick the door shut. It would be a talent, really, if it weren't such a fucking awful cycle."

"Well, it's a good thing I'm not going anywhere."

Cass scoffed and sat up.

"Hey," I said, grabbing her hand before she stood up completely. She didn't meet my eyes, but she stayed seated, and that was enough. "I don't say things I don't mean. You should know that by now."

"I don't need rescuing from my abandonment issues."

"Don't twist my words. You're not broken, and I've never treated you like you are," I said. She lifted her head wearily.

"Lucas, you really don't have to do this," Cass muttered.

"You can keep trying to kick the door closed, but it won't work." I gave her a winning smile. "You'll have to try a lot harder than that."

"Okay," she said hesitantly, giving me a small smile.

I exhaled and pressed a kiss to her forehead.

"We should head back," I said. "I don't want Kameron sending the search parties out."

"Yeah," Cassie said, her voice distant as she grabbed her clothes from the pile beside the picnic blanket. "I guess we should."

"Hey," I murmured once we were fully clothed. My fingers encircled her wrist and tugged her to me. "We go at your pace. Just like the first time."

Cassie kissed me, arms wrapping around my neck, our bodies molding together.

"I'll hold you to that," she whispered as we pulled away from each other.

"Good."

The Marine Corps reserve was an entirely different from what I was used to. It had been a long time since I'd been called at eleven at night. I sat straight up in bed, the book I'd been reading long forgotten as I picked up my phone.

"This is Morales."

"Hey dude, sorry to bother you this late. Needed a sign of life. I tried to text you several times, but you didn't respond."

I swore under my breath, only now seeing the three unread text messages from my squad leader's number.

"Just needed to know you're alive."

"Damn," I muttered. "Yeah, dude, I'm alive."

"Alright, just respond to my text next time, alright? I don't enjoy waking people up in the middle of the night, but I have to fill out this spreadsheet or they'll have my ass."

A baby started crying in the background, and the tiredness of his voice suddenly made sense.

"Yeah, man, I'm sorry. I'll take my phone off do not disturb."

I would at least set it up to where Morrow's texts and calls would bypass my settings so I didn't make his life any harder than it needed to be.

"Appreciate it. Have a good night."

He hung up before I could say you too, and with the chaos on the other end of the line, I decided that was for the best, anyway.

Morrow

> Forgot to mention this while I had you on the phone, but the ball is coming up in November. You got to the unit late, but just text me whether you have a plus one, I'll get you squared away

The message ended with a beer emoji.

Me

> Will do. Thanks for the heads up.

"Fuck me," I muttered to my ceiling.

The Marine Corps ball was a unique event. I barely remembered the ones I attended while on active duty because I was blacked out at just about all of them. The only ones I'd been sober at were the two I'd attended with Mallory, and those weren't memories I was keen on revisiting.

Would Cass come with me if I asked?

I'd have to go to the ball that weekend, regardless. I was

contractually obligated.

But it would be damn nice not to go by myself.

Chapter 22
Cassie

We were officially trying. As much as two people who still had a hell of a lot to say to each other could.

It still felt weird to speak it aloud in my mind, because Lord knew I was already jumpy. The last few weeks had been much of the same: Lucas sneaking into my tiny house or me sneaking into his.

We'd never stayed the night. Somehow that felt like a step too far, even though we'd already admitted that we had no desire to see other people, or somehow back out of the strange relationship we found ourselves in.

And then last night, we'd stayed up late to finish a heated game of Scrabble in the farmhouse. Everyone else had folded—I had kicked their asses past the point of return—but Lucas was determined to win.

He'd also been determined to make me come so hard I saw stars and had to bite the back of my hand so I didn't wake up the entire house with my scream.

That's also how I found myself in the farmhouse kitchen, making my morning coffee, when Imogen's screech tore through the previously quiet space. I practically jumped out of my skin, unable to control my reaction.

"Why in the ever-loving *fuck* are there panties on my coffee table?"

Oh, my God.

My cheeks heated so quickly I was vaguely dizzy as Connor and Kameron both appeared in the hallway, looking ready to kill.

"Christ, baby, you can't yell like that," Kam said, pressing a hand to his chest as if to stop his heart from racing out of his chest. Connor scowled at the bright pink thong lying there.

How the fuck had I missed that? We'd cleaned up the board game, wiped down the table, we'd—

Right. We hadn't stopped to double-check.

Because Lucas had then picked me up over his shoulder and marched me down the hill to continue his feast.

"What's all the racket—oh," Abbie said, closing the back door behind her. Bass came running through the dog door a second later, making a beeline for the coffee table.

To my horror, Bass put his front paws up on the table and leaned forward—

"Christ, don't do that," Kam groaned before the situation became a million times worse, picking Bass up and walking him towards the kitchen.

I was still standing there, frozen, holding my coffee mug with a white-knuckle grip and trying to puzzle out how in the hell I was going to explain this.

"Sorry, everyone," Abbie chimed in, looking bashful as she approached the coffee table and swiped the panties up, sticking them in her back pocket.

Connor's jaw hit the floor as he watched his pregnant

wife shrug her shoulders nonchalantly. "The pregnancy hormones have really been getting to me."

"Mercy," Imogen muttered. "Someone save us."

"Sorry," Abbie said, looking apologetic as she sauntered over to Connor and pressed a messy kiss to his cheek. "Love you."

Connor was looking at her with an incredulous expression.

He knew good and damn well those weren't hers.

A few seconds later, Abbie's eyes met mine from down the hallway, and she winked at me.

She fucking *winked*.

"Why does everyone look like they've seen a ghost?"

Lucas's voice rang out from the front door. He dusted his boots off on the mat and hung his hat on the rack, shaking out his black hair with one hand.

"The hell did I miss?"

"Abbie left her *panties* on my coffee table," Imogen said through gritted teeth, but I didn't miss the way her shoulders shook with silent laughter. She was putting up a tough fight, but she'd crack in the next few minutes, especially now that Lucas was back.

Lucas's booming laugh sent a shiver down my spine.

I was going to *kill* him.

Kam joined in shortly after, and even Connor stood in the corner, shaking his head in disbelief that this had somehow become his life.

Sure enough, Imogen cracked as soon as Lucas started laughing. Abbie re-appeared in the doorway, rosy cheeks a sign of how hard she'd been laughing herself.

"I'll be more careful next time," Abbie promised, wiping a tear away from her eyes in between fits of laughter. "So sorry for the drama, everyone."

Lucas's eyes were bright and mischievous when he looked at me a few moments later, but I looked away.

I was struggling to find the same level of humor in the situation. Shame and guilt sank like rocks in my stomach.

Everyone thought it was hilarious, but if Abbie hadn't stepped up to falsely take the blame, there would have been a series of very uncomfortable questions I wasn't ready to answer.

There were only three women in the farmhouse regularly, and it was becoming increasingly rare that the six of us were all here together. With Abbie's due date approaching, these weekends would become even rarer.

Lucas and I were getting careless. And that was something neither of us could afford.

"Relax," Lucas whispered when he came to stand beside me in the kitchen to make his morning coffee. "You look like Bass just took a crap in your coffee."

I wrinkled my nose in disgust. "Nice visual."

Lucas bumped his hip with mine as he turned the tap on to wash out his favorite mug.

"No one knows."

"Only because Abbie jumped in to save our asses," I hissed. "And in case you weren't keeping track, that's now two people in the house that know about us."

"Us, huh?"

"Don't start right now," I warned. "You know what I mean."

"Relax. We'll keep our trysts to the tiny houses."

"I should never have used that word in front of you," I muttered.

"That's true," Lucas said. He finished washing his hands and gave me a polite smile. I gave him a mocking one right back.

"Your vocabulary is just so much larger than mine," Lucas remarked. I pressed my lips together in a firm line to keep from grinning.

"Get away from me."

"As you wish," Lucas said with a mock bow before retreating towards the front door.

"This isn't *The Princess Bride!*" I called in a petulant tone.

"Thank God for that," Lucas called back.

"The hell is with you two?" Kam asked. Imogen's expression was indecipherable.

"Play nice," Abbie chastised. "It's good to have friends."

Abbie's smirk told me she knew good and damn well Lucas and I were more than just friends.

Luckily for me, she was also kind enough to hide her smugness behind her coffee mug.

I didn't trust myself to speak, so I simply shrugged and went back to sipping my coffee, allowing myself to dive headfirst into the pool of memory swirling in my mind.

The only way to kill the guilt is to tell the truth.

Those words rang through my head for the entire rest of the day. I wasn't ready to tell the truth about Lucas. It made me an unbelievably shitty person to keep this from her.

But I was greedy. I was greedy because I wanted to keep that just for us.

I found Imogen reading on her Kindle in one of the rocking chairs on the farmhouse porch. She was wearing one of her beloved lounge sets, legs tucked beneath her and a cup of tea next to her.

She looked so at peace. Comfortable.

And God, the sight of it made my chest ache.

"Can we talk?" I asked.

Imogen put her Kindle down on the table and nodded. I slid into the chair beside her, clinging to my cup of coffee like it was my lifeline. I should have been drinking decaf this late in the day, but I needed the extra bit of courage for this conversation.

"I want to tell you about Watford," I murmured. Imogen inhaled sharply.

"You don't have to. I was kind of a dick about it the other day."

"No," I said, shaking my head. "You were right. I needed a push in the right direction."

I took a sip of coffee and decided that there was no other way to do this.

"When I was sixteen, I spiraled out of control," I began. "Our parents were controlling as shit. Despite my perfect grades, all of my extracurricular activities, all the riding medals in the living room, I was always failing at something. Nothing I ever did was good enough. I finally snapped one day. Decided I wanted something for myself. For one night, I told myself, I could break every rule. I told myself I could do whatever I wanted for one night."

"I don't like where this going," Imogen muttered.

"You're not going to like it at all," I said. "I let one of the senior boys take me to a party. He'd been panting after me for months. But that night he left me to fend for myself, probably to go bum a smoke off some other loser. I didn't really talk to him again. But that night I drank myself stupid. I danced until the room spun. I don't remember the specifics, but I know I lost my virginity to a man who definitely would have caught a charge. I had sex for the first time on some random frat bro's floor."

Imogen's hand flew up to cover her mouth. "*Fuck*, Cassie."

"Strap in," I said, sinking deeper into the chair. "And don't say I didn't warn you."

I didn't meet her eyes as I launched into the second part of the story.

"Weeks went by, and I didn't tell anyone. I snuck back into the house after the party through the unlocked window in my room. Save for an absolutely massive hangover, I was fine. Until I wasn't."

Imogen's breath hitched. "Cassie."

"I had all the classic symptoms. But I was in denial about it. I was sick in the mornings before school like clockwork. My pants were tighter. I went to Watford General after school one day, fully expecting to steal a pregnancy test. But Abbie's mom saw me staring at them, and she took one off the rack and handed it to me. No questions asked. I took it as soon as I got home."

I blew out a long breath. "Those pink lines came up so quick, Imogen. The box tells you to wait a few minutes, but it was barely thirty seconds before the lines appeared. I told Mom, and it went about as well as you would expect. She blew up. Her eldest daughter was officially a statistic. But I'll be damned if she didn't buy me a bottle of prenatal vitamins and schedule my first ultrasound."

"God, Cassie, you let me yell at you on the phone about how selfish you were when it came to Carmen," Imogen whispered. "If I had known—"

"I made a lot of mistakes with you, Im. Just because something bad happened to me doesn't negate my being a bitch to you when I didn't have the right to."

Imogen sat back in her seat, pressing her knuckles to her mouth as she nodded.

"Mom picked me up early from school and drove me to the clinic the day of my ultrasound. I think I knew something was wrong before the tech did."

Imogen's face contorted in pure anguish.

"I lost the baby," I choked out, forcing myself to keep my eyes on Imogen as I finished the story that I'd held inside myself for so long. "I had an ectopic pregnancy. Apparently they're not as uncommon in adolescents as one would hope. And the worst part was I was finally coming around. I'd actually started to imagine what life would be like if..."

I couldn't finish the fucking sentence. Imogen's eyes welled with tears as she reached for me.

"I thought Mom... I thought you were going to say she asked you to—"

"No," I whispered. My throat was raw and scratchy from the effort of holding back my tears. "Remember when I said my relationship with Carmen was complicated? This is why. She was so mad when I told her, Imogen. I thought she might actually hit me for the first time in my life the night I showed her the stick with those two pink lines on it."

I exhaled a shaky breath, running my hand through my hair.

"She never once asked me to get an abortion. Not once. That was the only silver lining, because she took riding away from me as my punishment. She pulled all support for my extracurriculars after that."

My chest felt like it would cave in at any moment. My stomach twisted as grief, sharp and biting, slid through me.

"I was scared, Im. Fucking terrified. Who gets pregnant their first time having sex? I'd somehow convinced myself that one insane night out would kill the rebellious desire in me and I could keep going. I had no idea who the father was, and I was terrified of the implications of offering any more details because I knew there would be a legal case, and I couldn't handle that. And Mom—God, she was so fucking mad at me. But I'd still started thinking about what life would be like with her. I'd started thinking about how I'd make it work. How I'd still give her a good life. And then it was gone. Just like that."

Imogen didn't say a word.

She stood first, and I followed, and she wrapped me in the tightest hug.

I let myself truly sob then, releasing every ounce of the pain and heartbreak and confusion and loss that I'd kept to myself for over a decade.

"Did you know it was a girl?" Imogen whispered, holding my face in her hands. "You keep saying her, and I didn't know if you..."

I shook my head.

"I'll never know for sure," I said as she wiped my tears away. "It's just an intuition thing, I guess. Every time I imagined it, she was always a beautiful little girl."

"I love you," Imogen said, her bottom lip wobbling. "I love you so much, Cassie. I'm so fucking sorry."

"I love you too," I choked out before another wave of sobs wracked my body.

I let Imogen hold me until they subsided.

When Bass hopped up and pressed his paws into my knees, begging for pets, I pulled him into a hug. I returned to my seat on the porch, finishing my coffee while Bass made himself comfortable. He was content just to lay in my lap and let me pet him.

"I'm going to make us snacks," Imogen announced, wiping the tears from her eyes. "This calls for a movie day."

"Really?" I said, my heart kicking up another notch. Imogen nodded and headed into the farmhouse. I paused at the threshold.

You need to tell her.

This was the perfect opening.

My heart was already open and bleeding on the table.

If Imogen could sit with the truth of why I'd shut her out when we were teenagers, she could sit with the knowledge that I'd been falling in love with her best friend behind her back.

But I couldn't.

One conversation wasn't enough.

But for today, it would have to be.

Chapter 23
Lucas

I met Cassie at the barn days later. Early autumn had swept down from the Washington mountains, solidifying the chill in the air as an all-day event. I'd switched my wardrobe from lightweight cotton to thicker flannel.

My heart lodged in my throat. We set about tacking the horses for their morning ride around the pen.

This had become the best part of my morning: rolling out of bed, splashing some cold water on my face, grabbing a cup of coffee and downing it in the time it took me to get down the gravel path to the barn to meet Cassie.

Cassie was always beautiful, but there was something ethereal about her in the golden light of dawn.

The sun was just peeking over the mountains behind the barn, illuminating her tan skin in golden rays.

She was softer in the morning. Like there wasn't anything that could derail her day yet.

There was something about her that softened when she saw me. The knowledge that I was a safe place for her, the same way she was for me, sent my brain into overdrive.

This morning, though, I knew I was going to walk the line.

"I have a question to ask you," I said. We'd been working

together in silence for several minutes, and the longer we stood there together, the likelihood that I'd chicken out increased exponentially. "And I don't want you to get spooked or run off when I do."

Not as clean of a transition as I would've liked, and based on the way Cassie smirked at me, she knew I had not wanted to blurt it out like that.

"All right, ask your question," she said, giving me a flirtatious smile.

"Will you come to the Marine Corps ball with me?"

The question came flying out of my mouth before I could stop it.

And when Cassie balked, I immediately cursed my lack of tact.

"You want me to come to the Marine Corps ball with you?" she repeated.

"Yeah," I croaked out. "I just found out about it because I got to the unit late and this guy had to call me to make sure I was still alive the other night and then he texted me right after and said that he forgot to remind me to buy ball tickets and book the hotel block—"

"Wait, *wait*," Cassie said. "Back up. You want me to come to a formal event—like a very *traditional* formal event—with you?"

"Yes," I said, my voice ending on a question more than I would've liked.

Cassie said, "I thought we had agreed to keep this strictly physical. Going to an event together feels a lot like..."

She didn't have to finish her sentence. I knew exactly what it sounded like.

It sounded like couple shit.

And here I was, asking her to break all of her rules and come to an event where there would be alcohol and a bunch of drunk assholes, all because I really didn't want to go by myself.

My mind had justified this ask a thousand times over, but nothing had prepared me for actually putting myself out there.

"Plenty of people just bring dates for the night," I said, trying to lighten the mood and bring down the seriousness of the conversation. "I'm serious. Some people will bring their wives because there are a lot of married dudes in my unit, but other people will quite literally go on a dating app to find a date just for this event."

Cassie watched me cautiously. It's like she knew there was more to this than just a practical arrangement to keep me from socializing by myself.

I sighed, rubbing a hand down my face in frustration.

Sometimes baring my feelings to Cassie felt like I was constantly reaching my hand out, only to yank it back, scared I'd get bitten. I never knew what her response would be, only that I craved something—anything—from her.

"I want you to go with me because it kind of sucks going alone. I'm gonna get roped into doing a bunch of stuff I don't want to do. I don't particularly feel like helping and dealing with a bunch of last-minute bullshit and not being able to drink until well past nine p.m."

Cassie snorted.

"So, that's the real reason you want me there? So that you can start drinking as soon as the clock strikes seven?"

I shot her a wry smile.

"I would love to have a drinking partner," I said. "Someone to keep me in line, you know."

Cassie cracked a smile at that.

"Right," she said. "You do get a little wild when you drink."

"Oh, you remember that," I said, feigning indifference.

Cassie rolled her eyes at me.

"So are you asking me there as a date, or are you just asking me because there's no one else you want to ask?"

I bit the inside of my cheek as I considered my response. I needed to word this carefully.

I finally settled on, "Why can't it be both?

To my surprise, Cassie's gaze softened.

"Yeah," she said, "Okay. I guess both is fine."

My heart decided it was *not* fine. My pulse kicked into overdrive, and my palms dampened as I stared at the woman who had made me want things I didn't think I'd ever be capable of feeling again.

"Really? You'll come with me?"

"Yeah," Cassie said. There was a softness to her face that had me reaching for her. "Isn't that kind of every girl's dream?"

She didn't back away even as I took another step closer. Damn near magnetic in the way our connection drew me towards her.

I let out a surprised laugh at her comment.

"The Marine Corps ball is *not* every girl's dream. It's a bunch of assholes in uniform drinking too much and belting out *Semper Fi* by Trace Adkins at the top of their lungs."

"Hot assholes in uniform," Cassie said, giving me another

flirtatious smile. "Really, who doesn't want a handsome military man to ask them to put on their best dress, dress up like a princess, and then accompany them to an honest to God *ball*?"

I snorted, snaking an arm around her waist and pulling her to me. I wanted to tell her she was making it a bigger deal than it was. "Formal event" was a stretch description for the Marine Corps ball.

But then Cassie leaned in, just like she always did. Like being with me in this way was as easy as breathing.

If only it could be that simple.

"Cassie Phillips, you never cease to surprise me."

She tilted her head so that her face was pressed against my neck. Her lips grazed the sensitive skin there.

I was completely fucked over this woman, and I didn't have the words to tell her.

All I could do was show her. And I planned to.

Not just when I snuck through the back door of her tiny house after everyone in the farmhouse was asleep, and not just during the ball weekend where we'd finally—fucking *finally*—be able to be together without constantly looking over our shoulders.

I could practically feel Chesty's eyes on me from the stall. I fought the urge to mouth "look away" at the horse, who had already seen too much.

"So what else do I need to do other than find a dress?"

I shrugged. "Nothing, just mark it off on your calendar. I'll drive us there. I already booked the hotel and bought your ticket.

Cassie's eyebrows raised. "You already bought my ticket?"

Fuck me and my big mouth.

"I, uh," I trailed off, rubbing the back of my neck awkwardly, knowing she had me there. "You can buy a ticket before you give them your date's name, you know, for the guys that are using the dating app to find one."

Cassie nodded slowly, a small smile still playing on her lips.

"Right. So if I'd said no, you would have found someone from a dating app to take?"

"I wouldn't have asked anyone else," I said, glaring at her. "If you didn't want to go, I would have gone alone."

Cassie's lips parted.

"Is there anything else I should know? Things I should prepare for?"

I smiled and shook my head.

"Unfortunately, there's not much you can do to prepare for the Marine Corps ball experience. Just be prepared for a lot of sitting and standing, and people waxing poetic about service."

That earned a derisive snort from Cassie, but I didn't miss the faint blush tinging her cheeks.

"I'm sure Reddit has some interesting pointers," she said.

We settled into a comfortable silence as we finished grooming Chesty before leading him out to the paddock.

I finished my coffee, and Cassie turned to face me. I was surprised to see a slight blush on her cheeks.

"Thank you for inviting me," she said. "Sounds like an adventure."

"It will be," I murmured, mouth suddenly dry.

"Do you want to tell the others?"

The question clanged through me. Telling them meant opening a can of worms I wasn't sure I wanted to open. At the same time, I knew our involvement was a ticking time bomb. It would happen eventually. I was just being selfish about.

"I'll leave it up to you," I said.

Something acidic sliced through me at the thought of keeping yet another secret from my best friends, but I would let Cassie make that call.

Where she was concerned, I was fucking whipped.

Cassie chewed her plush bottom lip, and my train of thought derailed entirely.

"Do you think that they'll make their own assumptions about why we're going together? If we told them."

It was my turn to give her a flirty smile.

"Um, yeah, Cass, I would say so. You only invite a girl to the Marine Corps ball if you're trying to, uh... *hit it.*"

A laugh burst out of her, and my heart seized up at the sight of her eyes crinkling. A genuine laugh from Cass was worth its weight in gold to me.

"Ew," Cassie said, grinning. "Hip doesn't look good on you."

"Don't be rude," I chastised, but there was no heat behind it.

"Shall I send you a couple of dress options and you can help me pick one?"

My heart beat wildly in my chest.

"Yeah, Cass. I'll help you pick out your dress. And I'll help you get it out of it after."

"You're insufferable."

"You love it."

Cass visibly tripped. What anyone else in the world might have considered a flirty retort was a confession. As Cass's lips parted around a gentle 'oh,' I wanted to take the words back.

And just as I was about to try, Cass surprised me for the thousandth time by stepping forward. I held my breath as she pressed a palm to my chest. I didn't move, didn't dare reach for her in case I shattered the moment.

She stood on her tiptoes to press an unexpected kiss to my cheek.

And when she smiled and said, "I guess it's growing on me," all I could do was stare after her.

I watched her walk away, wondering how in the fucking world I was going to claw my heart away from her.

Because she'd stolen it and hadn't even realized.

Chapter 24
Cassie

"Can we introduce some color in here?" Imogen said.

Abbie, Imogen, and I were all standing in baby Harvey's nursery, covered in pale pink paint.

"It's pink," Abbie said. She currently had her feet up in the rocker, taking a well-deserved break.

"Abbie, be serious. This is barely pink. It's pink-tinged beige."

"I hear you feel strongly about the beige mom aesthetic. It's okay to feel your feelings."

I smacked a hand over my mouth when Imogen's mouth hinged open.

"Abbigail Collins Harvey, did you just try to *mom* me?"

Abbie shrugged and crossed her arms over her chest.

"Oh, she's good," I said between laughing fits.

"Don't you start," Imogen said, flinging the slightly wet paintbrush in my direction. I gasped indignantly as even more paint landed on my overalls.

"Speaking of starting," Abbie said, turning to me. "How did the job interview go?"

Right. I'd had a Zoom job interview at another law firm in downtown Seattle. I wasn't confident in my performance. It had been years since I'd had to interview for a law position, but Lainey had pulled some strings to even get me in the door, and they were nice enough to let me interview over video instead of in person.

"It was alright," I said noncommittally. "I should know something in the next week or two."

"Do you think you'll take it?"

I chewed my bottom lip. "I honestly don't know."

Imogen smirked. "I knew it."

"What?" I said, my heart lurching.

"Winding Road is growing on you," she said in a singsong voice. "I'm telling you, the place has magical healing properties."

"That's true," Abbie sighed. "It's a special place. With special people, I might add."

"Right," I said, not missing the twinkle in her eyes when she said it. My shoulders sagged forward in relief that she didn't say anything else. "Yes, Winding Road is definitely a special place."

"You know, the more we expand, the more we could probably use a lawyer on retainer," Imogen mused out loud. I whipped my head towards her.

"I'm a divorce lawyer," I said. "I've barely thought about contracts outside of that context since I was a 1L."

"Pish posh," Imogen said, waving a hand around. "You're one of the smartest people I know. We need smart people, not contract experts. You're already certified to practice law in Washington. We probably couldn't pay you as much as the big law firms in Seattle—"

"Imogen," I whispered.

"She's serious, you know," Abbie said, groaning as she adjusted in her chair. "You could stay with us. Lord knows I wouldn't complain about the extra hands."

I looked away when she started humming gently to her daughter in an effort to put her to sleep so she could sit without being kicked repeatedly in the ribs. It was getting harder to be near Abbie. Not because I was jealous.

Because it *hurt*.

Watching her with Connor opened something in me. A hole that would always be there, but kept reopening every time I watched her and Connor. I couldn't shake the distant, de-railing thought: *it could have been me*.

"You don't have to decide now," Imogen said, sensing the growing distance. "Just... think about it. Kam would be more than happy to talk to you about it."

"Thank you," I mumbled.

"Speaking of Kam, where are the boys?"

The boys.

Something about the casual way they mentioned them sent my stomach spinning. I knew Abbie and Imogen had clawed their way to the happiness they'd found now, but *fuck* if it didn't make me feel insane sometimes. The ease with which they navigated life in their little bubble felt so ridiculously out of reach for me.

"I sent them out for lunch," Imogen said. "They're picking up burgers at the Roadhouse."

That got Abbie's attention. "Seriously?"

"Yep," Imogen said before looking at me. "How long has it been since you had a Roadhouse burger?"

"Too long," I said honestly. "You guys can head into the

living room to wait for them. I want to finish this last window, and then I'll join you."

I adjusted the ladder to face the window so I could finish the trim there. I'd barely gotten anywhere when a low wolf whistle echoed from the doorway and I damn near fell off the ladder.

"Jesus Christ," I yelped, clinging to the metal to steady myself. Paint sloshed everywhere, and I swore loudly as I turned to face the culprit.

"Lucas, you can't scare people when they're seven feet up on a ladder."

"It was an instinctive reaction," Lucas said, throwing his hands up defensively. "Your ass looks so—"

"Shh!"

I threw my hands out in a *what the fuck* gesture and waved them wildly toward the door that was still very much open.

Lucas smirked and stepped into the room fully, closing the door behind him.

"Happy now?" he said as I delicately placed the paintbrush back in the paint container and descended the ladder. I crossed the room in two steps and raised my hands to push him out of the way.

"You are *insufferable*—"

In a heartbeat, Lucas snagged both of my wrists and pressed them into my chest instead. His thumbs gripped my wrists firmly, the pressure making my head swim in the best way. There was no anger, just a subtle reminder that made my stomach flip.

"Careful," Lucas murmured. My core clenched at his low

tone. "You know how much I like it when you—"

I cut him off with a searing kiss.

He released my wrists in favor of pulling me to him, long arms snaking around my waist and squeezing my ass. My fingers wound through his hair, keeping him close.

I vaguely remembered that I was covered in paint, but I didn't care. I lost myself in him.

I craved the white space in my head that existed only when his hands were on me. Like I didn't have to think about anything else. I could just *be*.

"As much as I would love to act out whatever scenario is playing through your head right now, our presence will be missed if we stay in here much longer," Lucas said, kissing me one more time before stepping away.

"Right. *Right*."

Abbie and Connor's house. Lunch. Imogen.

"Take a deep breath," Lucas said, squeezing my shoulders. "I'm sorry. I shouldn't have ambushed you like that."

"It's okay," I croaked. "It's just... *I'm* just..."

Not *okay*.

"I'm here," Lucas whispered. "You're safe."

I stepped into his arms and buried my face against his chest. He wrapped his arms around me and squeezed. I let out a shaky breath and clung to him as I said, "I lost a pregnancy when I was a teenager."

The words were out before I could keep them tucked away. Lucas stilled, his breathing faltering.

"Christ," he murmured. His grip on me tightened. "Cass, I'm so sorry."

"I had finally started coming around to the idea of being

a mom," I whispered. "That my life would look different. But then I learned I had an ectopic pregnancy, and my dreams were shattered. In an hour, it all just *vanished*."

I sighed and pressed my face against his chest again, listening to the sound of his heartbeat. "So it's hard sometimes. The closer we get to Abbie's due date. It's bringing up a lot."

"Thank you for telling me," Lucas murmured. His fingers hooked beneath my chin, tilting my face up towards his. "I don't know what to say, and I can't take the hurt away, but I can listen. I can carry part of this for you."

"Thank you," I whispered.

"I'll *always* be here to listen."

I didn't doubt that. I knew he would. Even if our romantic involvement ended one day, Lucas would probably always be a person I could lean on.

A steady presence. Something I wasn't used to accepting.

We finally broke away, and I headed to the bathroom to wash my hands of paint before joining everyone else in the living room. Everyone except Lucas and me was already digging in, so I slipped quietly into the kitchen.

"You have paint on you," Connor remarked to Lucas when he flopped down on the couch.

My hands froze as I reached into the bag to pull out the last bag of fries.

"Do I?" Lucas looked at his shirt, and sure enough, there were multiple swatches of pink paint down his front. "Oh, right. I fell when I popped into the nursery to see the progress."

"You fell," Connor repeated, deadpan and entirely unconvinced.

"Yep. Tripped and fell right on my ass."

Abbie pressed her chin into her hand to keep herself from bursting into laughter. I didn't dare move a muscle. Imogen rolled her eyes.

"You're a dumbass, you know that?"

"And you're so nice and encouraging to me," Lucas said, sticking his tongue out in Imogen's direction. Imogen flipped her middle finger right back. Kam just sighed heavily, like he'd accepted his fate a long time ago but still held some level of hope that eventually the people around him would mature beyond the age of fifteen.

"Dangerous," I whispered when Lucas passed by me in the kitchen to snag his food. Imogen and Abbie were discussing which cooking reality show to watch while they ate.

"I'm finding that I care less and less," Lucas murmured as he grabbed a handful of fries. "I told you I like you in denim."

Lucas drove us back to Winding Road that night. I hardly said a word, entirely lost in my mind. What the hell was I going to do? I had to decide about my job situation sooner rather than later. Savings only lasted so long, and I hated the idea of continuing to freeload at Winding Road for months on end. Especially when things were about to get complicated with the arrival of Abbie and Connor's baby girl.

I stood in the kitchen of the tiny house, rinsing off the

plate of chicken picatta Kam had made for dinner. I'd taken my dinner back to the tiny house, desperately needing the space to sort through the tangled mess of thoughts in my head. I reached for a clean glass just as a massive insect scurried from behind the metal rack.

"Fuck," I screeched, dropping the glass onto the counter. I stepped back and ran for the couch, keeping my eyes trained on the thing as I fumbled for my phone to call the closest person who could help me.

"Well, well, well, here I thought you'd give me the silent treatment all—"

"There's a big fucking bug in here," I interrupted. "Huge. *Help.*"

Lucas chuckled. "I'll be right there."

I stayed where I was on the couch, yelping when the bug briefly took flight and landed on the fridge.

Lucas stepped through the front door seconds later. I pointed toward the massive winged demon, and he made quick work of capturing the creature in the water glass I'd dropped minutes earlier.

Once he'd safely guided the bug back outside, he turned to look at me on the couch. My knees were tucked to my chest.

"Thank you," I said, exhaling a deep sigh of relief. "I don't do winged bugs. Normal bugs are okay. Spiders are fine. But insects with wings are a no fucking go."

"Good to know," Lucas said with a knowing smile. "Need anything else?"

"No," I said instinctively. "Wait, actually, while you're here, can you look at this dress and tell me if it's okay for the ball?"

He nodded and sat next to me on the couch. I pulled up a picture of the dress I'd ordered and turned my phone towards him. He pressed his lips together and inhaled sharply.

"*Fuck.*"

"Is that a seal of approval?"

"It's a reminder that I need to practice being on my best behavior. But yes, it's perfect. You'll look stunning."

I smiled and put my phone face down on the side table.

"Are you okay after earlier?" Lucas asked.

"Yeah. It comes and goes, you know? Sometimes it feels like I can't breathe. Like I'm mourning something I never truly got to have. And other times I feel ridiculous because I was sixteen. It wouldn't have been glamorous or exciting. It would have been fucking hard."

"It's okay to mourn a life you might have had. Even if it would have been hard. It would have been beautiful, too. Whatever you feel about it is okay. Have you told Abbie?"

"No," I said, shaking my head violently. "I'm not putting that on her. It's not hers to carry."

"Okay," Lucas said. At some point, his hand had made its way onto my thigh. Not in a sexual way. In a casual way that made me feel like he wanted to touch me simply because he wanted to.

Lucas liked being around me. And not just because we had ridiculously good sex. Because he thought I was funny. He enjoyed my presence.

I rolled my lips together and dug deep to find another kernel of courage to shell out for the day.

"Lucas?"

"Yeah, dream girl?"

I swallowed the lump in my throat and cupped his jaw with one hand, tilting his face towards me. He looked at me, brown eyes and rich, full lips so close to mine.

"Will you stay here tonight?"

Lucas's eyes went impossibly wide.

"I don't want to—" I huffed out a frustrated breath as I stumbled over the words. "I don't want sex tonight. I'm fucking exhausted. But I just—I want you here."

"Yes," Lucas said without hesitation. "I'll stay."

The invisible weight I'd been carrying crashed to the floor, long forgotten as I pulled my hair back and stood from the couch.

While Lucas changed and washed up, I yanked the sheets back and laid down, listening to the tap running while my heart banged against my ribcage. I wore a thin white cami and sleep shorts that could barely qualify as clothes, and when Lucas returned in nothing but his boxers, I felt that familiar sense of calm wash over me.

The kind that was only around when he was this close to me.

He crawled into bed next to me, and I turned to face him, our legs tangling together, our chests just inches apart. I took one of his hands in mine, and he propped himself up on his other elbow.

"Are you excited about it?" I asked as I traced the lines of his palm. "The ball, I mean."

Lucas smiled softly, content just to watch me. I'd stopped feeling off under the weight of Lucas's gaze. In a way, "It'll be an adventure. I'm glad I get to do it with you."

"Yeah," I said with a yawn. I hadn't been tired fifteen minutes ago, but evidently my body was ready. "Me too."

"You can sleep," Lucas murmured. The hand I wasn't holding slipped into my hair, gently running his hands through the curls. "I'll be here when you wake up."

My breath hitched in my throat, and remorse flooded me.

"I'm sorry I left that night," I whispered. I gripped his hand tighter. "I'm sorry I ran."

"Shhh," Lucas replied. He pressed a kiss to my forehead and murmured, "That was then."

And so, so fucking much had changed since then.

"I'm here because I want to be, Cass. I'm right where I want to be."

Sleep claimed me right about the time my heartbeat slowed to match his.

Steady. Present.

I too, was right where I wanted to be.

Chapter 25

Lucas

The next few weeks were a blur of activity. I had another drill weekend and spent most of my time on the farm preparing for harvest season. Crops didn't make up a huge portion of our revenue, and with the new Warrior's Grant on deck, Kam and Connor were discussing the possibility of not planting anything the upcoming year and re-imagining how we used that land.

Cass and Imogen were spending more time together. Watching the two of them gradually grow closer made my chest tight. Imogen and I had become fast friends, bonding over our shared love of heartland country music and dark humor. And Cass...

She'd become part of me. I didn't know where or how, but it had happened. The thought of spending an entire long weekend with her, just the two of us, no outside distractions or need to hide, was sending my brain into overdrive.

When the ball weekend finally arrived, I was all too eager to get the hell out of Winding Road and be alone with my girl.

I decided I'd skip the coffee making, not wanting to make a scene in the kitchen by making two cups and opening the door for questions than necessary. But as I rounded the corner of the staircase to refill my water bottle, I came face to face with none other than Kameron Miller.

"Mornin," Kam said, taking a sip from his coffee mug.

You had to be kidding me.

"Do you have a sixth sense for when I'm getting ready to do Marine Corps things and you post up at the kitchen table to ambush me?" I asked. I refilled my water and turned to face him. There was no use in trying to slip past him. I knew an incoming Kameron interrogation when I saw one, and there was avoiding it.

Kam shrugged. "A gentleman never reveals his secrets."

I huffed out a laugh. "So that's a yes."

"I just wanted to check in," Kam said, shrugging. "You've been extra busy these last few weeks."

"There's been a lot to do," I muttered.

"Right."

A long pause stretched between us.

"You're mincing words, Kam."

"And you're avoiding me."

I pressed my lips together in a fine line. "Not avoiding you."

"Try again," Kam said. He was always infuriatingly un-flappable. He really would sit here all morning, staring me down until I gave him something honest.

"I would ask you why you care, but we're past that point," I muttered. I leaned back against the kitchen counter and crossed my arms over my chest.

"Correct," Kam said. "Does it have something to do with Cassie?"

My head snapped up.

"Busted," Kam said, grinning like a maniac. "You're crushing."

"Yes, I'm *crushing*," I said through clenched teeth. "I've been crushing for a long damn time, trying to work through all my messy feelings about Mallory, adjusting to life in the reserves, and still going to work every day. So yes, I've been busy. And I promise I'm not trying to be a dick when dodging your questions every two seconds. I only have so much bandwidth to get through the day with."

Kam smiled.

"That's the first time I've heard you use her name."

"What?" I said, rubbing my temple.

"Mallory. You hardly ever say her name. But you did just then."

Huh. I had.

"Names have power," I murmured. "And she doesn't have that kind of power over me anymore."

I'd always avoided using it because even the mention of her name in casual conversation would rip the wound open again, as if it had never healed in the first place. Every time I talked to Imogen about it, we'd always substituted her name for another.

She, of all people, knew how empowering it was to take back control when that power had been ripped away from you by someone you trusted implicitly.

"I'm proud of you," Kam said, interrupting my thoughts. "It's difficult to get over that kind of heartbreak."

It wasn't, but it was a hell of a lot easier when you had something to look forward to.

I glanced at my watch and held my wrist up to Kam, tapping the watch face.

"I need to go. Would hate to be late for such an important occasion."

Kam waved me off. "You're free to go."

"Thank you for the friendly interrogation."

"Someone has to keep you in line."

"If only you knew," I muttered and headed for the front door.

"Behave yourself," Kam called after me. I flipped him the bird over my shoulder, smiling when I heard his booming laugh in response. I flew down the porch stairs and opened the driver's side door of my truck, frowning when I didn't see Cass sitting there like we'd planned.

Something rustled in the backseat, and my heart damn near leaped out of my chest.

"What the hell are you doing? Are you hiding in the backseat?" I asked incredulously, just barely pulling away before my training kicked in.

"What else was I supposed to do?" Cass whisper-yelled from where she was crouched on the floorboard of my truck. "Just casually sit in the front seat like we're not sneaking around behind people's backs?"

I rolled my eyes. "You're insane. Get up here."

Cass scowled at me, but dutifully climbed into the front seat.

"I'm entrusting you with the playlist for this trip," I said, handing my phone to her. "This is an enormous responsibility. Can you handle it?"

She smirked at me, eyes gleaming with mischief as she

clicked her seatbelt into place. "I can handle anything you throw at me, big boy."

Jesus, this woman and her mouth. "You're sassy today."

"Just excited, I guess," Cass said. She bit down on her thumb as she settled into the seat, scrolling through my mountain of Spotify playlists.

"Yeah," I said, unable to hold back my smile as I put the truck in drive. "Me too."

"Let's see what we have here..."

"One caveat," I said. "No judging the playlist titles."

"I make no promises," Cassie said. "This one's called *Winter Arc Era* with a lifting emoji."

I groaned and ran a hand down my face.

"Aren't arc and era sort of redundant?" Cass mused.

"I hate this already," I muttered.

"You don't," Cass said.

"I don't," I admitted with a sigh.

"Oh, what about *Cowboys Cry Too*? There's thirteen songs on here, holy cow—"

"You're done," I said, grabbing for my phone. She laughed and shook her head, clutching the device to her chest. She grumbled something about needing me to keep my eyes on the road and shoved my hand away.

"I love this so much," Cass murmured as she continued scrolling. "It's like all the different versions of you."

And then she paused, and I had a sinking feeling I knew exactly what playlist she'd found.

"Okay, before you freak out—"

"This one's called *C*, and the playlist cover is the Space Needle. Lucas, is this mine?"

I swallowed, tightening my grip on the steering wheel. "It's ours."

The words reverberated through the cab of my truck. Silence descended, and I had to physically bite my tongue not to fill it with an excuse that downplayed how seriously I took the curation of that playlist.

Every song that had reminded me of us over the last six months had gone on there. Songs that described my feelings for her, reminded me of that night in Seattle and all the days since.

It was my heart in twenty songs.

"You made us a playlist," she repeated, and I watched out of the corner of my eye as her face lit up. "*Lucas*."

"Play it," I said, voice rough. I didn't trust my ability to form words.

Cass didn't trust herself either, because she hit play on the playlist without a second glance, and laid my phone flat across her lap.

I watched her breath hitch when *Infinite Baths* by Sleep Token filled the speakers.

I felt the shift between us, inching closer to something we hadn't dared name, but was becoming harder to turn away from.

We planned to stay at the same hotel the ball was being held at, namely for convenience's sake.

We entered the opulent lobby, and I let out a low whistle. Towering plants and trees framed a breathtaking waterscape installation in the middle of the marble floor. I carried the two garment bags slung over my shoulder, one with all of my uniforms and the other with Cass's dress.

"Where's your head, dream girl?"

I watched her throat bob.

"Just... remembering."

Right. Because the last time we'd shown up at a hotel together, we'd been on the heels of the best fucking night of our lives.

"I'm already there," I murmured as I stepped past her. As we approached the check-in counter, I heard a loud, "Morales!"

"Get ready," I whispered to Cass. "It's starting."

"What's starting?"

"The chaos."

I smiled at the receptionist and rattled off my name and info. She slid two key cards over, and I handed one to Cass before turning around to face the music.

"Here he is," I said, smiling as my squad leader approached.

"Glad you made it safe," Morrow said, clapping me on the shoulder.

"Morrow, this is Cass," I said, gesturing to the man in front of me. "Cass, this is the guy who is the main character in every funny story I tell from drill."

Cass laughed and extended her hand to him. "Always good to put a face to the name."

"My wife is upstairs napping, but she's dying to meet you. Would you like to have dinner with us later? This hotel's Italian restaurant has the best carbonara you'll ever have.

Sera and I always eat there the night before the ball."

"That sounds great," Cass said. I must not have done a good job of schooling my expression because Morrow laughed.

"Some people actually like to spend time with others," Morrow said. I rolled my eyes.

"I'm not as antisocial as you make me out to be, you know."

"Yeah, yeah, whatever," Morrow said, glancing down at his phone. "I should let you guys check in. Enjoy your time."

"See you later," I said, and turned back to Cass.

"You sure you're up for dinner? You can say no. You're not breaking some unspoken rule by wanting a night to yourself."

"No, I want to," Cass said. She tucked a stray piece of hair behind her ear. "It would be fun to go out on a double date. Like actual couples do."

I was helpless to stop the grin that formed on my face. "Cassandra, are you asking me to be your boyfriend?"

"Oh my God," Cass muttered, grabbing her suitcase and my arm and dragging us toward the elevator. "You really are the worst."

"I'll take that as a compliment," I said. I pushed the button for up and rocked back and forth on my heels while we waited. Cass was still taking in her surroundings, and I was too damn whipped to do anything other than watch her.

The elevator doors opened. The room was on the fourth floor, a respectful distance from the elevator, with an amazing view of the mountain valley the hotel overlooked. A single king bed took up most of the space in the room, with a long couch pressed against the window. I hung the garment bags in the closet while Cass threw her suitcase onto the couch.

"What are you thinking about?"

"I'm thinking about the night we met," she murmured.

"Which part?"

"All of it."

I let out a long breath before walking over to her. I wrapped my arms around her waist, pressing a kiss to the space between her shoulder and neck. She shivered, but didn't pull away.

"Do you think about it?" Cass whispered. Her hands came to rest on mine arms, squeezing gently. "Because that night takes up a lot of space in my brain. I replay it more often than is healthy.

"I think about it every day, Cass."

Every. Fucking. Day.

Chapter 26

Cassie

Seattle, Washington
Midnight

Lucas swiped his keycard, and the door swung open. The hotel was everything I expected from downtown Seattle: vibrant, colorful throw pillows with matching tassels and a modern, crescent-shaped velvet couch that accented the king-sized bed.

"This place is stunning," I said. I set my purse down on the side table, chewing on my bottom lip. I approached the window that overlooked the busy city street below. Despite the late hour, there were plenty of people ambling about. Businessmen still in their suits, either heading to the bar or home for the evening. Couples wrapped up in each other's orbit, like there was nowhere else they'd rather be.

"It is."

"This hotel has gorgeous architecture," I blurted, suddenly nervous. "It's crazy that I've never been here, because—"

"Cass?"

"Yeah?"

"Shut up and let me kiss you," Lucas muttered, reaching for my waist. His hands gripped my hips, tugging me to him, and I groaned as our lips met again. Lucas's arms wrapped around my waist, hauling me against him, and I let him feel all of it.

"You can change your mind at any point," he said, his teeth skimming a line up my neck that sent a shiver down my spine. "Just say the word and we'll—"

"Don't stop," I whispered, fisting the front of his shirt. "Please."

His lips traced the shell of my ear, and I bit my bottom lip. I reached for the buttons on his shirt, fingers trembling as I undid the top one. One by one until finally my hands were on his bare chest, touching and stroking the hard lines of his abdomen. He shivered when our lips met once more, his tongue sliding against mine in a way that filled my brain with static.

"Fuck, Cass," Lucas murmured as I tilted my face towards his, catching his mouth in another languid kiss that had my knees buckling.

Soft. Sweet. Heady. Distinctly masculine.

"You might be the death of me," Lucas groaned, swiping his thumb over my swollen bottom lip when we parted again.

I turned around in the mirror, pressing my ass against him, my back molding to his chest. Lucas didn't miss a beat, wrapping his arms around my waist and tugging me against him.

"Help me take this off?" I asked, gesturing to the zipper of my dress.

"Not yet."

Lucas drank me in. I watched his gaze travel down my body, over full breasts and a round stomach, sculpted thighs and lean calves. His hands gripped my hips, fingers splayed wide as he looked his fill. I shifted my weight from one foot to the other, unused to this level of scrutiny before.

"You're staring," I whispered.

"I've been trying to be a gentleman," Lucas murmured. "All fucking night I've been doing my best not to stare. Forgive me if I take some liberties now."

"You're a gentleman," I confirmed, sucking in a sharp breath when his hands squeezed my hips again. "But I'd really prefer you weren't right now."

Lucas chuckled darkly as he swiped my hair off my shoulder, pressing a kiss to the back of my neck.

"You mean that?"

The words were a whisper against the curve of my shoulder, and my head lolled back against him of its own accord.

"Yes," I hissed as his hands continued traveling up and down my body. I squeezed my thighs together when he let out an appreciative groan.

He finally reached for the zipper of my dress, dragging it down slowly. The sleeves fell down my arms and the red satin pooled at my feet, leaving me in only my black heels.

"Fuck," Lucas muttered. "Nothing underneath."

"Not in that dress," I said, letting out a small, breathy

laugh.

His hands trailed up and down my sides, fingertips gently grazing the sensitive skin there. I huffed out an impatient laugh and grabbed his hands and brought them to my breasts. The action earned me another groan, a low, tortured sound I wanted to memorize and play on a loop every time I got off for the rest of my damn life.

He squeezed me roughly, kneading them in his hands like they were the best fucking thing he'd ever felt, and I let my head drop back against his shoulder again, watching him work his hands over my body. I couldn't remember the last time I'd been this turned on.

There was something about me standing there, completely naked, with his shirt unbuttoned and pants still on that sent a thrill through me.

"I'm keeping the heels on," I whispered, and Lucas groaned into my neck, grinding his rigid length against my ass. I turned around, wrestling his shirt off completely. I pressed my palms into his chest, gently leading him towards the bed. He sat down on the edge, his eyes raking over my body as I stalked towards him.

"You trying to kill me, dream girl?" Lucas murmured. His words had warmth spreading through my entire body, the tension coiling in my stomach winding tighter at the way his eyes darkened.

I placed my hands on his thighs and leaned down to kiss him once before sinking to my knees in front of him.

Lucas's eyes widened in surprise.

"You don't have to—"

"I want to," I said, adjusting my knees to a more comfortable position. I put my hands on his thighs again, practically salivating at the sight of his hard cock straining his pants. "I promise it's more for me than it is for you. I want you to fuck my mouth."

Lucas moaned in response, and the sound sent a thrill to me. He lifted his hips up and tugged his pants down and as soon as his cock was free, my mouth was on him.

Lucas's pants and low curses spurred me on, and when his hand wound through my hair to guide me even further, I moaned in encouragement.

I needed him to know I'd been thinking about sucking him off for the better part of the night. His grip tightened, and I squeezed his thighs.

Yes.

I could only imagine what I looked like, in nothing but my thong and heels, on my knees for him. My core throbbed with need.

When he muttered, "such a good fucking girl" as I licked him from base to tip, I finally slipped a hand between my legs to chase my own pleasure as I worked him. I was drunk on the feeling of knowing I was the one making him unravel, that I was the one he wanted this badly.

"Fuck, Cass, are you touching yourself?"

I hummed around his cock in affirmation, fingers circling my clit before slowly dipping inside. My entire body was a live wire, a spark on the verge of igniting. I finally dared to meet his eyes, pulling my mouth from him and pressing a kiss to the base of his cock.

"Christ," Lucas panted, swiping his thumb across my cheek as he looked down at me, his expression a heady mix of awe and lust. "Cass. Dream girl."

I almost fell apart beneath the weight of his gaze, his praise ringing in my ears like a promise I desperately wanted to keep. I slid my fingers in deeper, gasping when the palm of my hand brushed my clit.

"If you keep working me like that, this will be over too soon. I plan on taking my time with you."

Lucas grabbed my shoulders, pulling me into his lap. I groaned when my center dragged over his cock, my hips settling over his.

"You're so hot," I whined when he dragged me over him again.

"I've been thinking about this all fucking night," Lucas said. "You in my lap, just like this. Wet and needy."

My answering moan was closer to a pant. I dug my nails into his neck.

Every thrust of his hips, the drag of his skin against mine, made me dizzier. Sex had never felt this good. Not with my ex, and certainly not when it was just me. Lucas watched my every move like he wanted to know every damn detail, learning what I liked, trying new angles.

"You're so good, Cass," Lucas murmured, his voice a low, rough rumble against the shell of my ear. His hands trailed over my stomach, his palm splaying wide against my navel, so close to where I desperately needed him. "Are you going to come in my lap?"

"Fuck," I cried out when his fingers finally slid inside. There was no resistance, and I let out a relieved sigh, a sense of rightness setting over me because I knew this orgasm was going to take me out. Lucas curled his fingers and I panted.

"Yes, *right there—*"

His thumb circled my clit twice and I was tipping over the edge, toes curling against my heels. My lips fell open in a shaky gasp as pleasure speared through me again.

"God, I want to be inside you," Lucas said, his teeth grazing my collarbone. "You're so fucking pretty when you come."

"Please," I whispered, legs still shaking as I laced my fingers through the hair at his nape and tugged his head back. "*Please.*"

Lucas kissed me in answer, fingers tangling in my hair. He laid me out on the bed and searched for his pants, finally fishing a condom from his wallet.

"You don't have to beg," Lucas murmured as he climbed on top of me. "You can have whatever you fucking want, baby."

Words left me entirely as he entered me. I gripped the sheets, throwing my head back, eyes screwing shut at how fucking good it felt.

I choked on a moan as he slid deeper. The oxygen left my lungs in a breathy pant as I pulled him closer.

It was insane. The whole fucking thing was insane.

I'd started the day in a relationship and was ending in a one-night stand. I waited for the shame to swallow me, but it didn't get the chance. Because when I opened my eyes again, Lucas was there, anchoring me back to him.

"Don't think," Lucas murmured, tilting my face back towards his. My eyes met his, and I locked onto that connection, fumbling for purchase as I reached for him.

"It's too good," I said, letting another whimper escape as he fucked into me again and again, hips snapping and setting a brutal rhythm like he knew that's exactly what I needed. "It's—"

Wasn't it? These things didn't happen. Not to me.

Lucas's fingers trailed down my neck.

And then his fingers tapped gently against my collarbone.

Fuck, was he—

"Yes," I whispered, and when his fingers wrapped around my throat, the rest of it snapped into place.

He tightened his grip just hard enough, and I whined. Actually fucking *whined* at how overwhelming it was. My nails dug into the muscular planes of his back, and Lucas rewarded me with a sharp thrust, a silent signal that he liked it.

He squeezed tighter and then relented, just the right amount of pressure and heat that had me gasping for air. Somehow he knew where the line was without me telling him. I didn't have to worry he'd go too far, and I didn't have to ask him for more.

My gaze locked with his and, *fuck*, that was a mistake, because what I saw there obliterated me.

Awe and lust and a greed that made my heart fucking soar because it matched mine.

"God," Lucas growled. "You're going to ruin me."

I was already there. I'd gone over that cliff as soon as he'd kissed me in the park. Maybe even the first conversation we had at Rain's. Somewhere between that stupid basket of wings and kneeling in front of him, I'd lost it.

"Focus on how good it feels," Lucas urged, like he could

feel my mind slipping away. "I'm there with you."

Somehow the knowledge of him being just as fucked up as I was over whatever this was had me re-focusing my effort. I met his thrusts, pushing my hips against his. My nails dragged down his back, and he shivered, bracing one hand above my head. His hips slowed as he slipped his other hand between our bodies. I gasped.

"Lucas," I hissed when he stroked my clit. My hips bucked forward to meet him, core tightening. "*Fuck*, no one—"

"I'm not them," Lucas cut me off, shoving impossibly deeper. The air left my lungs. "You're going to come again."

What the hell was happening?

My thighs clenched around him as he stroked my clit in time with his thrusts. My jaw hinged open in disbelief, my fingers digging into his shoulders.

Lucas smirked like the smug bastard he was.

"Atta girl," Lucas murmured, keeping his right hand between my legs but bringing his left hand come up to squeeze my throat again. His grip was harder this time, like the smug bastard knew that's what it would take. "That's my girl."

I came again with a shocked, strangled cry as his words tore through me, my back bowing off the bed with the force of it as he chased his own release. My thighs still shook when he rolled onto the bed next to me. I took the opportunity to slide down the bed, already opening the folder of excuses why I wouldn't stay the night.

Lucas reached for me, fingers snagging on my wrist as he murmured, "stay."

Fucking *hell*.

"I should probably leave," I whispered. "One night, re-member?"

Lucas's breath hitched.

I could practically hear the walls being rebuilt in my head. How he'd knocked them down in the first place still escaped me. Not after I'd spent so long pushing people who made me feel any kind of powerful emotion away. I waited for the moment to shatter. Waited for the excuse to slam the door closed. I waited for him to argue with me. To put up a fight.

"Probably. But you don't have to."

Something twisted in my chest. I didn't dare look at him while I turned the question over in my mind. If I looked at him, it was over.

"Okay," I relented. "I can stay for a little while."

The relief that swept through him made a ball of emotion lodge at the based of my throat. I kicked my shoes off so I could lay down comfortably and settled my head on the pillow, letting out a surprised 'oh' when Lucas reached up to tuck a piece of my hair behind my ear. He was so close now. And in the well-lit hotel room, I could see every feature of his face. Rich brown eyes. Lightly tanned skin that was close to mine.

Devastating.

"Not bad for a first time."

"That was *not* your first time."

"No." Lucas smiled. He propped himself up on an elbow so he could look down at me. "It was my first time with *you*."

I let out a surprised laugh and pressed a palm against his chest. "I'm beginning to understand the flirty playboy past."

Lucas grimaced. "I haven't been that guy for a long time."

"Old habits die hard, though," I murmured. His eyes softened, like he knew I wasn't talking about him.

"So, what's the verdict on the shitty job?"

"I can honestly say I've never had a guy ask me about my job during pillow talk."

Lucas rolled his eyes. "I already told you. I'm not them."

I bit my bottom lip as the image of him wringing another orgasm from my body flashed in my mind.

"You most definitely are not," I agreed. "And I don't know. I want to quit, but what the hell else would I do?"

"Find something else," Lucas said with a shrug. "Seattle's a big city. You'd find something."

I hummed non-committally.

"Where's your apartment?" he asked me a few moments later.

"Close to here," I said with a yawn. "I could probably get an Uber or something."

"I'll walk you back."

"Oh no you don't," I said, smiling. "First of all, *one night*. Second of all, you'll use your masculine wiles on me and I'll invite you inside for round two, and Lainey will *flip* and demand to know your entire backstory. And Lainey is the last person you want knowing your entire backstory."

"Why is that?"

"She has friends in high places," I said. "And by high places I mean Etsy listings of the witchy variety."

Lucas let out a low whistle. "Best I stay here then."

I couldn't stop myself from grinning.

And that's how we wound up talking for two hours. Sometime in the early morning hours, we both fell asleep, with Lucas's arm thrown over my stomach and my head halfway onto his pillow.

Chapter 27

Lucas

I hung our formalwear in the hotel closet while Cass un-packed. We both rinsed off in the shower and changed clothes.

I took her hand in mine during our brief stroll around the hotel, admiring the towering palms, plush greenery, and waterscapes in the lobby. When we arrived at the restaurant, Julian and his wife were sitting on the plush couch outside. They rose to their feet as we approached.

"I'm Sera," the woman said, extending a hand to Cassie and then to meet. "It's great to meet you both."

"Likewise," Cassie said with a smile as the host led us inside.

We took our seats, Julian and Sera sitting across from us. Our waitress greeted us, and we ordered our first round of drinks. Sera ordered a fruity mocktail, and Cass excitedly followed suit.

"So, how did you two meet?"

Lucas smiled and gestured for her to do the honors. Selfishly, I was curious how she'd explain it.

"Kind of a weird story actually," she said. "We had a one night stand when we ran into each other in a bar in Seattle."

Julian choked on his next inhale, and Sera let out an amused laugh.

"That is not how I expected you to explain that," I said, shaking my head. I rested my hand on her thigh, my thumb gently stroking the sensitive skin there.

She shivered, and I bit the inside of my cheek to keep from smiling. I'd put a bruise there just before dinner, where I'd had my own personal feast.

Cass shrugged, her cheeks pink.

"Oh, I like you," Sera said as she took a sip of her water. "I heard through the grapevine that you're a divorce lawyer?"

"Yep," Cass said. "Although I'm on a bit of a sabbatical right now."

"Same," Sera said. "Not the lawyer part, but the sabbatical part. I was in finance, but we had our first baby last year. I never went back after my maternity leave ended. I just couldn't do it."

My hand instinctively squeezed Cass's thigh beneath the table.

"I can't imagine," Cass said, and gave Sera a genuine smile. "Can I see a picture?"

Sera's entire face lit up as she nodded and pulled her phone out of her purse.

"You've opened a can of worms," Julian said, waggling his eyebrows at his wife. I rolled my eyes.

"He just turned eight months," she said, showing her phone to Cass first and then to me. "That little fake remote is his favorite toy right now. He says mama and dada."

"Mostly mama," Julian chimed in.

"He's handsome," I said, unable to stop my smile.

Cass smiled too as she looked at the picture of their son. "His chubby little cheeks are so sweet."

I quickly averted my eyes. My chest tightened with something I couldn't place. My thoughts scattered. Somewhere between awe and confusion and heat that I was all too familiar with where Cass was involved.

Our server arrived, and we ordered appetizers and a fresh round of drinks before returning to the conversation. I launched into a conversation with Julian about something sports-related. I didn't keep up with football that often, but he did. It also gave me an excuse to listen in on Cass's conversation with Sera. The last thing I wanted was for her to feel overwhelmed.

"How are you finding military life?" Sera said.

"Who, me?" Cass said with a laugh.

"I mean, the constant back and forth. The late-night calls. It's like having a mistress that takes priority in all things," Sera said as she tore into a mozzarella stick.

Cass let out a strained laugh. "Right. Yeah. I like to keep myself busy, so..."

Her voice trailed off, and it was clear she didn't know what the hell else to say.

My thumb continued to rub an idle circle on her thigh. We'd been so wrapped up in each other, in figuring out this thing between us. Neither of us had dared upset the balance by asking about what the future looked like.

"That will serve you well," Sera said. "I didn't mean to spook you. Julian used to be active duty and transitioned out about a year ago. So, we're used to the military being at the center of everything. The reserves are different."

"Right," Cass said. Her thigh tensed beneath me as she shifted uncomfortably in her seat.

"That's part of why Julian and I hit it off," I interjected. Cass visibly relaxed. "I was on active duty for a while, too. I also took a *sabbatical* while I figured my crap out."

Cass shot me a wry smile. "A new big word for your vocabulary."

"Prepare to be sick of it," I replied.

"So when did you guys tie the knot?"

I choked on my sip of water. Cass sat up straighter.

Sera shot a scandalized look in her husband's direction, and while she didn't actually say *what the hell*, Julian heard the message loud and clear.

"We're not married, actually," I said, my smooth tone showing no sense of annoyance. Cass briefly looked at me to see my reaction, but I couldn't decipher it. Julian laughed.

"Sorry for the assumption," he said, pressing a hand to his smile to hide a smile. "You two argue like an old married couple."

Did we?

"I'm recently divorced," I said.

The words lingered there.

"He's right," Cass stepped in. "We're just enjoying our time."

And then she shifted in her seat, dislodging my hand.

I pulled it away slowly, giving her time to pull it back.

She didn't.

Luckily, we were both saved from having to come up with an alternate answer when our food arrived. The rest of dinner revolved around Julian and Lucas trading funny active duty stories.

"Oh, I meant to tell you. You'll meet our new staff sergeant at the ball tomorrow. He's been dealing with family stuff these last few drills, so I don't think you've crossed paths yet."

I sat up straighter. My jaw clenched of its own volition. "What?"

Julian shifted in his seat.

"He's coming from Pendleton. He's joining our prior-active duty club."

"What unit?"

Don't say it. *Don't say it.*

My pulse roared as Julian rattled off the numbers. Sera clocked it immediately.

"Is that your old unit?"

"Yeah," I said, clearing my throat. "It'll be interesting."

"No kidding," Sera mumbled into her glass. Julian nudged his thigh with hers.

I just knew the two of them were going to have the best conversation after this dinner. They were exactly the kind of couple I imagined had the best tea-sharing sessions.

"It'll be fine, man. He seems like a good dude."

My responses were shuttered after that. I still cracked jokes and smiled, but based on the way Cass kept giving odd glances, they never quite reached my eyes. The dinner ended on a high note, with Sera giving Cass a crushing hug and telling her to come find her in their hotel room if she needed anything before the ball tomorrow night.

When Cass linked our fingers together as we said our

goodbyes for the evening, my chest ached for an entirely different reason.

"I'm sorry if the divorce comment came out wrong," I said. "There's... never a good way to explain it."

"It's okay," Cass said, voice soft. "It just surprised me, that's all. Are *you* okay?"

We walked down the hall towards the elevator. I squeezed her hand.

"I'm alright. Just don't like when my past and future collide. I didn't leave active duty on the best terms with most people. There's a chance our paths never even crossed, but..."

"You're anxious about it," she finished for me when my voice trailed off. "That's understandable. I mean, I'm clearly not educated in the nuances of military interactions, but there's a gap there, right?"

I inclined my head towards her and nodded.

"You're learning," I said, grinning.

"My anxiety won't allow me to look like a complete idiot at a formal event, unfortunately," she said with a sigh.

"You'll be fine," I said.

Silence stretched between us during the elevator ride up to the hotel room. I swiped my key card.

Cass shrugged off her jacket and sighed, turning to face me.

"Do you feel like this is moving too fast?" Cass murmured.

"No."

Cass exhaled, slow and controlled.

"Do you?"

"Sometimes," she admitted. "Some days it feels like this

thing is moving at the speed of light, but then I look at you, and I don't want to stop."

I unbuttoned the top of my dress shirt. Her eyes tracked the movement.

"I am physically incapable of denying you anything."

Her eyes widened.

"Come here," I murmured as I finished unbuttoning my shirt. She stepped towards me, wrapping her arms around my neck. She slid my shirt off my shoulders, running her hands down my bare chest as I hooked my thumbs in the belt loops of her jeans, tugging her against me.

"You're distracting, you know that?"

I hummed in acknowledgment, dipping my fingers beneath the denim waistband to rub her smooth skin. She sighed contentedly, tipping her head towards the ceiling.

"What's on your mind?" I murmured, dipping my head down to trace the column of her throat with my nose.

"Nothing," Cass whispered. She shivered when I pressed a kiss to her jaw. "It's all just white noise when you hold me like this."

I tugged her closer to me, even as my stomach swooped at the insinuation that I was the place she could let her guard down.

"We have the night to ourselves," I said.

Cass smiled, and my grip on her tightened.

"I have plans for you, dream girl."

Chapter 28

Cassie

I was grateful Lucas had the forethought to bring us here a day early. Getting the time to adjust had proved important to my mental health. Lucas and I spent the entire first night wrapped up in each other, pausing long enough to eat a room service dinner and watch half of *Spirited Away*.

I woke up the next morning with Lucas's arm thrown over my stomach and the muscular planes of his back tempting me. This weekend alone with him was already an indulgence I shouldn't have afforded myself, but since I was already here...

I reached my hand out, stroking my knuckles up and down. I reveled in the feeling of his skin, like I was allowed to want him next to me like this always.

And God, did I want.

It still alarmed me just how much I wanted this man. What had started as a curious desire in a bar had turned into borderline infatuation. I'd never been able to shove Lucas into a box in my mind. He'd always had an in, a secret passage right to the very heart of me.

He groaned and arched his back slightly. My palm splayed

wide on the small of his back. The morning after Seattle, I'd run. I hadn't been able to come up with a good reason to stay. The want that had culminated in the best night of my life had scared the ever-loving shit out of me.

And now I was here, on the other side of the state, in the same place. The morning after.

Except this time I wasn't running.

This time, I wanted to play for keeps.

"If you keep doing that, we're not leaving this bed until you're hoarse from screaming my name."

God. I squeezed my thighs together. "You have to go to work."

Lucas groaned deeply into his pillow. "No."

He turned his head to look at me, giving me a soft, sleepy smile that was as sexy as it was sweet. It twisted the ball of emotion in my chest into a tangled mess.

"We have a few minutes," I whispered, leaning in to rub my nose against his. "If you want—"

"I *always* want to."

That made two of us.

I let out a contented sigh when he finally reached down, cupping my sex. I gasped when he rubbed his hand down, a slow drag of his calloused palm that set my body on fire.

"You're so wet for me, dream girl. I've barely even touched you."

"Don't," I warned as I ground myself against him, panting when he pressed his hand harder.

"It's fucking hot," Lucas murmured. He crooked his fingers, so it was his knuckles dragging against me instead, and I gasped. "Everything you do is so fucking hot, Cass."

I rolled my hips, pushing him towards the bed so I could straddle him.

"I love you," I whispered.

Lucas shuddered. "Cass."

"I mean it," I said again. The words burst forth from me, a flower blooming beneath his touch, a vine snaking around my heart and tethering me to him. "I love you, Lucas."

He flipped me onto the bed, cradling my face in his hands as he ground himself against me. All the air left my lungs as my back hit the sheets, the slick heat between our bodies enough to make me dizzy. My eyes fluttered open, and there was Lucas, staring at me, that beautiful jaw hinged open in what looked like awe.

"Say it again."

The command made me swallow hard. I wound my fingers around his neck and pulled him down to me so that our faces were only inches apart.

"I love you."

The words were barely out of my mouth before Lucas was pushing into me again, and the sheer perfection of it sent me spiraling.

"I love you, dream girl," Lucas said, kissing my cheek, my jaw, my collarbone. Everywhere his lips could touch. I cried out as he grabbed my hips, driving himself deeper.

I wanted to drown in this, in him. I wanted it every single fucking day for the rest of my life.

I lost myself in him. In the connection between us, that beautiful invisible string pulled taut.

"Fuck," he growled as I dug my nails into his back. I wanted to mark him again. Lucas shuddered when I bared my teeth against his collarbone, biting down when my orgasm crashed through me. Lucas quickly followed, groaning my name over and over again.

He pulled out of me and slid onto his side. He pulled me into him, and I went willingly, wrapping myself around him. My body shook with the force of what we'd just done, the full weight of it slamming into me as the last of the walls I'd perfected shattered into glass before my eyes.

"I'm here, baby," he murmured into my hair. "I love you, and I'm here."

"God," I croaked. "*Lucas.*"

"Now that I know I'm allowed to say it, I hope you're ready to be sick of it."

My heart pounded in my chest, and I pressed my face into the hollow of his throat.

"What do you mean now that you're allowed to say it?"

"I think I fell in love with you that first night, Cassie."

My eyes fluttered shut.

"I believe you," I told him, and meant it. For all that had hurt Lucas in love, he'd never stopped wanting it. He and Imogen were similar in that way. It didn't matter how hard they tried to turn away. That craving to be loved by someone in a soul-crushing, life-altering way remained.

I could say the same about myself, but in a more complicated manner.

"Does this change things?" I whispered after a few minutes of silence, nothing but our shared, rapid heartbeats echoing between us.

"The only thing it changes is that I now have a license to kiss you whenever I want. Wherever I want."

My stomach swooped low at the implication. "We're going to tell them?"

"Yeah, dream girl. Should have done it a while ago. But sometimes it's better to... be sure."

He hesitated over the words. My thumb stroked the sensitive skin at the base of his neck, reminding him I was already with him.

I glanced at the alarm clock on the nightstand and swore loudly.

"You're going to be late," I said, pushing away from him. Lucas reluctantly let go, rolling out of bed and running a hand through his hair.

"I desperately need a shower," he said.

"I do too," I sighed, flopping back against the pillow. I pulled the plush white duvet over me and regarded Lucas's naked form as he headed for the bathroom.

"Come with me?"

"Definitely not," I snorted. "You will never make it downstairs if we don't stop."

Lucas shrugged his shoulders and said, "Love you," before jumping into the bathroom and turning on the shower.

I pressed a hand over my mouth, unable to stop the small giggle that escaped me.

I had never been a giggler. Even now I bit my bottom lip to prevent the sound from slipping out.

Maybe I was understanding what people said about finding your person. I thought about the soft edges of Imogen's smile, the way she was still the same person she'd been before but with more peace. The quiet contentment of knowing someone was with you for all of it.

I turned onto my side and grabbed my phone from the nightstand, quickly clearing the email notifications away. I'd deal with them whenever I got back to Winding Road.

Instead, I navigated to my texts, smiling when I saw I had several unread messages from Lainey.

Lainey

FaceTime me this morning? I miss seeing your face.

Me

Call you in a few

Lainey

I'll be here

Waiting patiently

I rolled my eyes affectionately. That was Lainey-speak for 'I'm decidedly not being patient and am instead waiting by the phone for you to call.'

Lucas re-appeared from the bathroom just minutes later, toweling off his hair and tossing it toward me.

"Ugh," I said, wrinkling my nose and shoving the damp fabric off the bed.

Lucas smirked at me as he pulled on his pants, grabbing my ankles and yanking me down the bed so he could climb over me. I yelped in surprise but wrapped my legs around him anyway.

"Be good, yeah?"

My cheeks flushed. "Okay."

"And text me if you need anything. Stuff gets stupid on the day of the ball, so I won't be back until an hour before we need to be downstairs."

"I'll be here," I said.

"Lucas?"

"Yeah?"

"I love you."

His smile was wild as he leaned down to kiss me. I pulled away quickly, giving him a knowing stare.

Lucas sighed. "You just told me you loved me. There is nowhere else I would rather be than in your arms."

The words rocked me to my core, and I couldn't keep from grinning.

"You get to see me in the dress later," I said, flicking his nose. That got his attention. With one final messy kiss, Lucas got off me and finished dressing.

"Love you, dream girl," he called over his shoulder as he left the room. I threw the sheets back and hurried to the bathroom to shower before pulling on a lounge set and setting up my laptop at the small wooden desk.

Lainey picked up right after the first ring.

"Cassie!" Lainey squealed with delight. She pulled her legs up underneath her and sank into the couch cushions. My chest squeezed tight with affection as I watched her.

"How's the family?" I asked, noting the background. "Are you still there?"

"Yeah, I'm still here. There's a lot of stuff going on, and they needed me here. So I put my shop on vacation mode again and have been hanging out since."

Lainey worried her bottom lip between her teeth, and I frowned at the realization that I'd been a remarkably shitty friend to her over the last few weeks. I'd been so wrapped up in my crap that I'd barely spoken to her outside of a few random text exchanges.

"Everyone is wondering when you're coming to visit again," Lainey said. She clearly wanted to move on, and I didn't want to push her, so I let her continue. "They're kind of obsessed with you. My sister went on and on about how we're the perfect pair because we balance each other so well."

"Ah yes, the classic grumpy/sunshine presentation. I'm the grump, of course."

"Naturally," Lainey smiled. "It's good to hear from you. How's life in Washington State?"

"It's okay," I said, rolling my lips together as I fought a smile. "That's actually what I wanted to talk to you about. You won't believe this, but—"

"Oh my God, you found him again!" Lainey let out a delighted squeak. "The guy from Seattle! The dark, tall, brooding gentleman who you spent one magical night with. You reconnected!"

"How did you... you know what, don't answer that. Yes. Turns out he lives an hour from my hometown. He was in Seattle because he was going through a nasty divorce. His ex-wife lives there."

"Shut up," Lainey crooned. I could feel the joy radiating through the phone. "This is so much better than the Etsy witch told me it would be."

"You did not pay real American dollars to have an Etsy witch do a reading about my love life."

"I did," Lainey admitted with a sigh. "She said—and this is a direct quote— that you'd *have to return to your roots to find what had been lost."*

"You made that up."

"I swear I didn't!" Lainey said with a laugh, and I believed her. "I'm happy for you, Cassie. You deserve it."

"Thank you," I said honestly.

"I have an admission of my own to make," Lainey said, her voice quieter than it had been earlier. "I, uh... I'm going to be staying in Keelbay Harbor indefinitely."

The words shot through me like an electric shock.

"Wait, you're not coming back to Washington?"

"I'll be coming back to get my affairs in order, but I'm moving home. My parents are getting older, and there's an opportunity for me to expand my business... I just feel like I've outgrown Seattle. I did what I came there to do. And now it's time for me to come back home."

Come back home.

"Lainey," I choked out her name. "Did that Etsy witch say anything else about me?"

"No," Lainey said, drawing out the vowel in a confused tone. "Why? Should I book another reading?"

"I don't think I'm moving back to Seattle either," I said in disbelief.

"Oh thank God," Lainey groaned, and I could picture the relief that probably lined her face. "I was really hoping to avoid the whole 'helping you find a new roommate' thing. It just sounds like an awkward nightmare. I mean, *no one* can compare to me. Not even Lucas. I was the perfect roommate. I kept you on your toes, never drank the last of the milk or left dishes in the sink, always made sure the kitchen cabinet had condoms—"

"Okay," I cut her off. "Yes, you were the best roommate. And it feels very poetic that we're both moving on at the same time."

Lainey beamed.

"Well, I *did* book a reading about *us* about six months ago, so..."

I couldn't stop the grin that split my face.

"You knew this was coming?"

"My sources never lie."

The ball of emotion that had lodged in my sternum for months unraveled at the sight of one of my closest friends, knowing she was on the other side of the country, and would be for the foreseeable future.

This was a good thing for both of us. We were both moving on to a new chapter in our lives.

But God, it still *hurt* to know that things would never go back to the way they had been before.

"I'll miss you," I whispered. "So much, Lainey. You were my first real friend in Seattle. You were my rock. It'll be weird not sitting on the couch with you every Friday night, sharing a family-size takeout carton of pad thai and watching Project Runway re-runs."

"I'll still be there for you," Lainey said, voice soft and affectionate. "It'll just look a little different. Especially since you'll have a giant hunk of a man keeping you company."

"Jesus," I groaned, scrunching my nose in distaste. "He's not like that."

"Well, he sure looks like it," Lainey said wistfully. "It's always the quiet military guys who use humor as a deflection tool. You just know they're kinky as—"

"Alright," I said too loudly. "We'll talk logistics more soon, yes?"

"Yes, ma'am," Lainey said teasingly. "Love you, Phillips."

"Love you back, Ross," I replied.

I stared out the window of the hotel as I hung up the phone.

I finally understood what Kam and Connor had told me about Winding Road when they first met me. That little stretch of land, and everything that had been cultivated on it with love and sweat and tears, had a way of knitting people back together, stitching shut holes you didn't even realize needed patching.

I would stay for as long as they'd have me.

My eyes drifted to the red dress hanging in the closet.

Something in my chest tightened.

I texted Lainey.

Me

I told him I love him.

Lainey

you're just now realizing that??

Me

Shut up.

Lainey

quit texting me and go get it ;)

***

When the door opened hours later, signaling Lucas's return

from rehearsal, my shoulders sagged forward with relief.

Somewhere between the phone call with Lainey and the moment I'd told Lucas I loved him, my anxiety had spiraled to a fever pitch.

Could I really do this? Could I be the person Lucas needed me to be? Had we moved too fast? Did we actually know each other well enough for this level of commitment?

He hadn't asked me to marry him. Hell, he hadn't asked me to be his life partner.

But that's where this was headed, wasn't it?

My chest was tight as he walked into the room.

"Hey Ca—"

He didn't finish his sentence because my lips were already on his. The force of it pressed him back against the door.

"Hello to you too," Lucas said. "Miss me?"

"I always miss you," I whispered.

Lucas pressed a kiss to my forehead, and the world righted itself. "I promise I missed you more. Knowing you were up here lounging in those tight little shorts–"

"Is your mind always in the gutter?"

"When your ass looks that good, yes."

Lucas gave my waist another squeeze and stepped past me, grabbing his garment bag from the closet.

"Uniform time. Prepare yourself."

I laughed and shook my head.

"It's dress time. Prepare *yourself*."

Lucas's eyes widened, as if he'd forgotten he wasn't the only one getting dressed up. I poked him in the shoulder as I passed him. I reached for the dress and stepped back into the bathroom.

My fingers traced the satin fabric, the delicate stitching of the seams.

It so closely mirrored the dress I'd worn the night we met. That was the main reason I'd chosen it. The only difference was in the neckline and the length of the skirt.

I slipped into the dress, sitting on the edge of the tub to buckle my heels.

I barely recognized myself when I looked at my reflection in the mirror.

How many times had I stared at my face, thinking of all the things I'd change? Not just physically, but personality traits I lamented, comments I wished I could take back.

Tonight, I took a moment to stare at the woman in the mirror.

I exhaled shakily and stepped out into the small hallway.

"Oh, fuck," I said, my breath catching as I rounded the corner.

Lucas was running a lint roller over the sleeve of his blues jacket. He held his arms out and gave me an "I told you" smile before turning to examine his backside in the full-length mirror.

"Still got it," he observed. "My ass looks *incredible*."

"You're..."

"Believe me, I *know*," Lucas said, grinning like a maniac. "I clean up well."

"Lucas."

I leaned against the wall for support, not trusting the way my heart was cracking.

"Yeah, dream girl?"

"I need you to kiss me right now or I'm going to die."

"Always so dramatic," Lucas murmured, but he obliged me. In two steps, he crossed the room, massive hands sliding around my waist and tugging me towards him. We were pressed for time, and on any other day, I'd try to talk myself down from the ledge. Lucas's tongue slipped between my lips, his hands gripping my hips in the way that drove me absolutely feral, and I crossed the point of no return.

Not crossed. *Sprinted.*

I'd fucking jumped over the cliff's edge weeks ago, and I'd been in free fall since, determined to deny what my heart and body already knew.

Lucas was *it.*

With Lainey's words and the terrifying truth of my feelings for this man pulsing in my veins, I needed him.

"I need you," I said, clutching his sides. Lucas opened his mouth to say something, but he quickly shut it when he looked at my face, felt the desperate way I clawed at him, like he was my very center of gravity.

"Are you okay?"

No, I was the farthest thing from okay.

But the words didn't form.

"I *need* you," I whispered instead.

Lucas hesitated for a beat before saying, "You're going to have to help me out of this. Carefully, because I do have to wear it in an hour."

He laughed when I reached for the clasp at his collar to get the stupidly hot and insanely impractical thing they called a jacket off. I put it down on the bed.

"Breathe," Lucas murmured. He was standing in front of

me in just a plain white t-shirt and tailored pants, reaching for me.

He was *always* reaching out for me.

Lucas rubbed his hands reassuringly up and down my arms.

"Where are you right now, dream girl?"

Drowning.

I was fucking drowning.

Chapter 29
Cassie

Seattle, Washington
05:00

In the quiet dawn, I slipped out of the hotel room. I quietly gathered my clothes and dressed as silently as possible. I grabbed my phone from the nightstand.

I left.

Just like I'd always done.

I walked down the streets of Seattle like I had a hundred times before, but it felt different this time.

I had unlocked a part of myself that I couldn't shove into a box. And there was no going back.

I took my heels off in the elevator of my apartment building. Every part of my body was deliciously sore. I glanced at my reflection in the silver elevator door and gasped when I saw the faintest of bruises along my collarbone.

I looked down at my shoes until the elevator door opened

to my floor. When I entered my apartment, I slung my bag on the kitchen island and grabbed a glass from the cabinet.

"You're back!" Lainey said, smiling widely as she stumbled into the kitchen, still rubbing the sleep from her eyes.

"I'm back," I said, voice rough after hours of conversation.

"Fun night?" Lainey asked, yawning as she pulled a mug down from the shelf.

"Yeah," I said, nearly choking on all the words I couldn't say. "It was."

Later that day, when I saw an unnamed phone number written in the notes app of my phone, my fingers hovered over the delete button.

As if I could simply undo something as earth-shattering as the night before.

I could never bring myself to press it.

Chapter 30
Lucas

"**H**ey."

My hands gently circled Cass's wrists, holding them to my chest. She squeezed her eyes shut, and I knew she was trying like hell to regulate her heartbeat.

"Better?" I asked a few moments later. She nodded.

"Sorry," she whispered.

"You don't have to be sorry," I said, giving her hands a last squeeze before letting them drop. "Are you sure you're okay?"

"Yes," she said, a tad too brightly. "Just the classic anxious cocktail of excitement and nerves."

I wasn't convinced, but I also didn't want to press her. Cass would come to me when she was ready.

I slid my blues jacket back on. She helped me wrestle the clasp on my collar shut.

I pressed a kiss to her cheek, and the faint blush on her cheeks sent my heart into yet another tailspin.

"Ready?" I murmured, extending a hand to her.

"As I'll ever be," she said, and stepped out with me into whatever waited beyond.

I hated small talk, but Cass thrived on it.

It shouldn't have surprised me, considering her work experience, but watching her work the room in her red dress and black heels, charming every single person she met with ease, made warmth spread in my chest.

Inevitably we separated, Sera having grabbed Cass's wrists, citing that she needed to meet someone.

When I'd turned around to head for the bar, I'd run smack into the new staff sergeant I'd planned on avoiding the entire night.

"Hey, you're Morales, right?"

"That's me, Staff Sergeant," I said, plastering on my best smile as I extended a hand to him. "Heard you just arrived from Pendleton."

He nodded and took my outstretched hand, shaking it firmly.

"I was surprised that there was someone else here from 1/1 here. Why'd you end up transferring to the reserves? Sounds like you were doing well on active duty."

"I, uh, went through a nasty divorce."

I coughed and looked into my glass of whiskey. I'd been entirely unprepared for this conversation, even though the question was innocent enough.

"I just needed some space."

He nodded. "I get that."

Someone came up behind him, clearly wanting to talk to him.

Thank God.

"It was good to meet you, man," he said, extending a hand to me.

"You too," I replied, shaking his hand firmly before turning my attention back towards Cass.

She was seated next to Sera, laughing at something the woman had said.

I finished the last of my whiskey as I looked at her.

The way she laughed with Sera had brought a question I'd never considered to the forefront of my mind.

Would this life be too much for her?

We hadn't talked about the future; hadn't talked about whether Cassie would eventually return to Seattle.

Sure, she seemed comfortable at Winding Road, and I suspected that Kam and Imogen had already offered her a place there.

But would she take it?

Would it be enough for a woman who loved the city lights, who craved new experiences and excitement?

I swallowed hard.

I loved her, and we were racing towards a cliff.

I made my way towards her, stopping as my phone started buzzing in my hand.

I glanced at the caller ID, and my stomach dropped.

It was my sister.

My sister didn't call me. Not these days. The last time we'd spoken had been the day I called her to tell her my divorce was finalized.

After a moment's hesitation, I stepped to the side, standing near an empty table as I hit accept on the call.

"Lucas."

My name was a sob, and every nerve ending in my body lit up. I was going to kill whoever made her cry like that.

"Adri, what's wrong?"

Images from the last night she'd called me crying flashed in my mind, and my stomach rolled.

"It's Dad," she sobbed. "He had a heart attack. Lucas, he's gone."

He's gone.

Two words that unraveled me.

"What?"

"He–he died," Adri repeated, gulping down a breath.

He died.

"But he..."

My dad had never been the healthiest person alive, but he was sturdy. Strong. A heart attack seemed like such an undignified way for him to go. So sudden. Unexpected.

"I know I have no right to ask you this," Adri whispered as my thoughts spiraled away from me. "But we need you here, Lucas. Please. Mom is a wreck and I can't–"

"I'll be there."

The words were out before I could stop them. Even though I didn't know up from down, didn't know if there were any flights out this late in the night, I knew I would be there.

Not for me. That ship had sailed a long time ago.

I'd go home for them.

Because Adri was asking me, and there had been too many things in her life that I hadn't been there to protect her from. I'd been too lost to my own shortcomings to be there for my family how they needed me.

"Just–give me a few hours," I said. I finally looked away from Cassie. I couldn't breathe right near her on a good day, and I *couldn't*–

"I'll be there by the morning."

"Thank you," Adri whispered. She gave me a small run-down of the day–Dad woke up uncomfortable, the chest pain got worse, and then the heart attack happened. There was nothing to be done. There was no stopping it, no saving it or picking up the pieces.

I hung up after reassuring her I was coming home, and the room tilted on its axis.

"Hey man, are you okay?"

Julian stared at me. I hadn't even realized he was standing next to me. I quickly nodded my head, a knee-jerk reaction I couldn't stop, and sought Cassie again.

She frowned when our gazes met. I turned around quick-ly, heading straight for the door, suddenly desperate for fresh air.

"Lucas!"

I couldn't breathe. I reached my hand out to brace myself against the stone pillar.

He's dead.

We might have had a chance to fix what broke eventually. I'd always expected there would come a day where both of us could lay our cards out on the table and talk through all of it. My relationship with my father was complicated at best, tumultuous at worst, but he was still my dad.

I had just lost that chance.

And it was my fault.

I'd ignored the calls after Mallory had set fire to my relationship with my family. It had been easier to walk away entirely than to walk over hot coals, to dredge up every one of my shortcomings and admit where I'd gone wrong.

Now he was dead. And the last words I said to him would always be, "don't call me."

Cassie came up behind me, hand outstretched like she would grab me, make me face her head on.

"Don't," I asked, still facing away from her.

"Lucas, what happened?"

"My dad's dead."

Cassie inhaled sharply.

"What do you need?"

Her words opened the gash in my chest deeper.

Of course, she wouldn't leave. Of course she'd stand here with me while I completely lost it.

I needed to turn back time. I needed air. I needed the last ten minutes never to have happened. I needed her arms around me.

But none of those things could happen.

Because they weren't physically possible, or because they'd break me.

Cassie in my arms would break me in a way I couldn't handle.

"I have to go home," I said. I straightened my posture.

"Lucas, look at me."

"I can't. We need to go."

Cassie followed me quickly, but she didn't reach for me again.

I was burning alive from the inside.

Grieving something that had forever been lost. An opportunity not taken.

Selfish bastard. I was so fucking selfish.

And that's exactly why I kept Cassie at arm's length the rest of the night. I found Julian again and told him what happened. I got permission to leave early while Cassie got our bags from upstairs. She did the whole thing in heels and her dress, forever a force of sheer willpower I'd never compare to.

We loaded the car in silence. I changed out of my uniform in the parking lot and felt like I could breathe a little easier.

Mercifully, Cassie didn't push me.

Like she knew I'd break completely if she touched me.

Chapter 31

Cassie

"Are we going to do this the entire drive home?"

My question rang out in the quiet cab of the truck. Lucas was white-knuckling the steering wheel.

"I can't give you anything right now, Cass."

"Then be angry," I said, exasperated. "Fuck, Lucas, your dad died. You're allowed to be pissed."

He still said nothing.

I swallowed tightly as I stared out the car window.

"Fine. I'll talk then."

Lucas opened his mouth to say something, and I quickly cut him off.

"I've spent my entire life keeping up appearances and doing all the right things. I got straight A's and walked across the stage at graduation with a full-ride scholarship. I had the wall of riding medals and first place ribbons. And then you show up in Seattle looking like you've walked out of my wildest fucking dream. Every day since you sat down next to me at Rain's, I can't breathe."

Lucas's entire body shuddered.

"Cass."

A name. A plea.

I knew how he felt. He'd told me over and over again.

But I'd never told him just how much he'd meant to me. Not like that.

It was the only truth I had left to give him.

That was my last attempt at pulling him back from the edge.

"Let me help, Lucas. Please."

"I can't," he murmured. His death grip on the wheel tightened. "I just can't."

I didn't say anything else after that.

I knew this spiral all too well.

But this time, I was the ghost standing on the other side of the room, watching as someone I loved lost themselves.

And I was surprised to find that being on the other side of the room was just as fucking terrifying as being the person out of control.

When we pulled into Winding Road two hours later, Lucas got out of the car without so much as a second glance in my direction. Cold dread iced my veins as I hopped down from the car, cursing the fact that I hadn't taken two minutes to change out of my clothes.

I followed him into the bedroom of the tiny house, standing helplessly in the doorway.

"I'll come with you," I tried again. "I can—"

"You can't help me with this," Lucas muttered, turning away from me. "Please, Cassie."

I didn't recognize this Lucas. This version of him was

cold, internal. I reached for him one final time, grabbing his forearm with both of my hands and yanking hard, as if I could somehow snap him out of this.

"Stop for two seconds and *talk* to me."

"I can't stop," he snapped. "You of all people know why I have to go, and I have to go *now*."

I *did* know, and that's what made it hard to watch him, throwing clothes into his weekender bag, dress blues crumpled in the corner.

The eldest child panic was written into every hard line of his body.

That deep urge to run right back to the place it all started, to the people who needed you the most, fucking all the consequences in the process.

Someone could burn their life down that way.

I would know.

And that's why I reached for him now.

Trying to pull him back from the edge I knew like the back of my hand.

"Lucas, you're not thinking straight. Let's take twenty minutes—"

Lucas finally paused, his fingers stilling on the shirt that was shoved halfway into his duffle bag.

"Cassie, I am barely holding it together," Lucas muttered. "I'm not trying to be an asshole, but I need you to just—*fuck*."

My heart beat out of time as I turned his words over in my mind.

"Are you asking me to leave?"

The words were barely above a whisper. Because I was so damn scared of the answer.

That had always been the line in the sand between us.

If someone pulled the plug by asking the other person to walk away, we would, but neither one of us had ever dared do it.

Neither one of us had ever truly wanted to walk away.

Even when I pushed and Lucas pulled, we'd never crossed that line.

But as I stared at Lucas now, this devastated, distressed version of him, I realized this might be the moment it all fell apart.

Lucas sighed and shoved the shirt in the bag. He turned away from me and gripped the edge of the small dresser, knuckles white. The only sound in the tiny house was the small wall clock ticking in the kitchen.

It was a long moment before he answered.

"Yes."

The word *shattered* me.

It was almost comical how quickly those old feelings came rushing back.

Every thought of not being good enough, of pushing too far, of always being the one to go out on a limb only to be shoved away, shot straight to the surface of my mind.

I stepped back like I'd been physically struck. The verbal blow landed right in the center of my chest.

It wasn't enough. It hadn't *been* enough.

I wasn't enough.

"Okay," I whispered. "I'll leave."

I wrapped my arms around myself as I pushed past him.

His head snapped up and tears blurred my vision as I stumbled forward.

As if the spell had been broken, he let go of the dresser.

"Cassie, wait—"

I didn't wait to see if he followed me.

I pushed open the door of the tiny house and left it open.

My heels slipped in the gravel lining the uphill slope, unable to grip the shifting rocks. Any other night, I might have briefly contemplated the stupidly perfect metaphor.

But I didn't stop. I couldn't stop. If I stopped, I would completely fall apart.

I didn't stop until I got back to the farmhouse. My feet carried me there of their own volition. I was no longer in the driver's seat. Despair had taken over entirely.

I knocked on the front door with a shaking fist. My lower lip wobbled when it was Kam who answered. His confused expression immediately morphed into one of concern as he took me in. I was a sight to behold, still in my formal dress and black heels.

"I need Imogen," I mumbled, slapping a hand over my mouth as the first sob escaped me.

"I'll get her," Kam said without hesitation, opening the door for me to step inside. He gently grabbed my arm and led me over the threshold. "You're okay, Cassie. You're safe. I'm going to get Imogen. Just stand right here, okay?"

But I couldn't stand. I slid to the floor, the red satin pooling around me. I stared at the floor as the room tilted.

"Cassie?" Imogen's voice was full of concern. She cursed when she saw me crumpled on the floor, rushing over to kneel in front of me. "Cassie, what happened?"

"He... I..."

Confusion sank into Imogen's features. "Who?"

"Lucas," Kam murmured, and another sob shuddered out of me. Imogen's head whipped towards Kam.

"What the hell are you talking about?"

"Im—" Kam started.

"I love him," I whispered. Imogen's eyes widened. "It's my fault. I love him, and he told me to leave."

Kam muttered something that sounded a lot like, "I'm going to kill him," before he pushed past me, boots stomping down the porch stairs.

"Cassie, I don't understand," Imogen murmured.

The thought of explaining Seattle to her at this moment made my stomach roll.

"I love him," I cried. "I'm so fucking sorry, Im. I'm so sorry I didn't tell you. I was so scared of screwing this up, and now it's ruined everything."

Imogen's shoulders slumped forward with realization. She let out a weary sigh.

"*Fuck*, Cassie. Are you serious?"

I could only nod. And then the sobs started in earnest.

Imogen wrapped her arms around my shoulders and let me cry into her shoulder. I don't know how long we stayed like that before Kam reappeared.

"He's gone," Kam murmured from the doorway. "His dad passed. He's flying home."

Imogen closed her eyes, tilted her face toward the ceiling, and let out a long sigh.

"Lucas, you fucking *idiot*."

Imogen's grip on me tightened, the protective side of her taking over.

"Will you pull the spare bed into the side room?" Imogen

murmured a few moments later.

Kam nodded, giving her shoulder a squeeze as he walked past her and disappeared down the hallway.

I croaked out, "You don't have to—"

"I do," Imogen said, still holding my hand. "It'll be like old times. I have one condition, though. You have to tell me how in the hell you fell in love with my best friend."

The laugh that escaped me sounded more like a hiccuped sob.

"I'll do my best."

Imogen handed me a clean pair of pajamas, fuzzy socks, and told me to hand her my phone, as if she knew I was already making plans to try and reel the situation back. She made us hot chocolate and popcorn, and my eyes welled up with tears when she handed the mug to me.

"This is still your favorite snack?"

"Yep," Imogen said, giving me a dazzling smile. "Kam hates it, so I make it a point to watch a movie on the couch just like this once a week."

I snorted.

"We haven't really talked about it, but you two are good together. He's perfect for you."

Imogen smiled fondly. "He's kind of the best."

We set our snacks on the nightstand and pushed the two twin beds together.

After we finished eating, we laid side by side, staring up at the ceiling.

And I told her everything.

I told her about Seattle.

I told her about the magical night we'd shared. About sharing cookies the size of our faces and discussing the trips we wanted to take one day. About our walk in the park and the way I'd watched Lucas fall just a little bit in love with the city that would forever have a part of me.

I left out the finer details about how the night ended, which Imogen was grateful for. Instead, I talked about how shocked and terrified and elated I'd been when I saw Lucas again at the party. How insane it was that out of millions of people, my Lucas was the same Lucas in Imogen's friend group.

Imogen didn't interrupt me. She let me reminisce.

I let out a long sigh when I'd finally finished, wiping a tear from the corner of my eye.

"And now, it's over," I murmured. "Feels like a really shitty way to end things."

"It's not over," Imogen said. "You don't go through all of that only for it to fall apart now. I would know."

I didn't have a response. The weight of heartbreak still sat heavy on my chest, threatening to cut off oxygen.

"He'll come back," Imogen murmured a few minutes later. "He just needs to work through this first. Lucas has never had a good relationship with his family. It's always complicated. There's always a crisis. After he stopped talking to them, things got better. But with his dad having passed..." Imogen inhaled deeply. "There was no way he'd miss his dad's funeral."

I closed my eyes. "He told me to leave, Im. I wanted to

help, and he just shoved me out. Like we hadn't just been happy and in love that morning."

"Yuck," Imogen reprimanded, and I pressed my fingers to my mouth to keep from laughing.

"Believe me, Cassie, he will fucking pay for it," Imogen muttered, rubbing a hand over her face.

"I'm not mad at him," I said, resigned. "I'm mad at myself."

"For being a good girlfriend?"

My eyes widened. "We're not... we never talked about that."

Imogen sighed. "God, you two really are perfect for each other."

My cheeks reddened.

"He'll be back," Imogen said again. "And you better be ready when he is, because I have a feeling that man will drop to his knees and beg your forgiveness when he finally comes to his senses."

"Is this a pattern of his?" I asked quietly. "You would know."

Imogen shook her head fiercely.

"No. It's not. Lucas has worked really damn hard these last few years. I think this was just one thing too many, and he broke."

She paused before continuing.

"We all break sometimes, Cassie. And sometimes we break other things in the process. We hurt the people we love. We push them away or tell them to leave even when that's the opposite of what we want. But there's always space for repair. It takes time—years, sometimes—for people to come around, but it's possible."

I didn't realize I was crying again until Imogen handed me another tissue.

"Stay here tonight, okay?" Imogen murmured. "There's water, comfy sheets, and a spare toothbrush for you."

"Okay," I said, my voice cracking on the word. Imogen gave me one last big hug, piled our dirty bowls and mugs onto a tray, and left the room.

I stared up at the ceiling for a long time. Sleep eluded me until the early morning hours, when I had finally exhausted myself.

I dreamed of the waterfall.

Chapter 32
Lucas

"**M**orales!"

The sound of my last name had me gripping my keys tighter in my fist. Because there was only one person who consistently called me by my last name out of uniform. And judging by the tone in which he yelled the name, he was *pissed*.

"Gotta go," I called back. I opened the back door of my truck and threw the duffle bag in the back, and slammed it closed again. When the car door shut, Kameron was standing there, looking like he wanted to strangle me.

"Don't do this," Kam said. "Do you hear me? Don't throw away a good thing because you're spiraling."

"What the hell do you know?"

Kam didn't so much as flinch. If anything, he looked disappointed.

"I know that there's a girl in my house right now who is hysterical because you pushed her away. She cares about you, and she's worried about you, and you shoved her to the side to spiral on your own."

I closed my eyes. My grip tightened even further. So much so that I was worried I'd break the stupid door right off its hinges.

"My dad died."

"And that is fucking awful," Kam said, his voice imperceptibly softer, as if he was talking to rabid animal, trying to calm it down enough to trap it in its cage. "But you don't have to walk that road alone. Give me the keys, Lucas. Let's go inside. We'll make a plan together."

"No," I snapped. "You don't fucking get it."

"I do," Kam growled, and for a moment, I thought we might actually fight.

Kam leaned forward, pointing an accusatory finger at my chest.

"Don't forget who you're fucking talking to. I've watched my mom become a ghost of the person she was. And in case you forgot, my dad's dead too, asshole. So if you want to throw down, you can throw down with me. *After* you go hug the woman whose heart you just broke and tell her you love her, too."

Pain seared through my chest.

For a moment, the thought of Cassie in pain overrode the grief sitting like a boulder in my chest.

And then I remembered why I'd shoved her away. I thought about my sister, my mother, waiting for me states away. Their life was in shambles, forever altered.

"I can't," I said, shoving past him and unlocking the driver's side door. Kam let me go, but his face morphed into anguish.

I reached for the door handle, but Kameron shoved his body into the space, blocking me in. His palms splayed wide on either side of the door as he stared at me with an intensity I didn't think I'd ever seen from him.

"Lucas, if you leave now, there is a damn good chance there won't be anything for you to fix when you get back," Kam said. "*Don't do this. Not to her.*"

I clenched my jaw and ground my teeth as I muttered, "Maybe that's for the best."

I had never seen Kam so disappointed, and it cut deep. Deeper than I'd been expecting.

This was a man I cared about. A man I'd served with. Someone who had taken care of me, given me a soft place to land during a time in my life where everything was a wreck.

And I was throwing him away as if he meant nothing to me.

Kam didn't say anything else. He stepped away, letting me slam the door shut.

I cranked the ignition and tore ass down the gravel driveway.

I told myself this was for the best. If I'd burned this bridge, I'd make a new one somewhere else. I would make it work.

The grief in my chest burned like acid the entire drive to the airport. I used the last of my willpower to walk past the airport bar once I'd gotten through TSA. I slumped in one of the seats and stared out the large glass window, watching the planes land.

I didn't think of Winding Road. I didn't think of Kam, or Connor, or the horses.

I didn't think of Cassie. I couldn't.

Because people like me didn't get happy endings.

I returned home for the first time since I had filed for divorce.

My sister greeted me at the airport, bleary-eyed and exhausted. When she reached for me, I didn't hesitate to wrap my arms around her and let her cry.

I swallowed down the anger at myself for staying away.

Maybe there would have been a chance one day.

We might have repaired what was broken. Where we could have talked, man-to-man, about life and love, and what it meant to serve.

That chance vanished when my father's heart stopped beating.

My father was not a kind man.

The war had broken him. Broken all of us.

But he had raised me to be a man of honor.

A man who showed up for his family when they needed him.

So I held my mother at the gravesite. I let her wail against my chest. I held my sister's hand. I saluted as the rifles fired.

I love you, Cass had said. *I love you.*

Three words that had the power to give life.

And the power to take it.

I stayed on autopilot the entire weekend. Speaking only when spoken to. I shook hands and hugged the people that asked for it. I ignored the whispers, the stares, the murmured comments and questions about my sudden return that were somehow directed to anyone but me.

At the airport, I kissed my mother's cheek, and hugged Adri tight.

I promised my mother I would call.

And then I got on another plane.

I flew back to the only place in the world I wanted to be.

And prayed like I'd never prayed in my life that there would be something to fix when I got there.

Chapter 33
Cassie

I mogen kept my phone for the entire weekend. It was for the best, considering there was absolutely nothing on social media that would bring me any level of comfort.

And standing by the phone waiting for a phone call that wasn't coming wouldn't help either.

So, I worked.

I spent most of my time at the stables. I helped Kam deep clean every saddle and rein on the property. I blazed new trails in the woods, clearing the footpaths after the most recent thunderstorm.

I helped Imogen bake bread, and I listened to every intriguing domestic thriller in the "available now" section of the Seattle Public Library system's Libby audiobook catalog on 2x speed, determined to get through as many as I could manage.

I stayed out of my head. Or at least, I tried to.

Something inside me had cracked open.

Something I'd never be able to wrangle back into submission.

I knew what love felt like now. Knew what it was like to hold someone and be held in return.

There was no taking it back. Not the honesty, nor the confessions, nor the memories.

Mari had once told me everything happened for a reason. The words were wasted on seventeen year old me: a girl with so much anger and no place to put it.

Now that the clouds of anger had cleared, I could see the truth of those words laid out over the years of my life.

Every time a door closed, another opened somewhere down the line.

There was also a deeper truth I'd accepted: that the existence of a new door didn't make it hurt less when the first closed.

But there was an odd comfort in knowing that something else always existed, even in the moments where I couldn't see it.

Kam, Imogen, and I were lounging on the front porch when Lucas came home.

I stared at his truck, steeling myself for whatever came after.

"Lucas," Imogen said, quickly standing to her feet as Lucas got out of his truck.

He hadn't shaved all weekend. Dark stubble lined his jaw, and even from several feet away, I could see the dark circles under his eyes. He was completely wrecked.

And then I realized Lucas wasn't looking at Imogen, or Kam, or even Bass, who had run out to the porch to see what the commotion was.

He was looking at *me.*

And then he ran.

I opened my arms before I truly grasped what was happening.

Lucas ran right into my waiting arms, crushing me to him. He buried his face in my neck and I wound my arms around him, inhaling the deep, woodsy scent of him, because now I knew how painful it was to be without it.

His fingers tightened around my waist, and I closed my eyes, tilting my face to the sun. I wanted to memorize this moment. Immortalize it in my soul, somehow. To have him just like this, always.

There was a faint rustling on the porch behind us, bodies moving back inside the house.

"I'm sorry," Lucas murmured against my neck. "I'm so fucking sorry."

I just held him.

"I love you," Lucas said, cradling my face in his hands as if it was something sacred to be protected, to be cherished. "And I'm a fucking mess, Cass. I'm a mess because I want all of it with you. And I'm so fucking scared by it I can't breathe."

"I'm here," I whispered, pressing a kiss to the corner of his mouth. He shuddered, and I pulled him even closer. "I'm here, Lucas. I'm right where I want to be."

And then he dropped to his knees in front of me, holding the back of my legs so neither of us toppled over. I gasped, completely taken aback.

Lucas didn't kneel for anyone. He'd survived too much, had come too far.

But he was kneeling for me.

"You have me," Lucas continued, holding on to me like I was his only anchor. "You have all of me, Cass. You're it for me."

"You're it for me too," I choked out.

I felt the truth of it in my bones. Like the last key sliding into a lock.

Except this time I wasn't trying to keep something out. I was keeping him in.

"You're everything I've ever wanted," I murmured. "I'm not giving you up."

Lucas pressed his forehead to my thigh and let out a shaky breath. When he looked up at me again, the anguish on his face stoked a fierce protectiveness in me. He still clung to me, and I reveled in it. I relished the feeling of him against me, letting myself drown in it.

"But you don't get to do that again, do you understand?" I whispered. "*Never* again."

"Never again," Lucas agreed. "I'm so sorry, Cass."

I couldn't bear it anymore. I grabbed his shirt collar and hauled him towards me.

"We all break sometimes," I murmured, cradling his handsome face in my hands as I echoed Imogen's words from that first night. The scratch of his stubble against my palm was a familiar comfort. "But you hurt me, Lucas. I don't ever want to feel that again."

The rawness of Lucas's expression cemented my resolve. He wouldn't do anything like this again. Somehow I knew it like I knew the fierce way he loved me.

"Never again."

There was more we needed to talk about. But there wasn't any doubt in my mind that we would. We would talk about all of it, and step into a new chapter.

Together.

"I love you," I whispered, finally pressing a chaste kiss to his lips. "I love you so fucking much it scares me."

"I'm there with you, dream girl," Lucas said, taking my face in his hands and kissing me. Soft and gentle at first, then more urgent.

When we finally broke apart, dazed and slightly off kilter, I jerked my head toward the front porch, where Kam was leaning against the doorframe, expression stormier than usual.

"You owe some other people an apology too," I said. "I can't promise they'll be as nice as me. Imogen is *pissed*."

Lucas grimaced. "I earned it."

I took his hand in mine and led him towards the porch.

"I'm sorry," Lucas said, holding Kam's gaze.

Kam stared him down, and rubbed a hand over his face. But he nodded in Lucas's direction. An olive branch.

And then Imogen burst out of the house, bulldozing past a shocked Kam and shoving Lucas hard in the chest. He stepped back, letting go of my hand and slapping it over his chest. He frowned at her, rubbing the spot.

"You idiotic son of a–" another shove. "I ought to strangle you with my bare hands, Lucas Morales, I swear to *God*. What the hell is wrong with you? How many times have we been through this? You don't get to push us away, and you definitely do *not* get to break my sister's heart, you *imbecile*..."

"Do we need to intervene?" I asked quietly as I sat down on the porch steps.

Kam sighed heavily, taking a seat next to me.

I watched as Imogen continued to berate Lucas, who looked uncharacteristically sheepish.

"No," Kam murmured. "Give her another minute to get it out, and then they'll go back to being best friends. At least she's keeping her hands to herself now."

"She's terrifying," I remarked.

Imogen was still talking animatedly, pacing in front of Lucas, who kept shifting his weight from one foot to the other.

"She really is," Kam said, but I heard the smile in his voice even while keeping my eyes fixed on Lucas's sullen form.

A few minutes later, Imogen's bottom lip wobbled, and Lucas hugged her.

The tension vanished from both of their bodies as they stood there. Lucas murmured something to her that I couldn't hear, but Imogen was beaming when she pulled away.

"We'll be alright?"

It came out more as a question than I intended. Kam nudged my shoulder with his before standing to descend the porch steps towards his friends.

"Yeah, Cassie. We'll be alright."

Chapter 34
Lucas

We had barely been inside the house for an hour, partaking in peanut butter sandwiches using Imogen's homemade jam, before Imogen's phone rang.

"Hello, you're on speakerphone," she practically sang, hitting the speaker button and laying the phone on the table. She licked the knife in her hands clean and walked over to the sink to wash it.

"I hate to break up the party," Abbie said. I instantly sat up straight because she sounded completely out of breath. "But it's happening."

"What?" Imogen screeched.

"You probably want to make your way over here," Abbie said. "And please bring the guys with you. I don't want Connor making someone cry because he's being a menace over his wife."

Kam and I both winced.

"We're coming," I said.

Abbie let out a loud curse, and I cringed, bracing for the blow I knew was coming.

"Lucas Morales, I know you've probably already been yelled at, but you better believe I am going to kick your rear—"

Her tirade was cut off by a low, pained moan, and the scratch of fabric against the speaker, a sign that her phone had changed hands.

"See you in a few hours," Connor grumbled. "And don't take forever getting here, yeah?"

We didn't take forever getting there. Kam drove the four of us in his truck as fast as he could without risking a ticket or someone's neck.

Imogen and Cass paced the waiting room floor for the next several hours. They were on standby in case Abbie requested their presence in the delivery room. Kam and I made sure they stayed fed and hydrated, chuckling at the way the two of them mirrored each other's actions.

It had never been more apparent that the two of them were sisters: the anxious tucking of curls behind their ears, the animated discussions and talking with their hands.

A reminder of far they'd come over the last few months.

Imogen received a text from Connor in the late evening with only two words.

She's here.

Imogen and Cass screeched with excitement and ran for the nearest elevator. Kam and I were helpless to do anything but follow.

I'd never participated anything like this before, and I hung back, making it obvious to Kam that I was ready to jump in if needed, but that I'd let Cass and Imogen lead.

They entered the room first. Abbie smiled widely when she saw the two of them.

"We named her Talia," Abbie whispered as they approached. "Close to Tilly, but still her own."

Imogen inhaled sharply, and Cass's eyes watered. Kam squeezed Imogen's shoulders.

I hovered near the doorway, watching the scene unfold before me.

Imogen stooped down to take Talia from Abbie's outstretched arms, sitting down on the couch. Kam sat next to her, one arm wrapped around Imogen's shoulders as they both stared down at her.

"Hi baby," Imogen said, stroking the top of Talia's head with gentle fingers. They stayed like that for a few moments. Cass was at Abbie's bedside, holding her hand and asking her if she needed anything.

"Your turn," Imogen said, passing the tiny bundle to Kam as she stood to switch spots with her sister. Kam smiled at Cass, nodding once.

Cass's eyes widened.

I straightened, ready to go to her, but Cass took up residence in the spot Imogen had just occupied.

Imogen placed Talia in her arms, and Cass's body lit up.

"Hi Talia," Cassie murmured. Her voice was softer than I'd ever heard it. Cassie relaxed as soon as she sat back, gazing down at Talia's sweet face. Holding the tiny infant was as natural to her as breathing.

"I'm Cassie. Welcome to the world. It's kind of crazy around here, but you've got lots of uncles and aunts who have been dying to meet you."

I rubbed my chest as though it would help ease the sudden rawness there.

Imogen conversed softly with Abbie, who was reclined in the hospital bed, cheeks flushed with exertion and sheer joy. Connor was downstairs grabbing coffee, and I was staring at Cassie like I was helpless to stop it.

Cassie's eyes met mine, and there was so much written in her expression. So many words and questions that I didn't have the answers to. Even if I did, I didn't think I could voice them.

I stepped out of the room when the crushing sensation in my chest became unbearable. Kam followed me out the door.

We left the three women to fawn over Talia. I leaned back against the railing lining the hospital hallway. I fixed my gaze on a single chipped tile in the floor, like it somehow held the answers to all of the questions swirling in my mind.

"Yeah, I feel that way too."

I lifted my head to find Connor standing a few feet from me. The dark lines around his eyes were the only sign that he was tired. There was a peaceful quality to him that was new. I swallowed the lump in my throat and smiled.

"Fatherhood looks good on you," I said, straightening so I could pull him in for a hug. He begrudgingly accepted, giving me an awkward pat on the back.

Even now, it seemed like the only person who could get away with hugging him was Abbie.

"Congratulations, Connor. She's beautiful."

"She is," Connor agreed, smiling at the view through the small window in the hospital door. The mental image of what he was seeing—Imogen, Cassie, and Abbie speaking in hushed tones about Abbie's birth experience and gasping with delight every time Talia wiggled in her sleep in her tiny bassinet—set my heart on fire.

My blood family was a shitshow, but the one I'd chosen was as close to heaven as a sinner like me could get.

"Thank you for inviting us to come visit you here," I said. "It means a lot."

"You guys are family," Connor said.

As if the concept were so simple.

"Right," I murmured.

Kam came to stand beside us.

"This feels poetic," Kam said with a sigh. "Three couples. Three happy endings."

I rubbed the back of my neck awkwardly. "A dude can hope."

"As Connor has reminded me on multiple occasions, everyone works through their crap at their own pace. You two will be just fine."

Kam nudged my shoulder with his.

"I think Imogen read about this in a book once," Kam mused, gesturing to the three women—sisters, in all the ways that mattered.

"I'm not capable of making any comments right now," Connor muttered, throwing his hands up in a *don't ask me* gesture. "Wax poetic to me in a year when I'm sleeping again."

I shook my head, unable to stop the smile overtaking my face.

"This is a full-circle moment if I've ever seen one," I said.

At Connor's confused expression, I hiked my thumb towards Abbie's hospital room.

"If you two hadn't reconnected, neither of us would have what we do now."

Connor looked stunned, as if he'd never contemplated that. Even Kam looked taken aback, like he'd never fully stopped to consider just how insane it was that we'd all found each other.

"Maybe you're right," Connor said, smiling softly when Abbie waved at him and mouthed, *is that for me* in reference to the coffee he was holding in his hands, grinning widely when Connor nodded. "But I think the events of the last few months have proven that the universe works in mysterious ways."

My chest tightened, because he was right. Connor stifled a yawn and squared his shoulders back.

"Now, if you'll excuse me, gentlemen, the mother of my child requests her well-deserved caffeine."

That left just Kam and me standing in the hallway. I opened my mouth to say something, but snapped it shut again moments later while I tried to find the right words.

"Kam, I–"

"Don't say it," he said, choking on the last word. "I'm emotional as shit right now. If you say something nice to me, I might cry."

I barked out a laugh, shaking my head, unable to wrap my head around how this was my life.

My beautiful, messy, imperfect life.

Any day surrounded by my family was a damn good day indeed.

Chapter 35

Cassie

Watford, Washington
Midnight

I closed the door of the tiny house behind me, unable to stop my grin as my eyes landed on Lucas standing just a few feet from the porch.

"Ready?" he asked, extending his hand to me. I grasped it, linking our fingers together and pressing a gentle kiss to his cheek.

"Lead the way."

We walked hand in hand towards the barn. These late-night stargazing sessions had become a staple of our weekend routine in the last few weeks since returning to Winding Road.

Lucas laid out the plaid blanket under his arm on a smooth dirt patch that would give us a clear view of the night sky overhead. He laid down first and I followed, practically hopping into his arms.

"Every time we do this, I think of Seattle," I murmured, burrowing against his chest.

"It's a nice callback, isn't it?" Lucas replied. His fingers drifted up and down my arm, a barely there touch that warmed me.

"It's everything."

There had been so much darkness in our lives. So much hurt.

And we'd still ended up here.

"I love you," I murmured. They were the only words that came close to describing how I felt about the man holding me.

I pressed my face against Lucas's chest, tightening the arm thrown over his waist as he gazed at the stars above us.

"I love you more, dream girl," Lucas replied, pressing a kiss to the top of my head. "You are the best thing that has ever happened to me."

That night in Seattle changed our lives in ways we were still grappling with. And truth be told, there was a chance we'd always grapple with our pasts.

Nothing is ever truly linear, least of all healing.

But in the arms of the man I loved, I knew we would tackle it as a team.

We'd navigate stormy weather the same way we navigated sunny afternoons: *together*.

And that?

That was everything I'd ever wanted.

Kevin Phillips

Hey. I think I'm ready to talk now. Coffee at Blackbeard's sometime this week?

Epilogue

There are many bars in Seattle, in the same way that there are many barns in Watford County.

But there's only one bar with a polaroid picture of two lovers with a personalized note that simply says, "Thanks for the wings — C&L."

Just like there's only one stretch of farmland, nestled in the Cascades, with a newly renovated barn that brought two soul mates together again.

On that same acreage sits a tiny house where two people repaired their ability to trust.

Look beyond the treeline, and you'll find a clearing nestled near a waterfall, where two people decided to put their hearts on the line and *try*.

And at the center of it all is a white farmhouse, aged by wind and time, that stands steady, despite the creaky floorboards that lead to the front door.

A house that became a home not just for lost souls in need of an anchor, but a symbol of rebirth.

Of family. Of hope.

Of love.

Three women sit on the front steps of the farmhouse, sipping lemonade as the late summer sun gives way to the night sky. These days, they laugh freely, the tapestries of their lives intricately woven from strings of both their past and the future still to come. The highs and lows. All of it joined in the most treasured of ways.

They watch their partners play soccer with two children. The older girl takes after her mother, long brown hair and quiet brown eyes. The younger toddler boy takes after his father, dark hair and a boisterous laugh.

A white dog runs in between their legs, barking and yipping with excitement when someone scores a goal. They smile until their cheeks ache as the men hoist the children over their shoulders, whooping their excitement and en-couragement.

The children grin wildly, jumping up and down, spinning and twirling in the carefree kind of way that comes from a childhood surrounded by healing adults.

They're siblings in every way but blood, nurtured by the bonds of friendship forged between their parents.

Together. Happy.

At peace.

The color of the sky changes from dusk to dawn, and so it reasons that hope never fully disappears.

Not even in darkness.

For nothing is ever too broken to be repaired.

Acknowledgements

Most days I can't believe this book is actually published.

I've said it so many times, but I'll say it again: Lucas and Cassie put me through the ringer. Out of the three books in the Watford series, this was by far the most complicated book to wrangle. This book ripped me open and pulled things to the surface I'd had buried for a long time. These characters forced me to dig deep and push myself as an author. I'm giving myself flowers here for not giving up.

Thank you, dear reader, for coming on this adventure with me. Lucas and Cassie have both been beloved characters since they first appeared on the page, and I hope you loved reading their story.

To all of the Seattle natives who have stumbled across this book: thank you for giving me grace with the creative liberties taken with the layout of downtown Seattle :)

To my husband and son: you make me the best version of me. I love you more than I can ever put into words.

Emily, you're the best alpha/beta/ARC/reader/all around hype woman a girl could ever ask for. This military spouse life is a wild adventure on a good day, but knowing we have each other makes it easier to get through the hard days.

Thank you to my family and friends: a special thank you to my seester, parents, and in laws. Thank you for everything: all the childcare, snacks, coffee, and encouragement. I couldn't do any of this without y'all.

H—I don't know if you'll ever read this, but I will always be grateful for your presence in my life. Your HEA is out there. I love you.

To the readers who have been with me since *Under Pink Skies* was first published—especially Mackenzie, Tyla, Brittany x3, Kiara, Elsy, Vanessa, Katty, and every bookstagrammer/booktoker that's ever taken a chance on this series. Thank you for every comment, like, and DM. I'll never be able to convey how grateful I am.

Next stop: Keelbay Harbor, Maine. :)

About The Author

Hallie Anne writes romance stories with complicated characters working through tough problems and the love they find along the way. She lives in the Carolinas with her family. When she's not writing, she's curled up with a cozy blanket, a cup of coffee, and a romance book. Connect with her on Instagram at @hallieanneauthor, and join her Discord server for behind-the-scenes snippets and exclusive online events!

Sign up for my newsletter
to stay up to date!

Join Hallie's Heartstrings

S ick of the constant social media scroll? Me too. That's why I created a Discord server where we can hang out and connect on a deeper level—without being buried by the algorithm.

Join the Discord server

www.ingramcontent.com/pod-product-compliance
Lightning Source LLC
Chambersburg PA
CBHW010736310726
48971CB00010B/2845